Tha. V Esther for your support may God bless you Wanda

Inherited Sin

Wanda J. Manning

313-310-3868
WMANN30884@
AOl.com

ZOË LIFE
PUBLISHING
WORDS TO LIVE BY

Published by:
Zoë Life Publishing
P.O. Box 871066
Canton, MI 48187 USA
www.zoelifepub.com

All Scripture quotations, unless otherwise indicated, are taken from The King James Version of the Bible.

Take note that the name satan and associated names are not capitalized. We choose not to give him any preeminence, even to the point of violating grammatical rules.

Author: Wanda Manning
Cover: John Jorif II
Editors: Robert McTyre and Jessica Colvin

First U.S. Edition 2009

Publisher's Cataloging-In-Publication Data

10 Digit ISBN 1-934363-44-8
13 Digit ISBN 978-1-934363-44-7

1. Christian Romance

Library of Congress Control Number: 2009925763

For current information about releases by Wanda Manning or other releases from Zoë Life Publishing, visit our website: http://www.zoelifepub.com

Printed in the United States of America

v8 04 15 09

Dedication

To my darling brother Tommy Jr.
Your ability to face your
handicaps with laughter is an inspiration to our family and you're
the glue that holds us together.

Inherited Sin

Wanda J. Manning

Thou shalt not bow down thyself unto them, nor serve them: for I the Lord thy God am a jealous God, visiting the iniquity of the fathers upon the children unto the third and fourth generation of them that hate me…

—Deuteronomy 5:9

Contents

Chapter One

Like Father Like Son

Detroit, Michigan
July 1985

Early Sunday morning, Roc heard his mother's voice sound off like a siren. "Get up children, it's time for church!" At once, he wiped the wet spot from his mouth and tilted his head. Then he gazed at the imposing sun spilling in through his window in disbelief. It was morning already. At this rate he would never get enough sleep to grow tall like his idol, Julius Erving. Slowly he dragged his sleepy body out of bed. He hated that another boring Sunday had come around so quickly.

For a long moment, Roc stood slumped against the bedpost trying to recapture the fleeting dream he was having. It was the same dream he always had—to be an NBA superstar. For just one moment, he wanted to savor the sweet taste of fame, to hear the cheering crowd as he made the winning shot. But it was too late. The image was gone. In his tiny world, the dream of stardom consumed him. It was contrasted by church—his worst nightmare.

If he had wings like the chirping birds outside his window, he would fly away to a timeless place where Sundays did not exist. Even the Bible said the seventh day was supposed to be a day of rest, but Rockwell, affectionately known as Roc, never rested. Every Sunday, there were at least three church services at First Bethel Assembly—the sunrise, midday, and sunset services. Faithfully, every time the doors opened, his mother was there. She'd also, without any qualm, insist that everyone in the household go to every single one, even Roc's father.

"Are you coming this time, Rockey?" she called out. But, unfortunately, there was no response from her husband. Maybe he was still asleep. Most of the time, Rockwell Sr. would decline and stay in bed. Naturally, his son resented him for that. Why did being grown give his father the right to say no and sleep in?

Roc's family, like most of the people he knew, gathered at First Bethel Assembly, a small Holy Spirit-filled church just down the street from their home on West Grand Boulevard in Detroit. First Bethel was the cornerstone of his community, a fixture. For as long as Roc could remember the red brick structure had been a part of him. But nothing within its walls had ever interested him—not even the silly girls that called him cute.

As Roc heard his mother's hasty footsteps, he snapped out of his trance.

Sunday school always began promptly at nine-thirty,

but Sadie Mae, Roc's mother, had overslept. She had burned the midnight oil studying for this week's lesson, "God's Amazing Grace." Well prepared, she did not want to miss a second of class. She could not believe she'd overslept. In a panic, she eyed the clock. It was just before eight. Still, there was ironing to be done and the children had yet to take their baths. With one bathroom and five children, it was always chaotic.

"Hurry children and finish your oatmeal! Time has no mercy—it won't wait on us just because we're running late!" she yelled as she glanced at the pile of laundry. A taunting reminder of what she should've done last night. And even more than that, they were evidence that it took more than wishful thinking to get a maid. Truth was, she'd given up on wishes a long time ago. She needed more to help her cope with life—she needed God. He was her for sure thing.

In a nervous state, Sadie Mae found herself ignored amidst the girls' chatter, the boys' horseplay, and the roadrunner's loud "Beep! Beep!" which blared from the television. These common noises would not otherwise bother her if time were on her side. But in a bundle of nerves, Sadie Mae stomped across the floor, turned off the television, and demanded total silence.

"We do not have time for this today! Get ready for your baths now!" she barked.

Just as Sadie Mae starched the last pair of slacks, she heard Joey, her youngest, emerge from the shallow bathwater. Tickled pink, he chuckled, splashing puddles of water on the floor as he streaked, unashamed, soaking wet, down the hall. When she looked up, all she saw was a blur whisk by. Luckily, Roc interrupted his brother's stride before the suds that covered most of his body made contact with his eyes. To Sadie Mae's surprise, Roc was helpful today. She watched his odd attentive behavior as he towel dried his baby brother.

She watched the way he gained his sibling's attention. *A born leader,* she thought to herself. She watched him. He was the spitting image of his father—tall and lanky. At nine, his narrow body was only legs and arms. He had big curious eyes and if a person wasn't careful, they could get lost in them. Like his father, he had an engaging smile—when he flashed his pearly whites, the charm oozed out. He had natural pizzazz and he knew it.

For Roc's looks and charisma, Sadie Mae was grateful. But it was his inherited strong will, self-absorbed demeanor, and quick temper that kept her in constant prayer. For some time now, she'd been on her knees, talking to God about Roc's defiant nature. Judging by his attentiveness, God had been listening, she thought. Sadie Mae took one final look at the boys as she dashed off to her room.

As time continued to escape her, she rushed to get dressed. Occasionally she wiped away the sweat beaming from her brow and tugged at her tight clinging dress. The form-fitting material hugged her defined curves—definitely not proper church attire. She knew people talked, even saints. But her body—God's temple, would never be the object of gossip.

So she knew she had to make some adjustments. But because the rest of her wardrobe was as skimpy as this dress, she had to improvise.

First, Sadie Mae wrapped a long black silk scarf around her bare shoulders. It poured down to conceal her perfectly round hips. To hold it in place, she clasped the two ends together with a beaded broach similar to the one on her clutch bag. And then, a string of pearls with matching earrings added elegance. Finally a pair of sling back pumps gave more depth to the black ensemble. She marveled at the accessories. They were all second-hand items she'd found at a thrift store that she stumbled upon downtown in her quest for bargains.

Now she gleamed at the sophisticated image she saw in the chipped mirror. Roc was not the only one in the family with looks. Although make-up could have enhanced Sadie Mae's modest exterior, it was not necessary to capture her natural beauty. Even after five children, she still maintained a sexy body that turned heads.

Quickly, Sadie Mae grabbed her Bible, admired herself for the last time, and sighed as she watched her husband turn over in bed. It was time to wake him up. It only took him a few minutes to dress. Over the years, she'd learned he was not a morning person, and it was best to wake him up when everyone was dressed and ready to go. Sadie Mae was excited as she gently nudged his body. This Sunday he'd promised to attend church with his family.

"No church for me today Sadie Mae. I promise...next week," he grumbled with his eyes still shut.

Sadie Mae drew in a deep breath as she wrestled with disappointment. She wasn't going to get mad. She was beyond anger. Truthfully, she was not surprised by his announcement.

She'd figured as much last night, when she heard his bare feet creep across the floor; when she saw his tall body slumped over in the dark; when she felt him slide into bed, settle himself between the covers with his back to her—as if the guilt in his face could be seen in the dark. At four-thirty in the morning, he was not as invisible as he'd hoped. She saw his every move. She'd even smelt the stench of stale whiskey, tobacco and cheap perfume. And while the burning question of where he had been was on her lips, she dared not to move or make a sound. Sadie Mae had stopped asking Rockey who, what, and where a long time ago. When he was out in the streets, she learned to just thank God he had the good sense to come home.

Standing over him, Sadie Mae could've reminded him of all the broken promises he'd made, but why bother. She'd already put him in God's hands. And like her grandmother used to say, "When you hand your troubles over to the Lord, they belong to Him...and you can't go messin' with God's business!"

After nearly twenty years of marriage to Rockey, it was no secret, the pull of the fast life kept him in the streets. But Sadie Mae believed in the power of prayer, and that a change would come.

"Maybe so Rockey...maybe next week," she said. As Sadie Mae gripped the door, she fought to keep her faith. It was one thing to know what the Bible said about faith. It was another thing to actually live by faith.

When she walked down the small hallway leading to the

living room, she saw five neat, fidgeting, well-dressed children lined up along the wall. They were eldest to the youngest, waiting for her final inspection. As Roc stood in the middle, he admired his spit-polished shoeshine. It was true, he hated church, but like his father, he appreciated looking good.

At nine fifteen, Sadie Mae gave her approval. Just up the street, the church was only minutes away. However, the heat would make it an unpleasant journey.

"Go and get my umbrella Roc," Sadie Mae said. His slow response prompted her to say it again louder. She needed that umbrella. Time had only allowed her to have a few curls and her limp fine hair would lose those if exposed to the dry morning sun. While Sadie Mae and the others waited in the shade on the front porch, Roc returned to the house. It was not until he heard his mother say "Hurry" the second time that he truthfully did what she said.

The five-room unit they lived in was on the first floor of a two-story building. It had two bedrooms, a living room, kitchen and bathroom. The children's room was an oversized room divided by a partition. Two girls on one side and three boys on the other, but most of the time little Joey would sneak into the room down the hall with his parents.

It was an issue of privacy that made Rockey put a lock on the bedroom door. It was his way of preventing the kids from going and coming as they pleased. This morning however, after Rockey heard the front door slam, he assumed privacy was not necessary. His family was off to church. No one was around to overhear his phone conversation. He sat up in bed, lit a cigarette, and dialed his lover's number. In his coarse voice, he spoke liberally and intimately to the woman, unaware that Roc was in the next room.

When Roc heard the pleasantries coming from his parent's room, curiosity drew him to the door. Quiet as a mouse with the umbrella in his hand, he stood there, eavesdropping. Roc heard his father confess his love to the listener. He heard him laugh—something his family rarely heard. He heard him speak softly, not in the harsh tone he used with his mother. He heard him whisper "Baby" into the phone. Not the bad "B" word he'd so often called his mother. Roc hated when his father cursed at his mother. Usually, when it happened, she would go off in private and cry.

Furious, Roc had heard enough—he began to turn away unnoticed. But it was the kissing sounds made into the receiver that made him dare to be seen. With little effort, Roc pushed open the partially closed door. Exposed—his eyes met his father's. Beneath the hostile stare, Roc's anger kindled and hate for his father burned from within. Silently, he vowed to make his father pay for all the tears he'd caused his mother and the entire family to shed.

"What are you doing boy? How long have you been standing there? It don't matter, just get your behind out of here...now! And close that door," Rockey said as his demeanor suddenly changed. Practically to his feet, he gritted his teeth and shouted at Roc with his mouth away from the phone.

Although his father repeated himself twice, Roc stood brazen. The heavy voice with a threatening tone meant nothing to him. Even as his father approached him, he did not flinch. It was not until he heard his mother's voice that he moved.

"Roc! Hurry up and come out here...now!" she demanded. Her anxious voice penetrated and, through his anger, Roc hastened to her. When Sadie Mae finally saw her son, she angrily questioned him about taking so long. With no time to waste, she quickly gathered all the children and took off down the street. Roc trailed behind.

"Roc, come up here," Sadie Mae said, still walking. "Why do you look so mad? Are you upset about something?" And then she said what she always said that infuriated him, "Boy, sometimes you look and act just like your father."

Chapter Two

Cloud Nine

In church Roc was bored. As usual, he wished he were playing basketball. His feet and hands twitched, and his eyes wondered as they became fixated on a vision of beauty. That's when he first laid eyes on Sonya, a pretty black girl. Her skin was like rich, deep, dark chocolate. Yet it was not her obvious cuteness, but her hair that fascinated him. She must've had a hundred pigtails hanging everywhere and she was twirling them around her finger. She was the first girl he'd ever paid attention to.

Instantly, his young heart fell for her as he giddily longed to get her to notice him. She was just one pew over. However, still fresh in his mind was the sting from his mother's swift hand and her final warning.

"Roc," she'd said, after she caught him hitting at Chloe, "Church ain't no place to play. If you don't be still, I will whip your behind right here, right now, in church!" Then she gave

Roc a sharp stern look—the look. The glare that harkened him; the one he seldom got from his gentle-spirited mother. That rare stone-face impression sent a clear and direct message even he understood—defiant behavior wasn't an option, but the prelude to a painful ending.

Roc wanted to yank one of those dangling pigtails he'd already estimated to be within arm's reach. He seriously thought about the devilish thrill. Even as he considered it, a cold chill went down his spine. He shuddered, scratched his head, and chose not to act upon the intrusive impulse. It was safer to daydream about the chocolate angel in between basketball dreams. *One day she'll be my wife, and everything will be just perfect*, Roc imagined, immobile.

As he stole glimpses of Sonya, his heart became merry. It was the best he'd felt all day. Even the drudgery of church and the memory of his father's transgressions were evaporated in his joy.

He'd began to believe getting that pretty girl's attention was hopeless. It was a missed opportunity. But as he was underestimating fate, Sonya's big brown eyes made contact with him. In that defining moment, he thought he was in heaven. Only a perfect place like heaven could describe the utopian high he felt when she made her move. While her parents, Mr. and Mrs. Jones, stood in praise, it was a piece of cake for Sonya to slyly overstep her boundaries because the firm hands that held her in place a moment ago were now lifted. The once attentive eyes that watched over her were now shut. Like a skilled opportunist, she seized the moment. She did it quickly as her parents were in awe, totally captivated by the angelic voices of the choir. Sonya cleverly snuck an innocent wink and waved her tiny hand at Roc.

The small congregation of three hundred or greater clapped thunderously as the choir sang their final "Halleluiah! Halleluiah! Halleluiah! What an awesome God." The day was no exception for Genesis Voices, the church's award winning mass choir—they were exhilarating. The sopranos were high, the altos were low and the tenors were high and low, a crescendo of voices all on one accord. Each note sang keenly.

One by one the members stood in admiration as the singing ministered to their souls. Even at nine years old, young Roc appreciated the sound as he listened from cloud nine.

Chapter Three

Growing Pains

September 1991

Sadie Mae had been working since Joey, the youngest, turned six and Rockey had come down with pneumonia, forcing her to work. It was only to be for a short time, but she reveled in her newfound independence. The temporary arrangement became permanent even after Rockey returned to his job at a small manufacturing plant.

In spite of the dual income, they were still plagued with hard times. Even with unanticipated car repairs, rent increases, and appliances that die two days after the extended warranty expires, it was difficult, but Sadie Mae managed to tuck away a nice nest egg. Soon, there'd be enough for a down payment on her dream. To Rockey's disappointment, the vision his wife had was not a car. He'd spotted some candy-red Eldorado white drop-top Cadillac that he'd hoped for.

Which, by the way, he'd seen all the way on the other side of town—and what he was doing there, Sadie Mae wasn't so sure about. But he wasn't going to get it anyway, not before she had her house. That was her number one goal. She'd lived all her life as a renter moving from place to place. Now was the time to fulfill her dream and become a home owner. It was an opportunity to claim her piece of the American pie. Sadie Mae would tread in the snow, work long hours, even some Sundays, enduring the menial labor as a maid—all to conquer her dream.

More times than not, because of car problems, Sadie Mae got to do just what she did today— share a brisk walk with her children as they headed for school. She enjoyed it, and the children never complained or felt embarrassed that she tagged along. As a matter of fact, when it came to her kids and school, Sadie Mae had a lot to be grateful for. They were ambitious and dedicated to pursuing higher education. Sadie Mae believed it was because she kept learning entertaining with good books. She and Rockey did not agree on much, but together they insisted that their children would read after chores and before playtime. The children read fiction books that challenged their imaginations and "how to be successful books" that created an awareness of their futures. Sadie Mae especially understood an idle mind was the devil's workshop.

As a teenager, when her eyes should've been looking at a book, they were watching other things—things that eventually made life hard for her. But she was determined to create an environment conducive to learning in her home. Interestingly, her children shared the same views, so even when Sadie Mae came across as being strict, she received few complaints.

Of the five children, Roc was the only one that played sports. But he always made sure he put academics first. He hit the books, studied hard, rarely missed school and never skipped classes. Learning came easy. Roc was naturally smart, but he went the extra mile because of pride—he wanted to be above the norm and never be mistaken as a dumb jock.

Woodward Avenue was Sadie Mae's first bus stop. It took two long bus rides to get to her employer's house. As she and her children parted ways, Sadie Mae waved goodbye and secretly blew kisses. Alone, she looked up and down the street. There was no sign of a bus in the busy traffic. She checked her watch. If she was lucky, she'd missed the thunderous young crowd.

Unfortunately, in less than five minutes, the isolated area became inundated with over-zealous, giddy teenagers—some with familiar faces and some with weird spiked hair, jheri curls, or visible tattoos—none of which she cared to see.

A young boy and girl, just babies in Sadie Mae's opinion, greeted, locked jaws and engaged in a passionate kiss. There was a slight chill in the air, but the little girl didn't seem to care. She had on a mini dress that exposed most of her body. She could not have been any more than thirteen, Sadie Mae thought, and the same age as her Regina—who, by the way, was still playing jump rope and had just gotten rid of her Barbie dolls. Sadie Mae thanked God for her teenage daughter's innocence.

The couple fondled each other openly with little shame. Sadie Mae twisted her face prudishly and turned away. To be honest, she was not sure if she felt disrespected or if she hated to be reminded of the missing passion in her life.

As she rode the second bus, it was a more peaceful ride. Most of passengers were older and probably going to work as she was. She sat where she always sat, in the back of the bus. It was ironic that even when given a choice, it was where she preferred. From the rear she had a good view of everything.

As the crowd cleared, she observed the regulars doing what they always did. There was the elderly woman up front who crocheted. The colorful afghan that now overflowed from her shopping bag was no bigger than her hand several weeks ago. The young man three rows to her left slept and the businessman one row in front of Sadie Mae read the newspaper.

Occasionally he'd give Sadie Mae advice about purchasing property, but his conversation was always short and direct. She did not know the man's profession, but his tailored suit and wingtip shoes suggested he was a lawyer or a stockbroker. And each day before he'd disappear in the shadows of tall buildings and the hustle and bustle of downtown, he'd grab his briefcase and coat, and then turn to hand Sadie Mae the real estate portion of his paper.

"Miss, happy hunting," he would say briefly before he left. And although he was a man of few words, his soft eyes always greeted her with a friendly silent hello.

As the buildings became land, and the land became houses, Sadie Mae nestled into her seat and gazed out of the window at all the beautiful homes. She rested the paper in her lap. Later it would be a resourceful tool for information, but for now, the outside view was too riveting to miss. Although it was the same charming community she'd seen the sun rise and set upon many times, it was always like the first.

She looked out at the endless rows of lovely homes. There were colonials that appeared as big as the White House, and cape cods that resembled castles. Even the ranch style homes seemed to stretch for miles. Funny, most of the ranches reminded her of the character J.R. from the television series, *Dallas.*

Sadie Mae also appreciated how the meticulous landscape captured the colors of each season. It was autumn and the mums were in full bloom. Hundreds of multi-colored leaves danced about, waltzing with the breeze. Soaking it all in, Sadie Mae marveled at the perfection of God. It was the brush strokes from His magnificent artistry that painted the beautiful earth-toned scenery.

What a lovely view, Sadie Mae thought as she continued to check out all the homes. She saw the huge chandeliers that hung from the open windows and imagined that the foyers were spacious with marble floors just like the Smith's residence where she worked. In fact, their breath-taking vestibule was larger than Sadie Mae's living room.

When she felt the bus halt, she knew it was the last stop—her stop, Rochester road. The sign "Welcome to Clarkston Courts" was in the middle of a flower bed. Just behind it, there was a small pond bordered by limestone with a sparkling fountain as its centerpiece. As Sadie Mae exited the bus, she looked at her watch. She was right on schedule. Mrs. Smith did not tolerate tardiness. And although she was not running late, she took long strides. Her employer's house was less than a block away.

When she approached the home, she heard an explosive sound of gunfire followed by sirens which seemed to come from inside. The noise made Sadie Mae stop dead in her tracks. Then gingerly, she walked toward the servant's entrance. The closer she got, the siren became ear-piercing. It was a common sound that echoed day and night in *her* neighborhood, but this was Clarkston Court, a quiet suburban tree-lined community. Then suddenly the foreign sound was shushed by the familiar voice of Mrs. Smith.

"My goodness, Bill, the neighbors are going to think you're trying to wake up the dead with that television so loud!" Mrs. Smith said as she turned the volume down to a whisper.

When Sadie Mae entered the house, she greeted Mrs. Smith with a warm smile. In a habitual manner, Mrs. Smith sluggishly responded to Sadie Mae as she hung up her coat. As usual, in that same worn-out tone she made very few good-natured remarks and hardly any eye contact as she fussed over her husband.

The puffy bags that drooped from Mrs. Smith's eyes could not be hidden with make up; although it was clear she'd tried to do so. Perhaps, Sadie Mae thought, she's had another rough night with Mr. Smith. His condition was worsening. Three years ago when Sadie Mae was hired, Mr. Smith was in the beginning stages of Alzheimer's. His signs of dementia were forgetting his car keys in the car, repeating himself four or five times, and forgetting names, faces, and reasons for doing things. And though his level of intellectual reasoning was fair at best, there was no need to disclose his illness. But soon, his strange behavior and disappearing acts forced Mrs. Smith to inform her staff of what was going on.

From the many photographs that filled the house, Sadie Mae could see that Mr. Smith was once a handsome man, and the various awards framed in the room that was once his office suggested that he was also once a powerful businessman. He'd worked his way up from the mailroom to the boardroom acquiring an executive position at a huge marketing firm. In his early days with the company, his aggressive leadership was quickly noticed. He was promoted to supervisor over the finance department before he'd even received a college degree. Once he obtained his Master's, there was nothing to stand in his way. Gradually, he climbed the corporate ladder and he did not stop until he reached the second-highest level as Vice President. But now the pale man with protruding blue veins and thin flyaway hair was only a ghost of his past.

When Mrs. Smith bent down to fasten Mr. Smith in his chair, Sadie Mae noticed nasty bruises on her chest and arm. It was not uncommon that her husband would strike her. Sadie Mae never discussed any of the Smith's personal affairs. The Smith's were her employers, the line was drawn in the sand, and it was made clear that no one should cross it.

It was obvious Mrs. Smith was embarrassed by her husband's illness, and pride kept her in total darkness, fearful that his former colleagues and associates would learn of his condition. Sadie Mae did not understand why her boss associated shame with his sickness, but she wasn't getting paid to understand, only for her duties, which consisted of cleaning, and informing callers that Mr. Smith was unable to talk because he was tied up with business matters.

Sadie Mae could identify with the Smiths' pain, but not their shame. She remembered when her mother was diagnosed with Alzheimer's. She was too busy asking for help to be ashamed. Her mother had to be watched around the clock. At that time, Sadie Mae had a young family that demanded her attention, so she had no choice but to ask people for help. She reached out to everyone for aid: government agencies that offered federal funded programs, state assistant programs, and even churches. If it had not been for the Lord and a few kind-spirited people, Sadie Mae did not know what she would've done. She thanked God everyday how He made Himself visible through the members at her church. Even the many times she thanked them, it never seemed to be enough.

As she continued to dust, Sadie Mae watched Mrs. Smith fuss over her husband. Having been blessed with a humble spirit, she thanked God. However she wished Mrs. Smith possessed the same uninhibited openness. Right then, she prayed, asking that God give Mrs. Smith the willingness to reach out to others.

Roc sat on the bench waiting to see if he'd made the team. More than anything, he wanted to play basketball for Riley High. And who wouldn't? Being on the varsity basket ball team was as close as anyone could come to celebrity status at his high school. And if you were good, like Roc believed he was, it was even better. A chance to be scouted, the publicity, scholarships, and all the cuties you wanted. *Oh yeah...all the girls,* Roc salivated. The thought of girls made Roc's body react in a way he had no control over. Embarrassed, he put his gym bag on his lap. To his surprise, when he moved the bag, it was open and a few of his belongings fell out.

Quickly he picked up the book, "The Scarlet Letter," off the floor before anyone could see it. He'd become fascinated with Nathaniel Hawthorne's writings after he read his short story, "Young Goodman Brown." The story was about youth, purity, and temptation. And lately, having forbidden desires was something Roc could relate to. He looked around. One person in particularly he'd hoped to see was his girlfriend, Sonya. She was the squad cheerleader captain, and he could depend on her cheers to motivate him. As he continued to look around, he spotted her within the huge crowd. The bench was full with quite a lineup of boys waiting to hear their fate.

During the scrimmages, Roc was confident, but not conceited. He'd gotten the coach's attention, but Roc wondered if the coach was impressed or if he'd remembered cutting him from the team last year. Roc remembered that Coach Beard had said he didn't' need a cocky freshman on his court, that what he needed was a team player—not someone to showboat with a lotta mouth. It took Roc a year to change his game. This time, he tried less lip and more trips to the hoop.

When the coach stood up and said he wanted to see some one-on-one, Roc thought it was déjà-vu. But this year he would not fly off like a loose cannon. No fancy footwork either, just skills. Coach Beard scanned the faces, checked his clipboard, and called twenty-nine—Roc's jersey number! Roc reported to the floor and took in a deep breath that filled his nostrils with the aroma of sweaty tee-shirts and gym shoes. The musty smell was thick in the air after hours and hours of practice. Then, before Coach Beard took his seat on the sideline to observe, he called Roc's opponent, number seventeen, to the floor.

During practice Roc had watched number seventeen playing. His game was alright. But the dude really thought he was all that, and in Roc's opinion, he'd just fat-mouthed himself through the competition.

On the court, before the whistle blew, the guy tried to show off. He did some fly moves—some Magic Johnson, Dr. J stuff. And then he started bragging, but Roc was not intimidated. *The win's a given*, he thought.

"Man, did you come to talk or play?" Roc said.

"Time will tell, blood," the dude said twirling the ball on his fingertip.

Roc could see the brother had game, but still, he was not threatened by him.

Finally when the referee threw the ball in the air, Roc leaped from the floor and stretched his long arms to gain possession. With finesse, he dribbled the ball down the court for an easy two-point lay-up. Roc said a triumphant, "Yes!" to himself. Then he heard Sonya scream from the stands, "Go Roc! Go Roc! That's the way you do it!" Roc did not look, but it sounded like she had the whole cheerleading squad shouting with her, like it was a real game or something. Roc felt confident, but to his surprise the opposition was not the easy win he'd anticipated—twice, the game was tied.

When the score was eighteen up, Roc stood at half court. He went for the game and missed the three point shot and then lost possession. An "Ooooh" came from the crowd. And before Roc could make his next move, he saw a tall brown blur fly in the air and swoop down into the hoop. "Nasty! Nothing but net!" someone shouted.

The slam-dunk put Roc in a do or die situation. He zoomed in and got the ball. Again at half court, he aimed, shot, and said, "Game!" before the ball had even gone through the net. Excited that he'd won, he basked in the cheers.

After waiting for what seemed like hours, Coach Beard stood to announce the final cut. Only fifteen out of fifty made the team. Sweating bullets, Roc was the ninth player to be called. When he heard his name and not a jersey number, it felt good. Recognition. Finally he was on the road to fulfilling his dreams. He was flabbergasted to be a *Riley's Cougar*. As he gathered his things, he saw the coach talking to number seventeen, who did not make the team. Roc imagined the kid was getting the same speech he'd gotten last year. Roc made a mental note to talk to the guy, because from a distance, he could see he was disappointed with his head slumped down. But when Sonya came up and planted a wet kiss on his lips, the thought flew out the window. She had his undivided attention, and he never even noticed when the guy left.

"Congratulations!" Sonya said. "This year I'll be saying all my cheers just for you."

Roc smiled, turning her around to check out her cheerleading outfit. *Her cute little shape is fitting it,* he thought, grinning with approval. Then he pulled her close and they embraced.

"Come on, I'll walk you home," he said.

As they walked home, Roc thought of the conversation he'd had with his boys. They'd talked about what they always talked about. His boys bragged about how all their girlfriends were giving it up. At fifteen, he thought he and Sonya had to be the only virgins alive.

"Hey, when can you sneak me in your room again?" he said as he bent down to kiss her forehead.

"Never," she pushed him away. "The last time...things went too far and you know I'm not ready for that."

"Sonya, I've known you since we were nine years old. When are we going be ready? You know we're going to get married when we get grown."

"You know, sometimes you're just too sure of yourself. Who says I want to marry you, anyway?" She paused. "Roc, I told you...I'm not the one. Now, if you want to go all the way, then you need to find you a new girl."

Roc looked at Sonya. He'd heard all this before. First,

she'd say good girls waited. Then, she'd say fast girls got pregnant. At times, Roc felt like Sonya thought she knew it all. Still he was infatuated with her. He could never forget the first time she kissed him and stole his heart. It was a sunny day. A gang of kids gathered behind the church to play hide-and-seek. When it was his turn to be sought out, he purposely made himself visible so he could be caught by Sonya. "Gotcha!" she said with pride. Then she gave him a peck on the cheek.

Roc didn't expect a kiss, but he was glad to get it. The childish affection was more than enough back then. But now, he was maturing and his needs went deeper than puppy love. He needed some real love. However, Sonya was a good girl and he respected that. But, if she was not going to put out, maybe it was time to find someone who would.

"A new girlfriend, huh?" Roc replied. "Remember, those words came out of your mouth not mine. I agree. It's time to move on. I'm tired of this kiddy girlfriend and boyfriend relationship. One minute you say yes and the next minute you say no. You're a tease! I got needs! So what I need to do is find somebody who can handle that. It's time for me to deal with a real woman and not a little girl!" he said, unleashing his built-up frustration. The words were blurting out so forcefully and quickly that he didn't have time to think. When he realized what he'd said, it was too late. He couldn't take it back.

Immediately, Roc could see the hurt on Sonya's face. She looked at him—hard and long. Her cold stare pierced his heart. At once her big baby doll eyes welled up with tears as she turned and ran into her house.

Roc looked at the closing door and then the darkening sky. It was getting late. It didn't matter to his parents if it was winter or summer. When the streetlights came on, he had to be in the house. Roc was not sure what he should do—go after Sonya and apologize, or rush home. His parents were strict, especially his father. It did not take much to make him angry.

Roc knew that if he was late he'd be punished, and that could interfere with after-school basketball practice. That could jeopardize his potential starting status. In an instant, the answer to stay or leave became apparent when Roc quickly took off and left Sonya's fluffy red and white pom-poms lying at her doorstep. With supernatural speed, he stretched his long legs and ran down the street. His lanky shadow cascaded in the dim streetlights which were glowing brighter and brighter.

Luckily by nightfall, he was standing at the door when his mother opened it.

Midway through the season, Roc was excelling on the basketball court. He virtually never missed. His jump shots, free throws, and his speed made him the coach's start player and the crowd's favorite. This stardom, along with his good looks and personality, made it easy to find a replacement for Sonya. Every week it was a different girl on his arm. But the one that really made him feel important was Sherri. She was a fair skinned sister—a sexy senior, with a cute face and a grown-up shape. Sherri had taken Roc under her wings as if he was her prized possession. She also had a lot of attitude, and a reputation. But the fact that she was known to be easy did not bother Roc.

On their first date, at the drive-in, Sherri made it very clear in the back seat of her daddy's station wagon how she got her reputation. She was the first real girl Roc had ever seen nude, and her body was more beautiful than those he'd seen in racy magazines.

When Sherri found out she was his first, she handled him with kid gloves. And she was nothing like Sonya...Sherri never said no! But the fling with her was brief. Aside from her being a real air-head, it started to trouble Roc that she'd been with most of the boys in school. Rumor had it, even some teachers.

Easy come, easy go, Roc thought as the chase was on to find someone new. But he made it his business to avoid Sonya when he was with other girls. Even though they were not together, he felt uncomfortable. One day, after a big victory game with their rival, Roc saw Sonya at her locker. He admired her from a distance. She was still the prettiest girl he'd known, and for a moment, he wished they were together again. Maybe, if he could just say hello and they could talk, it would be nice. He missed her friendship. Truthfully, he hadn't had any fun with another girl or decent conversation since they'd split. When Roc got up the nerve, he walked toward Sonya. As he got closer, he tried to think of an opening line.

Preferably something funny enough to make her laugh, and smooth enough to make her forget he'd made her cry.

When he got within earshot of Sonya, Roc realized she was already laughing. In fact, she was hysterical. Then, he saw she was talking to another guy. He couldn't believe it! He knew he didn't have a right to be jealous, but he was hurt.

After that shocking moment, he could not eat or sleep, and he could barely breathe. His pain even interfered with his performance—both on the court and in the classroom. The only thing he could do without effort was think of Sonya. He desperately wanted her back. He called her home several times, but she refused his calls. In school, she treated him as if he was invisible. And just when he thought things could not get worse, Sherri came to his locker after school one day and, in tears, claimed she was having his baby.

Chapter Four

Choices

When the doorbell rang after ten o'clock on a school night, Sadie Mae knew there was a problem. Dressed for bed, she walked to the window, leaned against the worn out blue sofa, and parted the curtains. It was a full moon, and in the lucid brightness, she was startled to see a young girl standing in the dark, alone, as if no one cared. Quickly, Sadie Mae swung open the door. As she turned on the porch light, she also saw an older couple—a stout black woman and a plump round bald white man. The three stood on the porch in grim silence surrounded by clutter, but Sadie Mae had no thought to apologize for her children's toys. She felt as if time was standing still as she tried to analyze the situation. The strangers had a sense of anger and urgency, and she wondered what brought them to her doorstep at that hour. Feeling her heart palpitate, Sadie Mae began to feel nauseous.

Roc, whose curiosity had beckoned him from the

kitchen, felt a sense of foreboding that made him shiver with fear when he saw it was Sherri and her parents. His clammy hands tightly gripped the glass he held as he tried not to drop it. But there was no hope to regain the strength lost in his knees. Shaking, he yielded to the wall for total support.

"Is this the boy?" the disgruntled man said stridently, making eye contact with Roc through the screen.

Sherri held her head down. She looked like a mess. Her signature well kept coiffure—the short and sassy cut that most girls envied, was disheveled. Her eyes were puffy, and it was the first time Roc had ever seen her dressed so sloppy.

"Did you hear me?" the man said.

"Sherri, answer your father," the woman said.

In the dark, Sadie Mae could see the girl had been crying and the man had a tight grip on her arm.

"I'm sorry, Miss. We hate to bother you so late, but our daughter is pregnant, and she says that your son is the father. And as parents, I think we need to talk," the woman said.

Pregnant? Sadie Mae thought. Instantly, her eyes welled up. The color vanished from her auburn cheeks, and she felt a stabbing sensation—a dagger deep in the depths of her heart, as the tears streamed down her face like a waterfall.

At will, her voice could not speak. The lump in her throat had cut off the necessary air supply. She swallowed hard; hoping even a portion of her stability could be summoned. She had to tell these intruders, these liars, to leave her home at once. It was a mistake; her son was a good boy. He was a straight A student. He went to church every Sunday—he was on the usher board and even sang in the choir, for goodness sake.

"Come in," she could not believe she heard Rockey say, after he put down the can of beer he'd almost choked on. And then he turned off the television. The only ebullient sound that filled the room, an intense game between the Knicks and Lakers, was now silenced.

She was still in shock—Rockey had calmly allowed these people into their home and offered them a seat. She wondered what was wrong with him. She'd seen him curse out people for less offensive acts than accusing their son of taking advantage of a girl, who'd looked to be no more than thirteen or fourteen. These people did not deserve his kindness.

Rockey looked to be afraid, but in Sadie Mae's opinion, it was too late to show concern. Over the years, he'd been totally apathetic in raising the children. From the beginning, he was not there for the small victories: the first time they'd tied their shoes, rode a bike, and memorized the alphabet or when they'd learned to count from one to one-hundred. He was always too exhausted from work or running the street to get involved in their lives. Even with his three sons, he'd shied away athletically. So it was Sadie Mae who first showed the boys how to throw a football, catch a baseball, and how to dribble a basketball. Now practically grown, his children were strangers. Rockey had only been a provider, and now Sadie Mae resented him standing with her as a parent. She loved him, but he did not have the invested emotion to handle this quandary.

"Are you sure it was my son that did this to your daughter?" Rockey asked.

Of course it was not Roc, Sadie Mae thought. “I think we have heard enough from these people,” she said. “It’s time we heard from Roc. He should know if he has slept with this girl or not.”

She walked over to Roc, looked up, and stared at him right in his eyes. She searched for traces of betrayal, a sign of disobedience, and there was none. But he had changed. Not only was he taller, he had grown facial hair, something that had never caught her eye until now. The contour of his face was thinner. He’d lost his cuteness, and he was strikingly handsome. Right before her eyes, her fifteen-year-old baby had become a young man. But still, she was not convinced he could father a child.

“Rockwell James, Jr.,” she paused. “Are you having sex?”

When Roc did not respond, her heart began to race.

“I’m going to ask you one more time. Are you...”

“Mama, I’m not the only one she’s slept with.”

It took a second for his response to formulate, and before Sadie Mae knew it, she had grabbed Roc’s neck and pulled him to her. “What did you say?”

“Mama...I know it was wrong, but I had all these feelings inside of me, that I couldn’t control. And besides, Sherri told me if she went to the bathroom after it was over, she couldn’t get pregnant,” Roc said, breaking free from his mother, bumping into the recliner as he quickly retreated to the other side of the room.

“She said what? And you’re telling me you believed

that? Get out of my sight!"

"Mama...please don't be mad. I didn't mean to get in any trouble...all my friends were doing it. Mama...I didn't mean to hurt you...I'm so sorry. Sherri was a senior and she promised to show me a good time."

"A senior? How old is she?" Rockey said

"I'll be eighteen in just a few days." Sherri said. Up until that point she'd been renascent and allowed her parents to do all the talking.

"Did you know my son was only fifteen?" Rockey said.

Sherri shamefully resumed her head-bowed position.

"Oh God...Lord, what has my son gotten himself into? She's a grown woman." And before Sadie Mae knew it, she was hysterical. She paced the floor mumbling, incomprehensible. The dagger in her heart had returned, stronger. She sat down, stood up, and then repeated the same act twice before she finally sat down for good. She took in a deep breath and exhaled, hoping the fresh oxygen would relax her. She held her chest. It was filled with excruciating pain. She massaged it until the hurting eased up. The relief felt good, and soon the labored breathing subsided.

After the anger, she grieved for Roc's lost innocence. *How did this happen?* she wondered. Her children were not supposed to make the same mistakes she'd made. She had taught them better. She had taken the necessary precautions: church, strict boundaries, and open communication, and still it was not good enough. Life had no guarantees.

"Okay Sadie Mae, enough of the theatrics. We still

don't know if the baby belongs to Roc, so before you have a heart attack, let's get that straight," Rockey said.

"It's not mine!" Roc said.

"And how can you be so sure of that young man?" Sherri's mother demanded.

"Because, Sherri has slept around with everybody, even some teachers," Roc said.

"You don't know that for sure! That's just cheap gossip from jealous people. But the bottom line is, true, I'm no virgin, but I know this is your baby, Roc...I'm sure." Sherri felt her stomach. "It is March and I have not been with anyone since we stopped dating in November. I'm four months."

"Four months, already?! I knew it was just a matter of time. Now this stupid girl has gotten herself knocked up like a fool. And if we got any sense, we will do something before it is too late," Sherri's father said loudly and angrily.

"George, please," his wife said.

"Well...let's cut the bull. The reason we're here is...I know a good doctor on the east side who can take care of this. But the cost is too steep for our budget right now. So we figure, you being the boy's parents, we can split the expense," the man said.

"No Daddy, please!" Sherri cried out. "I can feel it moving inside of me! Please don't make me kill my baby!"

After ten minutes, the curious, clamoring voices that searched for answers and solutions began to fade into deafening silence. Then finally, a decision was made. Tonight, Sadie Mae would pay her portion by check, and tomorrow

Sherri would go to the clinic. And in a matter of minutes, the time of the procedure, the whole ordeal would be behind them.

Even after the disturbing late visit was over, Sadie Mae still heard the weak cry of the young girl echo in her mind, pleading for her child's life. But the adults had made a decision. At seventeen, how could she know what was best? Sadie Mae vehemently objected the notion to terminate a life. But her voice was overruled by Rockey, the girl's parents, and her fifteen-year-old son who cried and said he did not want to be a father. It was yet another unexpected expense that sliced away at Sadie Mae's dream.

By the time midnight came, the house was calm, but Roc's life was anything but peaceful. He sat on the end of the couch, heavy in thought. He deeply regretted getting involved with Sherri, and he promised himself never to get caught up in a situation like that again. He had fun being with Sherri, and the other girls, but it was never worth losing his freedom, and most of all, jeopardizing his dreams of college, becoming a basketball legend, and being with Sonya.

When Rockey came into the kitchen to get a beer, something he'd hope would relax him, he saw Roc with his head hung down and assumed he was still crying.

"Boy, stop that crying. You were man enough to make a child, now be man enough to accept the consequences," he said with the refrigerator door open. "This time you were lucky. Next time you might not be. You better think about what you're doing...the last thing you want to be is married and stuck."

Rockey had no idea Sadie Mae was behind him, but she was too mired in the madness of everything to be offended by his view of marriage. She just looked at him toss back a gulp of beer, and when he had disappeared, she looked at Roc. She wanted to find the compassion to console him, but she was drained. Perhaps tomorrow she would be stronger to deal with it all...

The restless night haunted Sadie Mae all through the next day. At work, she fought to stay awake between the laundry and ironing. During the noon hour, her usual time of prayer, she found the faith to pray for forgiveness. She pleaded with God to hush the girl's cry that still echoed in her head. Earlier, before she left home, she gave strict orders to Roc to contact her if something went wrong. When her workday ended and there was no contact, she assumed the abortion had been successful.

Sadie Mae had two long bus rides to think about that young girl and the decision that was forced on her. She knew what it was like to be young, pregnant, and afraid. She felt tears roll down her face in the chilled March wind. What saddened her most was she had taken part in destroying her own grandchild.

Finally, when she arrived home, the first thing she noticed was the porch was cleaned and organized. The children's bikes were standing upright in the corner; the toys were put away in the toy-box. And finally, the wooden floor had been swept down. She'd constantly complained about everyone tracking salt into the house, but now the crystal-like chips were gone.

When she went inside the house, it too was meticulous. And then when she saw Roc cleaning his room, she had to ask what was going on.

"I skipped basketball practice," he said. "I knew it was time to do some early spring cleaning."

"Have you heard from Sherri or her parents?" Sadie Mae asked.

"No," he said, resuming his cleaning.

All the children, except for Regina, her oldest girl who was cooking, participated with the cleaning. Her children doing their chores without being asked, Sadie Mae thought, was definitely strange. But this was no ordinary day.

And just when Sadie Mae had doubts that the day held any certainties, she saw her youngest, Joey and Chloe, galloping through the house, leaving destruction in their paths. She waited patiently to hear the others complain of their horseplay, which came after a few seconds.

"Chloe and Joey stop playing around before someone gets hurt!" Regina shouted from the kitchen.

And then Sadie Mae heard the horror in Roc's voice as he said into the phone receiver, "What do you mean...Sherri is missing?"

Chapter Five

What the Future Holds

1994

Sherri had been missing for nearly three years, and still the rumors were disseminating on her whereabouts. A cancelled check was the only paper trail to justify the brow-raising anecdotes of her midnight escape across the state line. Some said she fled with her lover, a teacher and married man, to avoid the inevitable scandal of her pregnancy. While some disagreed and said there was no romantic get-away and it was just happenstance, the teacher quit soon after Sherri disappeared. Some thought she really ran to Hollywood, where she would abort her baby and then become a porn star. Then finally, it was said that she ran to protect her lover's honor.

When the news hit Bethel Assembly, Sadie Mae never got involved with the gossip, even when her son's name came up. As far as she was concerned, Sherri had found a safe haven for her unborn child, and it did not matter what people said. A life was spared.

One day, about six months after Sherri was gone, Sadie Mae saw the girl's mother. The stout woman sat alone on a park bench outside the post office. She appeared to be in high spirits reading a letter. And then the woman held what looked to be a photograph to her chest and chuckled. The two had not spoken since the night of Sherri's disappearance, and Sadie Mae wanted to know if there'd been any news. As Sadie Mae drew near the bench, her view became obstructed by the sudden presence of a man—Sherri's father.

Sadie Mae stepped back. The man did not look approachable. His demeanor had not changed since the last time they'd met. He showed disinterest in his wife's feelings, as he displayed no concern in the letter she held, but instead flew his hands back and forth angrily. His lips moved in the same manner. In a fury, he snatched the paper, tore it into pieces, turned, and walked away. The woman bent down to salvage what the wind had not blown away. And when a fragmented image blew over to Sadie Mae's feet, she didn't hesitate to pick it up. Although it was hard to discern, it appeared to be a photo of Sherri holding something. This explained the man's anger.

Rumor was Sherri and her father couldn't get along. He'd even pressed theft charges on her the night she'd escaped in his car with his money.

Senior year was a breeze for Roc. It was no surprise

when he was appointed as valedictorian for the class of '94.

Even through the incident with Sherri, during his sophomore year when he was bombarded with a mélange of emotions, he'd maintained a 4.0 average. The baby scare did not hinder him, but engendered in him a stronger sense of responsibility and conviction as he left his callow days behind.

Roc scored high on his SATs, and the college offers poured in to recruit him. When he chose Michigan State, for athletic reasons, it was a disappointment to Sadie Mae. She'd hoped he'd follow in his siblings' footsteps and attend a strong black institution like Morehouse in Atlanta with Raymond, or Prairie View A&M in Houston with Regina. But he did not want to pursue medicine or law. He'd dreamed of going pro in basketball, and he had a better chance to be scouted as a key player for the Spartans. The university had more media coverage. Besides, he would be riding on a full scholarship, *and* it was the college Sonya had chosen. They'd gotten back together and they were inseparable.

On senior prom night, Roc pulled up to Sonya's house in a leased red Corvette. He was the third to receive such a gift for graduation weekend. Sonya's house was lit up, and there were a few strange cars in the driveway. When Roc rung the doorbell there was a loud chime, and then an unfamiliar woman opened the door. "You must be Roc, Sonya's date," she said. "I'm Sonya's aunt. Just call me Aunt Lucy."

Roc smiled, and instantly three flashes exploded in his face. After he'd adjusted his sight, from the corner of his eye, he saw a pudgy girl with a camera in her hand run down the hall.

"I got a picture of him! He is cute Sonya!" the girl said.

"And that's Mary, my twelve year old daughter," Aunt Lucy said. "I hope we're not making you nervous. Sonya's parents just invited some of us over to be a part of this big night."

"No madam, I'm not nervous," Roc said, walking along side her.

The reception Roc received from Sonya's family was gregarious. He was escorted back to the living room where Sonya's father was watching the evening news. Mr. Jones was a quiet man with a calm spirit. His daughter showered him with adulation and Roc had always respected him. Mr. and Mrs. Jones had something special that worked. Sonya said that they made it a habit to read the Bible together daily. They had a successful marriage—even the house had an air of peace and love. Roc liked that.

Mr. Jones rose up to shake hands. "Hello young man," he said. "You look nice in that tuxedo."

"Thank you, sir," Roc replied.

"I hope you children have a nice time tonight. Sonya has been planning for this night for weeks."

"I've been excited about it myself, Mr. Jones."

Mr. Jones looked at Roc, and then leaned over to say something, but he was interrupted by loud clapping, cheers and snapshots as Sonya entered the room. She was radiant in her shoulder bearing ice-blue gown. As she walked toward Roc, he was breathless. The silk caressed her body like a glove and the mystery of what was beneath aroused Roc.

"Sweetheart, isn't our daughter beautiful?" Mrs. Jones said.

Mr. Jones went over and kissed his wife, then his daughter, and then he looked at Roc.

"Son, I trust you to take care of my daughter tonight. She's a good girl," he paused, "and I want to keep it like that."

And while the last statement made Roc feel uneasy about having certain thoughts of Sonya, it did not make them go away. He just cleared his throat and said, "Yes sir. You can trust me."

With the exception of Sonya's pledge to give up her virginity, prom night was mildly uneventful. After the dance, Roc and Sonya cruised around the city looking for the perfect place to consummate the promise. Roc was excited but concerned that he was doing all the talking. He gave Sonya compliments, even tried small talk, but she did not open up. She just stared out the window. And while his efforts to vie for her attention failed, it did not provoke his temper. He knew she was nervous. Soon Sonya's curiosity was piqued by Roc's attention toward her. Instinctively, they looked at each other and smiled.

"Are you nervous?" Roc asked.

"No, I'm scared!"

Roc pulled over, turned down the soft music, leaned across the console and kissed Sonya.

"You think I'm going to hurt you?"

Sonya shook her head, no.

"But...what about marriage, Roc? We don't talk about that anymore."

"Sonya, we're too young for that. We will get married, but I don't think we should rush it—maybe after college, when we're more mature and financially secure to start a family."

"But you think we're old enough to have sex and handle all the emotions that come with it." She paused. "Roc, we can get married and live on campus as husband and wife. Who says we have to start a family? My parents married young and they're still in love. I just think sex without security is risky."

Roc looked at Sonya. Her unrealistic ideas of marriage spooked him. Now, he wasn't excited to be intimate anymore. Strange, he thought of his father's haunting advice. The last thing in the world he ever wanted was to be tied down at a young age. He did not want to make the same mistake his parents made. It was important to him to always love Sonya, and he wondered if Rockey had ever felt that way about his mother. It was hard to tell. There was always heated tension between them.

Roc knew he could not explain his fears of marriage to Sonya. She would not understand, coming from such a stable environment. At this point, he was prepared to take her home, but then Sonya apologized for her jitters and insisted that they go through with the plan.

Excitedly, they drove around in search of the right hotel. Finally, they found it—a well kept low budget hotel situated on a busy road across from a huge park. The stars glistened upon the body of water that surrounded the park. It was a romantic night. As Roc and Sonya entered the hotel, holding each other's hand, they felt grown. Roc was familiar with hotels. He'd gone as a child when his mother wanted to splurge, but he'd never been to one before with a girl.

As Roc approached the front desk to ask about the rates, Sonya's nerves caused her to bow her head and stand behind him. The desk clerk glanced at Roc, then at Sonya.

Uneasy, not knowing what to say, Roc turned around to put his arm around Sonya and pulls her closer. It was then that he noticed another couple in the lobby. There, like a deer in headlights, stood his father with room keys in his hand and a woman—not his mother—on his arm. The woman was quite young and her curvy body was in no way concealed by her black racy dress—one no decent woman would wear in public. Her seductive walk told Roc instantly that she was the reason for many of his mother's tears.

Infuriated, Roc could feel the hairs on the back of his neck rise as he met his father's eyes. Gasping for breath, with his fist clenched, he demanded to know who his father was with, but Rockey did not respond.

"Who is this?" Roc asked again, louder.

"Who are you yelling at?" his father responded. "Oh you're a man, now. Talking to me like that...all swollen up, like you're ready to fight. Boy...let that air out of your lungs—this is just a good friend of mine, from out of town, and I was just walking her to her room."

"Out of town, Rockey, what are you talking about? Who is this?" the woman said.

"I'm his son!" Roc shouted.

"Your son?" the woman demanded heatedly, looking both men up and down. The resemblance was obvious.

"Kelly, I'll take care of this. Go to the room. I'll explain everything when I get there," Rockey said.

"You won't be explaining anything to me—you liar! You said you didn't have any children. I told you, Rockey, I don't need any drama in my life," she glared. "So don't call my house again, don't send me flowers, don't try to find me at the club—just leave me alone!" And with that, she twisted away.

"Kelly! Kelly! Woman come back here!" Rockey yelled.

The woman threw up a hand as she strutted away. Without looking back, she disappeared down the hallway.

"I'll be," Rockey said, exasperated. Then he looked at Roc. "Now, I suppose you're going to run home and tell your mama what you think you saw and get her all upset for nothing. The woman was just a friend of mine. No big deal!"

"No big deal? You're cheating on my mother and it's no big deal!? Nothing that matters to us has ever been a big deal to you," Roc said with fire in his eyes. "So, is this what it's all about? Is this why you got all dressed up? You leave my mother alone, and ride your women around in the car she scraped and saved for? And after you've wined and dined them, you bring them here? I will never understand what my mother sees in you! I hate you!"

"Okay...boy, you said enough. I think it's time for you to be quiet and go somewhere and cool off,' Rockey said, gesturing for his son to leave.

But the rage inside Roc had escalated, and he was not about to cool off. Instead, he drew back with all his anger and might, and slammed his fist into his father's face. The blow was so fierce that Rockey nearly lost his balance, and almost fell to the floor. Rockey quickly composed himself, shook it off, and then he collared his son. And when he did that, Roc's anger became uncontrollable. It was the spark that ignited a lifelong battle. Instantly, a flurry of punches began. The two tall men trampled over furniture, knocking over everything that wasn't nailed down. The intense brawl did not stop until Sonya and the desk clerk broke them free.

Roc's face was drenched in blood; his youthful body was no match for his father's street skills and quick hands.

"Boy, don't you ever think you're man enough to take me on. If this ever happens again, I'll seriously hurt you!" Rockey shouted. He had his face shoved so close to Roc's that their noses almost touched. "You want to be a man? Go ahead, be one! Stop being a mama's boy and get out from under my roof!"

Now at a distance, Roc studied his father—his moves, his behavior, his countenance—and he loathed him. He watched him bend down and pick up his straw hat, straighten out the brim, and put it back on his head. And in a smooth manner, he walked over to the desk clerk, laid money on the counter and said, "This should take care of the damages." Then he left. Never once did he look back at his son, but it didn't matter. Roc never wanted to lay eyes on his father again.

Chapter Six

Passion

Rockey came in after midnight. He crept quietly through the hall and gently opened the bedroom door. He woke Sadie Mae with soft tender kisses and stroked her back until her eyes were completely open. She stared into her husband's face. In the dim moonlight, he looked burdensome. His eyes were drained and hollow. The muscles in his face were tensed and tight. Again, Rockey kissed her, over and over, and she felt him relax. They shared the kind of kisses she thought he'd forgotten about—the passionate kind they exchanged when their love was young and forbidden.

Completely enveloped in his arms, Sadie Mae escaped to a time when love was exciting and desirable—she longed to stay there. Mired in his passion, she felt safe and secure, and expressions of love came naturally. "I love you. I will always love you no matter what," she whispered in his ear. His warm breath rushing down her neck was intoxicating. This was the Rockey she loved: passionate, warm, and unselfish.

Chapter Seven

About last night

Sadie Mae watched the sunlight beam down on the dry pavement. Although it was hot and sticky, she took tiny steps to reach the Smith's house. It was a cool retreat, but she was in no hurry for the nine-hour day to begin.

A stroll was what she needed. Some time to sort out her thoughts. Last night kept replaying in her mind. What had come over Rockey? He had not been that romantic in a long time, not since that scarlet flame was still burning in their hearts as inseparable teenagers, enticing them to run away and get married when they were too young and impetuous to consider the consequences. Often, Sadie Mae grieved the lost love. That's why last night meant so much.

This morning when Sadie Mae walked into the Smith's, she was glowing. As usual, Sadie Mae took a quick inventory. Her employer's residence was dark, cold, and lifeless. It reminded her of a museum filled with antiquated objects on display to be shown, but not touched. Everything in Sadie Mae wanted to draw back the thick curtains and let the sunlight pour in, but she feared her boss would disapprove.

As far as bosses went, Mrs. Smith was alright. Her fastidious nature was bothersome, but not unbearable. She recognized her workers' birthdays, gave paid vacations, and awarded Christmas bonuses. When she had a complaint, she never lashed out or spoke insensitively. But she was not personable. Her unfriendly character was intimidating to most, but not to Sadie Mae.

When she entered the kitchen, Sadie Mae's hollow footsteps against the ceramic tile were not heard by Mrs. Smith as she spoke adamantly on the phone. Although the conversation she overheard was low, Sadie Mae detected the sadness in her employer's voice. Mrs. Smith's refusal to an apparent offer to go shopping with an old friend was a dead giveaway to her underlying pain. Her weak excuses were no cover-up. Mrs. Smith hardly left the house and Sadie Mae felt sorry for her.

Hanging up the phone, Mrs. Smith turned around. "Good morning Sadie Mae," she said softly as she opened the blinds. She stared outside. "It's beautiful out. Perhaps you can serve me and my husband breakfast on the patio. Some morning sunshine will do us both some good. June is such a beautiful month."

"I'm sorry Mrs. Smith, but I overheard your conversation, and I would be more than happy to care for your husband while you step out for awhile. You see, I've had experience with a person affected with dementia before. My mother suffered with it before she passed."

"I appreciate the offer, but my husband is a hand full, and I would not be comfortable leaving him in anyone's care."

"I understand, but if you change your mind, I'm here."

"How long ago did your mother pass?"

"Over ten years ago. She was involved in an auto accident."

"I'm sorry to hear that. Now if you will excuse me—"

An hour or so later, when the phone rang again, it was Mrs. Smith's friend calling back to insist that she get out of the house for a while. Her friend even suggested a nursing facility that could come to the house to care for her husband.

Mrs. Smith did not have many friends. Actually, this "friend" wasn't even really a friend. She was just the wife of Bill's former business associate. The news of her husband's illness had surfaced and he'd abdicated his position with the company. The luncheon engagement was nothing more than a sympathy date, but Mrs. Smith did not care. The thought of getting out sounded more and more irresistible. With much thought, she reconsidered the offer from the woman and then reluctantly asked Sadie Mae to watch over Mr. Smith.

After Mrs. Smith left, her husband continued to nap for at least an hour before Sadie Mae heard his bell ringing. Sadie Mae prepared Mr. Smith his lunch. As she fed him, he looked in her eyes and studied her before he asked for his wife.

It was a good day and Mr. Smith carried on a halfway descent conversation with Sadie Mae. They talked about children, work, and finally Sadie Mae talked about their beautiful home.

"I love this home, I always have," Mr. Smith said. "One of these days Betty and I will move a few miles down the road into one those big estates in Clarkston Court. Now those are some beautiful homes."

Sadie Mae understood. In Mr. Smith's condition, he often spoke this way. The Smiths were already living in Clarkston Court and they owned a beautiful home in the area. As he began to ramble, Mrs. Smith came in. She'd only been gone two hours and she fussed over Mr. Smith as if she'd taken a week's vacation. She dropped her bags, wiped his face and straightened him up in his wheelchair.

"Thank you so much, Sadie Mae. I really needed to get away, but I must admit I felt guilty the entire time."

"Your husband didn't give me any trouble."

"Betty, tell this gal we do not live in Clarkston Court. We live in Palmer Hills. She won't listen to me."

"Honey, we moved from Palmer Hills years ago. Don't you remember?"

"Now you're talking just as crazy as her. Take me to my room," Mr. Smith said angrily.

Later on after her husband was resting peacefully, Mrs. Smith took a break. She sat down at the kitchen table, routinely running her finger across the shining marble top, inspecting it for dust before she relaxed. Then she invited

Sadie Mae to join her. It was apparent the spotless house did not need any more attention.

It was late afternoon, much too late for coffee, but Mrs. Smith anxiously got up from the table and made a fresh pot anyway. If the caffeine didn't keep her up, her husband probably would.

After a few sips of black coffee, she gave Sadie Mae some history about the lovely home in Palmer Hills. It was their first home after many flats and apartments. The suburban dream house was affirmation of the financial security Mr. Smith had worked hard to gain. The quaint hilltop Cape Cod was a short distance from the road, but the trail leading to their doorstep was a lonely one with few visitors, and no children to fill the open fields with laughter and noise. The seclusion became too much for the Smiths, so they decided to move to Clarkston Court where there was evidence of life—active neighbors on both sides with young children and far less trees to obstruct the scenery. In fact, Mrs. Smith said the Palmer Hills house was still in their possession; they just never got around to selling it. By now, there was so much work needed, since the maintenance had been severely neglected, and Mrs. Smith said her plate was too full to think about it. Besides, the hilltop mansion set so far back from the street that no one ever complained.

She doubted if anyone knew if it was empty or not. "Maybe one day we'll finally get around to selling it," Mrs. Smith finally said with a nonchalant look on her face. It was obvious, at that point, she really wasn't concerned about it.

Sadie Mae marveled at the Smiths. *They have two beautiful homes. How blessed they are,* she thought.

When Sadie Mae arrived home, Chloe and Joey, having been in the house all day, begged their mother to let them go play. Just as soon as Sadie Mae began to give them a nod, the two immediately bolted to the park down the street—Joey with his basketball and Chloe on her bike. Sadie Mae didn't even get a chance to thank them for cleaning the house and taking the chicken from the freezer.

With the house empty, Sadie Mae slipped out of her black and white uniform, freshened up, and began to prepare dinner before she sat down to rest. Soon Roc would be home and he would tell her all about last night. She could hardly wait to hear about the prom. She pulled the black cast-iron skillet from the cabinet and placed it on the stove. It would be quicker to deep fry the chicken instead of baking it as she had planned to do earlier. She filled the skillet with grease and turned the burner on high. She chopped fresh vegetables, flicked on another burner to boil water and dumped in a cup of rice before she adjusted the heat. Although she'd worked all day, she enjoyed cooking for her family.

Hours passed and still no Roc. Sadie Mae assumed he was joy riding in the sporty Corvette. But if he did not come home soon, she would try to contact him. She had not heard from him all day, and that was not like him to miss a home cooked meal.

When Rockey came in, Sadie Mae was resting on the couch. She was not sure if the affection he'd shown last night was an isolated incident or not. She waited for his lead.

"Hey baby," Rockey said, giving his wife a juicy kiss and plopping down on the chair next to her.

Sadie Mae wanted to ask about the sudden change, but she feared what would happen. She figured she should just enjoy the moment, so she just said, "Are you hungry?"

Before her husband could answer, she was up and heading for the kitchen just as Roc came in the door. Immediately she saw his face and gasped for breath. His eye was blackened and his lip was swollen. It was obvious he'd been in a fight.

"Roc! What happened to you?"

"Nothing...Mama...it's nothing."

"Boy...what do you mean nothing? I'm locking at your face!"

It took a few minutes for Roc to calm his mother down, but finally she understood when he expressed the fight was necessary to defend Sonya's honor. He hated to lie, but he watched his father's actions as he spoke—the truth would've been explosive. Soon Rockey worked his way to the kitchen. To vie for his wife's attention, he affectionately patted her on the behind. When Sadie Mae gave a bashful grin, Roc left the room.

"Roc, honey, are you hungry?" Sadie Mae called, still smiling. When she got no answer, she headed for Roc's room.

Rockey yanked her back, "You need to stop babying that boy. He is too grown for all that. If he's hungry, he knows how to come and eat."

"I think you need to stop being so hard on him."

"Mama," Roc said from the back room, "thank you for

speaking up for me, but I don't need you to. He's right. I'm a man now and it's time I move out on my own," Roc said. His voice was strong and confident as he walked into the kitchen, holding a suitcase.

"Roc, what are you talking about?" Sadie Mae sensed something was wrong. "In September you're going to college. Until then, you're not going anywhere."

"Mama, I'm leaving tonight."

It was not until Sadie Mae noticed the suitcase in Roc's hand that she took him seriously. She demanded an explanation, but Roc's only response was to say, "It's time." Sadie Mae wanted to protest, but the look in Roc's eyes made her feel defenseless. Still, she tried to convince him to stay. When she got nowhere with him, she tried to make her husband talk some sense into his son, but Rockey was silent.

Sadie Mae was angered by his nonchalant attitude, but now was not the time to focus on him. Her mind was on her son. She begged and pleaded with him to stay. But even her rare display of tears did not make an impact. Sadie Mae knew there was something wrong, but Roc refused to tell her.

"Roc, you're just a child. Stay here and work it out—whatever it is you're going through. Once it is over, then you can leave! But it don't make sense for you to just strike out on your own like this, like you're running away from something. Don't you trust me with your problems? I promise you I won't judge you. Tell me what is wrong! Whatever it is, it can be fixed," Sadie Mae cried.

Roc looked at his father and then his mother. He knew

not even Mama's kisses could make this all right. He had to leave. It was the only solution to avoid more conflict.

Before he left, Roc put the keys to the Corvette on the table and walked out the door. The sound penetrated through the silence like Roc's cries did when he was a baby. To calm him down, Sadie Mae would lay him against her chest. *Why can't it always be that simple*? she thought. And she watched Roc walk away.

"When I get my own place, I'll be back for the rest of my things," Sadie Mae heard him say as he walked down the street. On the front porch, the evening sun exposed her tear-filled face. But her neighbors were too busy to notice. The peaceful blue skies were settled across the city and it was the perfect weather for yard work and late spring cleaning.

After Roc disappeared, Sadie Mae stood, paralyzed with shock. Rockey came out of the house eventually. Suddenly, he had something to say. In as few words as possible, he explained the transition from boyhood to manhood. Then he reminded Sadie Mae that he was only a young man when he left home when he was thrust into the role as her husband and a father.

Sadie Mae listened carefully. She expected to hear her husband rant as usual about the unexpected pregnancy that began their young family. But Rockey remained calm. Even more peculiar, he continued to display the same affection he'd shown since last night. He held her close, then closer. He wiped away her tears. His tenderness was supportive, but surprising. It was then that Sadie Mae realized he was hurting too.

Roc walked around for hours, not sure of where to go or what to do. He'd always had his future mapped out. But he didn't anticipate it would all happen so fast, overnight. Before he knew it, he was at Sonya's doorstep. When he rang the doorbell, Sonya peeked out the window. Seeing her face was an answered prayer. He wasn't sure if he could handle seeing anyone else.

Sonya had not seen Roc since last night. She became angry when she saw his wounds had worsened. His face was puffy and swollen. She couldn't tell if his eyes were red from the fight or from tears, but she thought it was best not to ask. Silently she just hugged him.

Immediately, all Roc's cares were lost in Sonya's embrace. He knew she was the only perfect thing in his life and he never wanted to be apart from her. He responded to her touch by drawing her nearer. It was safe to love her and now he needed her more than ever. He knew his desires went deeper than physical needs. Even though he and Sonya did not sleep together last night, he still felt something strong. He had never experienced this connection with any of the other girls. He held Sonya so tight he thought he might hurt her.

"Roc I love you. Everything is going to be alright," Sonya said as she looked into his eyes and then down at his suitcase.

"I had to do it...I left home," Roc said.

"Come over here and sit down."

When Roc sat down, Sonya slid his suitcase beneath the patio furniture. It was best that her parents did not know what was going on with him.

"Baby, I'm going to school early to work something out. But Sonya, I don't want to be alone right now. Will you come with me?"

"With you—" Sonya paused and thought about the serious question. "I don't think my parents will allow that," she said, pushing the suitcase back even further.

"Sonya, I need you—" he paused. "Will you...will you marry me?"

Sonya could not believe her ears. Instantly she lit up like the scintillating sun and started to laugh. The sound seemed to echo for miles. She'd waited for this moment since the first time she'd laid eyes on Roc. Now that it was here all she could do was let out a big yes. To say she was excited would have been an understatement of her joy. She was ecstatic.

Sonya was not naive. She knew Roc's decision had something to do with the tension between him and his father, but she had enough love in her heart to make their marriage work.

Passionately they held each other close. Once Sonya accepted his proposal, she thought of her parents. She believed that she and Roc's marriage could be just as strong, and the two of them would always be in love.

Chapter Eight

A Day in the Future

Six months later

Winter 1994

December 31st, a winter wedding will be perfect, Sonya thought as she gazed at her wedding gown. In two days, she would be Mrs. Rockwell James Jr. She must have doodled "Sonya James" on her notepad at least a thousand times before she went over her final checklist for the wedding. Everything was flowing smoothly. Today, she had to pick up her mother's dress and her father's tuxedo. Her parents had paid for the entire wedding. Although they'd planned for this day since the day she was born, Sonya was still grateful for their financial contribution. It only took six months to plan such a beautiful wedding, and no one was more surprised than Sonya of the outcome.

Sonya looked down at her watch—it was ten thirty in the morning. The rehearsal dinner wasn't until six. She had plenty of time to run her errands and be back on time to get dressed for dinner if she hustled.

Slipping into her coat, the phone rang. It was the caterer she'd hired for the rehearsal dinner; there were minor complications to discuss. The otherwise calm Mother Allen sounded frantic. The door to the fellowship hall at First Bethel Assembly was locked and the maintenance man with the key could not be found.

"I need to get in to setup everything as soon as possible. Six o'clock will be here before you know it," the woman said excitedly.

"I'll call you back," Sonya said.

It only took one phone call to Sonya's father, a deacon at the church, to solve the problem. Sonya let out a sigh of relief and bundled up in her winter gear as she headed for the bridal shop.

Meanwhile, Sadie Mae sat at the kitchen table with a notepad and her bank book. The elaborate Ritz reception had put a strain on her. She was not financially prepared for the lengthy guest list—two hundred people at thirty dollars a plate. Her life savings was in jeopardy. It looked like there'd be just enough left over to help Roc get through college. She'd learned with Raymond and Regina, even a full scholarship did not cover the day to day expenses. Practically broke, she would have to start from scratch to replenish funds for Chloe and Joey. As far as her dream house, well that dream went up in smoke six months ago when Roc said, "Mama we need your help."

Sadie Mae added and subtracted for another hour or so, and still the bottom line figure never changed. When the doorbell rang, she hurried to the door. It was a delivery man. She signed for the package he'd brought and looked at the name of the sender, Mrs. Betty Smith. It was an unexpected surprise. *How thoughtful of her,* Sadie Mae said to herself. The package was light. Smiling, she wondered what was inside. She placed the package with the other gifts that adorned her living room floor. Over the past week, there'd been a steady flow of packages, all shapes and sizes. The mountains of gifts stretched across one end of the room to the next. It seemed each day, they accumulated higher and higher.

As Sadie Mae went back to the table to do more calculating, out of nowhere, Rockey made a foray to the kitchen from their bedroom. He looked grouchy, but his surly temperament was no surprise. When Sadie Mae said, "Good morning," sarcastically he replied, "If you say so," as he opened the refrigerator door. He then took a quick glance inside, maneuvered his hand around the crowed shelves and grabbed a cold drink before he swung the door closed. He then eyed all the palatable dishes of appetizers Sadie Mae had prepared for the rehearsal dinner on the kitchen counter. Each platter was embellished with green garnishments and colorful fruit. The picturesque dishes came from a magazine that Sadie Mae had tried her hand at imitating. She was pleased with the results.

Still silent, Rockey began to sample everything in sight. He scooped up some spinach dip from the vegetable tray, cheese and crackers from another tray, and finally he took several slices of potatoes skins. There were noticeable vacancies left in each dish when he finally sat down. Sadie Mae assumed Rockey was experiencing a hang-over, and his head and stomach were irritable. Usually after a night of drinking, he either hated the sight of food or needed food depending on what he'd had. Because he was hungry, Sadie Mae surmised vodka was his drink of choice last night. A couple of weeks after their son left, Rockey resumed his late night prowling, putting a halt to the affection he'd so suddenly displayed.

"The rehearsal dinner is at six. Will you be able to make it?" Sadie Mae asked.

"I'm not sure. I'm not feeling too good. Maybe I'll feel better after I have something to eat. Is there any real food around here?"

Before Sadie Mae could respond, she heard someone at the door. She rushed to the entryway assuming it was another delivery. But the door barged opened before she could reach it. Startled by the unexpected intruder, she let out a gasp and stepped back. When she realized it was Roc, she smiled from ear to ear, pleased to see him. A week had gone since his last visit.

Towering over her, Roc greeted his mother with a kiss, and wrapped his lanky arms around her. But the same affection was not extended to his father. He never even looked his way. The tension was still strong between them. Sadie Mae begged for answers, but got nowhere. Both men were stubborn and insisted nothing was wrong. She hated that they were so much alike.

"Thank God for the strong wind that blew you by," Sadie Mae chuckled.

Roc smiled. "I just wanted to see you before tonight Mama—to see if you needed anything and if everything was alright," Roc said as he watched his father getting food from the refrigerator.

Sadie Mae was more than alright, she was happy her son was becoming a man, a husband. She, however, was the only one excited about the wedding. The rest of the family felt they were too young. Sadie Mae felt the same way until Roc told her that he and Sonya were planning on living together on campus even if they did not get married. When Sadie Mae could not convince Roc to change his mind, she concluded it was better for them to live right before God than to live in sin. Sadie Mae was totally against shacking up. As far as she was concerned, it was just another counterfeit blessing the devil had to undermine God's plan. Besides the Bible says, "When a man findeth a wife he findeth a good thing." It didn't say, "A girlfriend acting like a wife...."

Roc surveyed all the gifts in the living room. He picked up a few, trying to judge the content by their weight. He even shook a few hoping the sound would provide some insight. "Towels...iron...toaster?" he guessed.

From a distance, Sadie Mae smiled at her son. Surveying all the gifts, he looked like a kid on Christmas morning, contemplating which one to open first. *He is just a boy,* she thought. It was time for them to talk, to discuss marriage, love, and most of all, God. She'd been meaning to talk to him, but he'd been so busy and his rare visits didn't help. Now was the perfect opportunity.

"Sweetie, you know marriage is not about gifts and a big wedding. It's about commitment and love," she said, removing a box from his hand as she guided him to the kitchen table.

Roc just gave an "I don't want to hear this" look.

"Well, why don't you sit down and indulge me for just a little while? I mean after all, in two days you're getting married and we might not have this chance again."

Roc looked at his watch and then down at his mother. He hadn't planned on staying long, and besides that, he didn't think he could stand being in his father's presence for any length of time. But his mother's arms were folded and she had that "I won't take no for an answer" look. So he agreed to stay, but only for a little while.

Roc and Sadie Mae sat at the table sipping on soda, laughing and talking about the good old days for at least an hour. It was longer than he'd anticipated, but he was okay with it. Actually, he really enjoyed it. The walk down memory lane was good for the soul. He'd forgotten all about the spotted haircut he gave Joey, and the time he put Regina's shoes in the oven after he'd made a mistake and dropped them in the toilet.

At the time, he thought if they dried, no one would know. But the farcical stunt backfired when the patent leather melted in the extreme heat and bubbled up. It was funny to remember, but there was nothing funny about the whipping he got for nearly ruining the oven and destroying a pair of good shoes.

But the memory that was the dearest, they agreed, was of Joey finding Roc's book stash and selling all the classic treasures to his elementary classmates for twenty-five cents a book. The whopping three dollars Joey earned, he gave to Roc for his birthday. Furious, Roc had demanded that his little brother get his books back, but Joey was crushed and he cried for hours. He said it made him look like a bad businessman and it was the only way he could afford to give Roc a birthday gift.

As long as Roc could remember, his family had struggled to make ends meet. He'd always promised himself when he became a rich basketball player that he would take care of his mother and his siblings. If he had his way, they would never want for anything ever again.

Sadie Mae and Roc thought of more stories to tell and the laughter continued. Roc could've reminisced with his mother for even more hours, but then she got serious. She asked if he was having any anxiety about getting married. Roc looked at her, swallowed hard, and savored the question. He thought about how his parents were sitting at opposite ends of the house. They'd been together for over twenty years, and he never saw them happy with each other. His greatest fear, he could not disclose, was that his marriage would end up like theirs. But then, how could that ever happen? He loved Sonya. When he told his mother he had no fears, she was pleased.

Like a game of ping pong, the conversation went back

and forth. When enough was said it was time for Sadie Mae to have the last word. She would end on her favorite subject—Jesus. "Have faith," she said with conviction. "Can't nothing like God enhance your marriage." Then for the first time, she expressed some regrets she'd made. Not having spiritual unity with Rockey, she felt, was her greatest mistake.

From the living room, Rockey could hear the conversation even though he was scarfing down pasta salad—more rehearsal dinner sampling. He surfed the TV channels, trying to curtail his boredom. His dullness peaked when Sadie Mae said the foundation of marriage was rooted in trust and faithfulness. The subject of do's and don'ts in a marriage was the last thing he wanted to hear. As a matter of fact, he'd heard enough. Dramatically, he dropped his fork, got up from his chair, and went to their bedroom.

Sadie Mae watched Rockey as he left. She could never understand his mood swings and why he was so irritable at times. He wasn't satisfied unless he made everyone feel the same way. *Misery loves company,* she thought.

Although she never sensed that things would change in her marriage, Sadie Mae was not bitter toward the institution. Her advice to her son was reflective of her genuine feelings. The truth was, secretly she still believed God would one day bless her with the kind of marriage she believed in.

After Sonya arrived home with her mother's dress

and her father's tuxedo, she realized the zipper in the beige sequence dress was broken, and her father's cummerbund was missing. But they were minor problems in comparison to the news she'd just gotten when Renee called. The matron-of-honor told Sonya that two of the bridesmaids' gowns were missing. Somehow, they hadn't been delivered to the bridal shop after alterations.

Sonya looked at her watch. It was four o'clock. She only had two hours to track down the gowns and get to the church before six o'clock. Up until that point, everything had gone as planned and she had no reason to panic, but the pressure was getting to her. Instantly, tears ran down her face and she cried out for her mother. Mrs. Jones heard her daughter's outburst and rushed to her side. When she asked what was wrong, Sonya was crying so hysterically that she couldn't even understand what she was saying.

"Everything is going wrong! Mama, what am I going to do?"

"First of all, sit down, take in a deep breath, and tell me what's wrong," her mother said. When Sonya told her about the dresses, she did not appear to be nervous.

"Honey, it is too late in the evening to worry about something that tomorrow will solve. The bridal shop has the solution to all your problems, and early in the morning we'll go and everything will be taken care of."

Mr. Jones heard the commotion from the other room. He went in to help settle Sonya. He didn't get through to her at first, but eventually she listened and calmed down.

"Mama, I can only hope that my marriage will be as strong as yours."

Sonya's parents had married young and understood the urgency of love. But they'd hoped their daughter would've at least finished college before she plunged into marriage. For one thing, they didn't want their daughter to experience a financial crisis like the one they had faced because it had put such a strain on their young marriage. If it had not been for God to pull them through, there is no telling where they would be.

"Honey, I just want you to know, if you're not really ready for this awesome responsibility, it's not too late to change your mind," Mr. Jones said.

"Daddy, I know this is not what you want, and you think I'm too young, but I never wanted anything as bad as I want to be Mrs. Rockwell James Jr.," Sonya replied.

"We just want to make sure you don't feel trapped," her mother said delicately.

"Mama, for the last six months, you and Daddy have clearly let me know you're not happy about my plans to get married. I understand you feel this way. But for the last time, I'm not going to change my mind. This is what I want. Please be happy for me," Sonya urged.

When Sonya's parents saw the sincerity in their daughter's eyes they knew the battle was over and there was nothing they could do to stop the wedding. Even though they had spent a fortune on the wedding, they were willing to take a loss if Sonya had backed out at the last minute, but now they realized that would not happen. So instead of any further protest, they decided to give Sonya some advice. After all, the most important thing was their daughter's happiness.

Sonya's parents said a mouth full, and their daughter took it all in. They even went to the Bible and wrote down scriptures that blessed them when they were in trouble. Sonya took notes and put the passages in her Bible, which was also filled with different prayers her mother had given her over the years.

The rehearsal dinner went well. Rockey did not show up and it seemed only Sadie Mae was hurt by it. Roc was glad to see his older siblings again. They'd come home for the wedding and to everyone's surprise, they'd made it home in time for the rehearsal dinner. Also, when Sadie Mae showed up at the church with Chloe and Joey, she had a package from the bridal shop in her hands. It was the gowns. They'd been delivered to her home by mistake. It seemed everything was working out and Sonya's anticipation grew for a day in the future...

Chapter Nine

The Wedding Day

Finally, the day Sonya had dreamed about for years had arrived in full splendor. Outside, the snow fell slowly. The picturesque December evening resembled a winter wonderland, complete with frosted pine trees, glistening icicles and long, outstretched branches that hung heavy with snow. Just before six o'clock, a lovely gray nightfall bid the day farewell, and the darkness was magical.

When Mrs. Jones placed the beaded veil upon Sonya's head, she looked like an angel crowned in glory. The full veil, hand-stitched crystal laced chiffon, swept down the designer gown. The white princess-line satin wedding dress was also gracefully accented with beads and crystal, which trailed along a lengthy train.

Sonya's long hair was pulled up into a French roll, with the exception of a few spiral curls that framed her face. The sparkling diamond stud earrings she wore could not overpower her glow.

She stood radiantly before the full-length mirror, and all agreed, especially her parents, that her beauty was breathtaking.

"It's time to hustle, Mrs. Jones. The ushers are waiting to escort you in," Sonya's wedding planner said as she entered the dressing room. Mrs. Gray had come highly recommended from the bridal shop owner, and she was working hard to keep everything and everyone in place. "Well," she looked at her watch, "everything is on schedule. Let's keep it moving!" Mrs. Gray paused and gave the blushing bride an admirable stare. "Sonya you look beautiful..." she whispered with a smile. She'd seen many brides and there was always an air of beauty that surrounded them, but Sonya's glow was so exceptional even Mrs. Gray had to stop and give her a second look. "You look simply gorgeous, and so does your wedding party, who, by the way, is waiting to make the grand entrance." Continuing to scurry about, Mrs. Gray prepared Sonya's father. "Father of the bride, remember, immediately after the song, "You Light Up My Life," is over, "The Bridal March" is played. The guests will stand and it is time to walk your baby girl down the aisle."

Sonya took her father's arm and he escorted her behind the wedding party where she waited patiently in line. The flowered altar, the procession of five pretty ladies wearing black sequined gowns and five handsome gentlemen wearing black tuxedos, taking measured steps to the beautiful voice echoing through the church made Sonya's eyes misty. But she could not restrain her tears when she saw the most handsome man of all, Roc, standing, waiting to take her hand in marriage. The flickering candlelight that filled the church created an ambiance which reflected their undying love. No dream she'd ever had could compare to this surreal moment.

"Don't cry," she heard her father say as he passed her his handkerchief. Funny, from a distance, she'd seen him cry earlier. She wondered if his tears were from happiness as well.

At the altar, the march halted and Sonya's quivering knees stiffened. When he received his cue, Sonya's father gave her a kiss, released her hand, and allowed Roc to step in next to her. In that instant, he became the most important man in her life.

After they exchanged vows, their marriage was sealed with a kiss and the church roared with cheers and applause.

At the reception, Mrs. Gray continued to be on top of everything. There would be no unattended guest on her watch! In secret, Sonya had shared with her a nightmare she'd had of Sherri showing up and crushing her wedding day. But everything was going as planned—no suspicious activities occurred and the guests appeared to be quite entertained. In fact, the atmosphere was flawless. Even during the isolated time the wedding party took pictures in the studio down the hall, Mrs. Gray kept everyone in good spirits. There was live entertainment, hors d'oeuvres, and champagne to keep everyone happy.

After taking pictures, Rockey became edgy. He didn't think the apologetic photographer would ever stop taking retakes. While everyone mingled—waiting for further directions from Mrs. Gray, he snuck outside for a cigarette. The night air was fierce. Temperatures were barely in the teens. Rockey quickly lit up. In his opinion, nonsmoking facilities were the pits, especially in the depths of winter. From the spacious rooftop landing, he peered out at the downtown area. The alluring bright lights beckoned his uneasy spirit. It was New Year's Eve—the granddaddy of partying nights. Downtown was live. He could see the excitement pulsating in the streets.

People dashed in and out of clubs. Most of the women wore sparkling evening gowns, and Rockey knew he could fit right in with his tux. Desperately, he wanted to be a part of the action. But instead, he felt like a child being punished, trapped, forced to stay inside.

Rockey sighed, took in a long draw of nicotine, inhaled deeply and for no other reason than boredom, he exhaled smoke rings and watched them disappear. His son had gotten married and the two had barely spoken. The whole evening, they'd only exchanged cordial words in passing.

It was a hostile situation and if it hadn't been for Sadie Mae, Rockey would not have gone. There were a million places he'd rather be...with Kelly, for starters. She knows how to have a good time, he thought, as her image became fixated in his mind. Yeah, Kelly was a piece of work. It took some apologizing to get back into her good graces after the prom night incident, but eventually she succumbed to Rockey's persuasive charm.

In the cold his mind wondered. The urge, to get into something he knew he shouldn't intensified even though he knew it would cause some more friction at home. But if he had a dime for every time he'd caused tension and disappointed his family, Rockey would be rich. The thing of it was, he never meant to do wrong. It was just something that always happened. Like a dark force was manipulating his footsteps or something, and all the guilt in the world couldn't override the thrill of living for the moment. He'd be the first one to admit his sexual appetite was intense—too much for one woman to handle. He also knew his sordid affairs compromised the sanctity of his marriage, but he could not be committed to just one woman. It wasn't normal. Besides, even if he wanted to live right, something inside would not allow it. That evil force greater than him was always at work. Rockey did not go to church much, but there was a passage in the Bible he could relate to. The scripture had always stuck in Rockey's mind because the day the pastor said it, it was as if he was talking to Rockey.

"Are you feeling the same pain and confusion Apostle Paul was experiencing when he wrote the profound words of Romans 7:15, 'I do not understand what I do. For what I want to do I do not do, but what I hate I do'? This Scripture is the one that made Paul seem as if he was bi-polar..."

It was weird because at the time, the church was crowded. It was the climax of the message. The Spirit was moving and the people were shouting when Rockey felt like he and the pastor were having a one-on-one conversation. Even at that point, nothing and no one could distract him. Rockey had never felt anything like that before—naked, like the window to his soul was exposed and God was trying to tell him something.

Rockey remembered, at the end of the service, an altar call was made. He wanted to go up like a few surrounding people did, but it felt like his feet were planted to the floor. Even when the man next to him nudged him to get by, Rockey felt paralyzed as his body barely moved. He knew the opportunity to turn his life around had presented itself, but he couldn't take it—fear, mostly. But the other thing was, something inside made him feel hopeless, dirty, and ashamed for all the bad things he'd done and was still doing. At that moment, he remembered drowning in a sea of negative thoughts—thoughts of being unworthy of God's grace.

Ironically, no matter how much Rockey tried to forget that day and that sermon, he couldn't. Deep down in his soul, he really did have the desire to honor his family, but he allowed his cardinal rule, "If it feels good then do it," to overpower him. But still, he had intense inner turmoil from having a kinship with the Bible passage and knowing what was right, yet still doing what was wrong.

Church was a passing thought that Rockey wanted to quickly dismiss. He took the last long draw from his cigarette, thumbed the butt into the air and then looked at his watch. Eight thirty-five. *The sooner the reception ends, the better,* he thought. Waiting inside were just too many people to smile at. He especially hated mixing with his son's new snotty in-laws. Good thing his poker face was polished.

But when he walked to the door and pulled it open, all his objections about the boring night instantly faded away.

Suddenly the scales of fortune tipped in his favor. A vision of beautiful perfection graced his eyes.

"Excuse me sir, do you have a light?" the woman asked as she stepped away from Rockey.

As Rockey accommodated her in the dim light, he recognized she was the same server he'd seen earlier in the kitchen with some other hotel staff. She was arranging the silverware and napkins on the trays. At the time, he'd been fascinated by her attractiveness. Suddenly inspired to light up again, Rockey remained outside. While he checked the lady out, he could not help but notice she was shivering with only a thin uniform standing between her body and the bitter cold.

"Aren't you cold?" Rockey said.

"Heck yeah," she said, "but I only have a couple of minutes for a smoke. That's not long enough to get my hat and coat—I just need a couple of puffs for now," she said rubbing her hands up and down her bare arms, trying to generate heat.

The woman's lips never stopped moving. She was attractive and talkative. In less than three minutes, between puffs, she'd practically told Rockey her life story. She was a recent divorcee, mother of two sons, who lost custody in a nasty battle with her ex (surprising to Rockey, she didn't say why). She was new in town, lonely, and looking for some action. Rockey took this as his cue. "I know a couple hot spots," he said smoothly. "Can I show you around town? Just as a friendly gesture, of course. Nothing else," he quickly assured her.

"Sure," she said. Then she disappeared. Seconds later, she dashed back. "Can you be back here in an hour? I'll give you my number...and who knows what else," she said flirtatiously, receiving the look she'd hoped to get from Rockey.

Rockey's imagination was running wild, thinking about what else he would like to get from her. He kept looking at her chest. She was definitely his type.

"Yes," Rockey said, stuttering like he always did when he was up to no good. But after his words caught up with his thoughts, he spoke smoother, then agreed to her request and looked at his watch.

Then out of nowhere, the waitress got serious and asked Rockey if he was married. The question took Rockey by surprise after her obvious flirting. His mind was not prepared to suddenly see Sadie Mae's face running around in his fantasy. No wonder it ended abruptly. Rockey began to shift uncomfortably and his eyes twitched nervously.

"Don't worry man. It don't matter to me. I'm just looking to have a good time, no commitments, just excitement."

Rockey was relieved by her lighthearted attitude. "Yes, I am."

The lady looked at his tuxedo.

"Did you just get married today?"

"No...oh no. I was a part of the wedding party."

"Look, I'm running late, and I'm freezing. In one hour, man, I'll be back."

Rockey gave an approving nod and watched her walk away. Maybe the night has *possibilities after all,* he thought.

After the traditional first dance, Roc broke away from his lovely bride and asked his mother for a dance. During the craziness of everything, he'd neglected to tell her how beautiful she looked, and how grateful he was for everything she'd done. Sadie Mae glowed with adulation as she soaked up all his compliments. It was good to be flattered. Her husband had not done anything but complain the whole day, and never once said she looked nice.

After the dance with her son, Sadie Mae wondered about Rockey. She hadn't seen him since the picture session. Where was he? Just as she looked around with a suspicious glare, Rockey appeared with an odd grin on his face. And before she could take her seat, he guided her back to the dance floor. They stole the show, dancing to Luther Vandross' *Always and Forever*. Rockey's smooth moves made Sadie Mae look like she was gliding.

Roc looked at his parents as they graced the dance floor. They looked good together. If love were as simple as a ballroom waltz, their life would be blissful. But Roc understood the nightlife was his father's element and his mother was a homebody, and often, very often, the two worlds collided.

"You look good tonight, Sadie Mae."

"Thank You, Rockey...you're looking quite handsome in that tuxedo."

"Thanks, but I feel strange in this monkey suit."

Sadie Mae patted him on the butt. She'd finished her third glass of champagne and was feeling sexy. "How about some monkey business later on big daddy?" she teased as she gave him a seductive wink.

Rockey smiled at his wife's advances. He figured she'd had something to drink. It didn't take much to get her tipsy. But he dismissed Sadie Mae's coquetting and just gave her an endearing kiss on the forehead and kept dancing. Although he was turned on by her flirting, he wanted some excitement tonight. Not that his wife wasn't exciting, but being with her was familiar, almost predictable. Tonight, he wanted to feel the conquest.

After Luther played, Barry White's, *You're My Everything* followed and Rockey's feet never missed a beat. He and Sadie Mae kept moving. He held her close. Sadie Mae's body fell in line with him and when he squeezed her closer, she felt safe in his arms. She wished the dance could last forever. It wasn't often that they stepped in unison. The rare closeness was stimulating.

Eventually, Rockey got disinterested and returned to the table. After nearly an hour had passed, he looked at his watch for the third time. His obsession with time did not go unnoticed by Sadie Mae. Even though she was enjoying the evening festivities, her eyes were on him. Finally, when the moment came for Rockey to make his move, he excused himself, said he needed some fresh air, and left. As usual, Sadie Mae assumed he was bored, so she gave him his space. Besides, she was getting nowhere with her aggressive affection and his rejection had become painfully obvious. The last straw was twenty minutes ago when he refused to dance again. His mood swing was sobering. It was typical of Rockey, she thought, as she realized there'd be no home fire burning tonight.

Rockey was on his second cigarette when the waitress showed up. This time, she was wearing a coat.

"Did you think I wasn't coming?" she said as she went into her pocket and pulled out a silver flask.

Rockey wanted to say, "I had my doubts," but he didn't want to sound anxious. "No, I just got here myself," he said as he watched the flask freely go back and forth from her lips. "You know, for someone who has occupied my mind for the last hour, I should at least know your name."

"Carmel—they tell me my mama had a sweet tooth when she had me, but I think it's kinda corny myself so my friends call me Candy," she said, in between sips. Then seconds later, she threw her head back and did not stop swallowing until the silver container was empty. "Wow! That's what a girl needs to knock the chill off," she said, shaking her body. Smiling, she walked toward Rockey, leaned against him, and in a soft sexy whisper she asked his name.

"Rockey," he said.

Candy broke away, unbuttoned her coat and started to dance, provocatively. "In my hometown, I was an exotic dancer," she said, turning her back to Rockey and moving her hips slowly from side to side. Rockey could not believe what he was seeing. She was hot. When a few people came out to smoke, Candy closed her coat and stood still.

"Follow me...I know where we can have some privacy."

When she took Rockey's hand and led him away to a secluded place, she turned and asked him a question that invoked a naughty grin.

"So Rockey...tell me...have you ever made out in the snow?"

Sadie Mae grabbed her coat. Rockey had been gone for over thirty minutes. She walked out on the deck and saw a few people smoking, but there was no sign of Rockey. As she prepared to return to the reception, she noticed another smaller deck off to the side. It was more private with very little lighting. Out of curiosity, she stepped down two small steps and peeked unto the other side. Visibility was not the best. A little spooked, she backed away and accidentally tripped up the stairs. She felt frightened and clumsy as she struggled for her balance in the dark.

"Are you all right?" Sadie Mae heard a female say and then she heard the woman giggle. *Oh my goodness,* Sadie Mae thought, *I'm not alone*. Instantly, she became mortified. She'd been caught snooping around. When she adjusted her eyes to the dimness, she was devastated by the sight. Fumbling in the dark to hide his disgrace was Rockey and some woman with her breasts completely exposed. Sadie Mae began to tremble in anger. She couldn't believe what she was seeing. She felt sick. Her sudden blurred vision made her lose her balance and she completely fell to the cold pavement. When Rockey rushed to her aid, she broke free from him and wiped the hindering tears from her eyes, immediately stood up, and slapped him across the face.

Her reactions were pure instinct—if she'd thought about what to do, she would've tried to kill him. The hit was not nearly as intense as her anger; although, the impact was so hard, it made her hand hurt. Like always, his actions caused her pain. Swiftly, with her head spinning and her mind racing, she ran back into the building. Rockey chased her down, and caught her within inches of the ballroom. The few people that stood at the reception entrance must've assumed Rockey and Sadie Mae's embrace was a display of affection, because they never stopped talking about how beautiful everything turned out. Even when he shouted, they didn't seem to be alarmed.

"Wait...wait... it's not what you think. She was just an old friend! Someone I know from the club. It was nothing. Don't get all excited and ruin our son's wedding," Rockey said. He waited for Sadie Mae's usual gullible response, but she kept uncharacteristically quiet. Rockey's nerves escalated and he began to shift around.

"Have you no shame?" Sadie Mae demanded finally with disgust, looking him straight in the eyes.

When Rockey came near her, she escaped before they made contact again. In tears, she stormed into the ladies room and locked the door. From a distance, Roc saw the commotion and went closer to observe. Both he and his father were standing at the bathroom door when Sadie Mae disclosed her pain.

"You're sick!" she said, "how could you embarrass your family like this?! You were practically having sex with her...I hate you! I have spent most of my life loving you. Have you ever loved me? Have you ever thought how much pain you've cause me...and your children—or are your selfish needs so great you don't even consider us when you get ready to do your dirt!? Oh God...Is sorrow my eternal fate because I'm stupid enough to love a low-down sleaze like you, Rockey?"

Roc looked at his father, and had a flashback of prom night. He wanted to clench his hands around his father's neck and ring the life out of him, but first he had to see about his mother. He knocked on the door, hard, then harder. When there was no answer, he pushed on the door with all his might, but to no avail. The door did not budge. Finally, he forced the door open with one strong kick. And when he saw his mother on the floor bawling in tears, he became furious. This was it. He'd seen her cry for the last time because of that cheating, selfish, poor excuse for a man.

"I'll kill him!" Roc screamed, charging at Rockey.

It took all Sadie Mae's strength to restrain her son. She begged him not to do anything. She said she would be more embarrassed if everyone knew what happened.

Standing at arm's length, Roc relaxed his fists and took in long deep breaths, and just eyed Rockey. "Okay Mama, have it your way, but I want him out of here—now! As a matter of fact, I will see to it that he leaves!"

Roc approached his father. Rockey looked his son up and down and stepped away from him. He did not want another altercation. But he could see his son was agitated and the slightest action would trigger him.

"Look Roc, calm down I just need to talk to your

mother. I don't want any trouble, just let me say something to her and I will leave."

"So help me, I'll kill you if you ever go near my mother again. You have hurt her for the last time. Now leave. I mean leave now!" Roc said as he held back his tears.

Rockey looked at his son and felt uncontrollable anger rising up in him.

"Boy...who do you think you're talking to? Get out of my way!" Rockey said trying to make his way to Sadie Mae.

"Look...if you don't leave, one of two things is going to happen—either you're going to have to kill me or I'm going to kill you!"

Roc's cold stare gave his father a sick feeling in the pit of his stomach. He considered his options—kill or be killed. He didn't hate his son and in a strange way, he understood Roc's anger.

"Roc, please don't allow us and our dysfunctional marriage to ruin it for you and your bride. Today is your day. Please go back to your guests," Sadie Mae said, standing between the two men.

In the midst of chaos, Sonya came running with her face all aglow.

"Roc, I've been looking for you all over. They're ready for us to cut the cake."

There was dead silence. Sonya looked at Roc and then his parents and sensed something was wrong, very wrong. When she inquired, the silence remained. And then out of nowhere, Candy showed up. She looked like a staggering alley cat with most of her chest still exposed.

"Oops, this must be your wife," she said laughing, looking at Sadie Mae. "Look man...I didn't mean to cause you no trouble; I was just looking for some fun. And I just want you to know it was a pleasure meeting you. Now if you all will excuse me, I've gotta clean myself up and get back to work, my break is almost over with." She looked at Sadie Mae, who had tears in her eyes. "Well maybe I'll go to another bathroom." And for the first time, Candy moved gracefully as she closed her coat and walked away.

Sadie Mae just stared at her and felt more pain. It was obvious she was young, but she had no respect for herself, and Rockey chose to be in some dark secluded place with her, a person like that, someone he didn't even know, rather than to be with her. She looked at herself in the mirror and felt old, ugly, fat and undesirable.

"Roc, you mean it has happened again?" Sonya said.

"Again?" Sadie Mae asked in horror.

When Sonya began to explain, Roc interrupted her. There was no need to expose his mother to anymore pain—learning about Kim was not necessary.

"What are you trying to say Sonya?" Sadie Mae asked.

"She means we're arguing again Mama," Roc said.

"Well...you don't have to worry about us having anymore arguments, not tonight anyway because if your father doesn't leave, I'm leaving," Sadie Mae said.

Rockey looked at Sadie Mae and said, "I'm sorry." Then he left.

Sadie Mae, still in tears, turned away and said nothing.

In spite of everything that happened, miraculously, the reception turned out fantastic. Shockingly, the guests never even knew about the disturbance and when Rockey left, his presence was barely missed. In fact, it was a relief for most of the guests because it was obvious he was not happy.

"A toast, everyone!" Mrs. Gray announced. "May the spirit of tonight forever bless the lovely couple. Congratulations Roc and Sonya!"

Chapter Ten

I Will Survive

Sadie Mae heard her alarm go off and realized it was time to get ready for work. She turned off the intrusive sound and sat straight up in bed without the usual yawning and stretching. It was Monday morning and she hadn't seen or heard from Rockey since the reception two days ago. He had never stayed away from home this long before. The latest was five in the morning following a late night of whatever. Even that was disrespectful, but she'd come to accept it. Now, was this something new he was trying to force on her? He'd even missed the opportunity to say goodbye to Raymond and Regina as they returned to school. Her best guess was that his disappearing act was because of sheer embarrassment. And if it wasn't the case, it should've been.

For a second, Sadie Mae wondered if something had happened to Rockey, then she wondered if he even deserved her concern. Why should she be worried about him anyway...

because she loved him? The thought came without hesitation. The bitter truth made Sadie Mae feel awful. She did not want to love him and hated herself because she did. It must be *convenient,* Sadie Mae thought, *to have the power to turn your feelings on and off just like that, without the slightest consideration for others.*

Reluctantly, she then looked at a nearby photograph of the two of them embracing and smiling. She could fool herself and say it was during happier times, but were there ever any happier times when their love was built on a lie? The lie he'd convinced her to believe—that he loved her? She quickly turned away, took in a deep breath, and eased out of bed.

Before she went to work, she walked down the hall and checked in on Joey and Chloe as they slept. In a few days, their Christmas vacation would be over, and it was back to school.

She stood at their door awhile just watching them sleep. They looked so peaceful. The rich joy she received from motherhood could not compensate for the emotions lacking in her marriage, but her children were compelling reasons not to hate Rockey. She saw him in them. Joey had his eyes, Chloe had his determination, Raymond had his walk, Regina had his smile, and everything about Roc, unfortunately, was like his father.

When Sadie Mae arrived at work, Mrs. Smith was waiting at the kitchen table. She wanted to hear all about the wedding. Over the past months, their relationship had gradually evolved into something special. While their association was more engaging than the typical boss and employee's rapport, they did not share the intimacy of friends. Neither had yet to speak of deep matters of the heart. However, every morning the women spent several minutes together, before Sadie Mae would begin her chores, just laughing over trivial small talk.

Habitually, as care taking for others was their inherent nature, the women subconsciously served each other. Sadie Mae poured the coffee and Mrs. Smith sliced the danish. As their laugher permeated through the silent corridors, the cold and still estate was filled with warmth—eliminating the eerie presence of lifelessness that loomed about.

Although Mrs. Smith appreciated the informal friendship, she wished it could be more endearing. Certainly she needed a shoulder to cry on. Her husband was getting worse. His fragile bones were deteriorating and now he was permanently confined to a wheelchair, which gave even more credence for his irritable temperament.

Neither she nor her husband had immediate family to call on. She had only a stepbrother that she'd met once, who lived somewhere in California. Their so-called fair weather friends were becoming less and less so with each passing day. It was funny to Mrs. Smith how personal hardships disclosed people's true feelings. It seemed when Mr. Smith was a thriving businessman, their social calendar was filled, but now the invites were few and far between, if any. And as if she did not have enough things to deal with, now she was getting pressure from the community to do something about their Palmer Hills estate. It had become an eyesore. She'd never dealt with legal matters and at this stage in her life, Mrs. Smith was not mentally prepared to start. If she was not afraid Sadie Mae would object, she would gladly lay her problems at her feet, though there was a time when she wouldn't have opened up to anyone like that. But recently, God had given her a change of heart.

Mrs. Smith listened to Sadie Mae talk about the wedding. Everything sounded so grand. Strange, her employee had only a fraction of what she'd possessed, yet Sadie Mae's life seemed so much richer than hers. She had children—which Mrs. Smith had always longed to have. Sadie Mae was married to a man she still loved after many years of marriage. Mrs. Smith knew this was true by the way Sadie Mae's face lit-up when she talked about him. They were childhood sweethearts and they were still together, and in love. How romantic, Mrs. Smith thought. As far as she and her husband went, they were just *together*. Even before Mr. Smith became ill, the romance had long left their marriage. They'd slept in separate bedrooms for years, gradually slipping away from being husband and wife, now living as roommates with separate lives altogether.

Sadie Mae also had spiritual peace which Mrs. Smith admired—until recently, she'd thought religion was nothing more than a crutch for weak-minded people. But Sadie Mae had started giving her deeper insight about God. Discussing Bible verses had become a part of their morning conversations. And from time to time, Mrs. Smith even caught herself praying, and believing that her prayers could actually change things. There was something else Mrs. Smith esteemed about Sadie

Mae, even envied—her youthful beauty. The woman looked as if she'd found the fountain of youth. It was obvious Sadie Mae didn't have many problems to fret over, Mrs. Smith thought.

When Mrs. Smith saw Sadie Mae look at the clock and stand up, she knew their morning talk was over. She could've listened for at least another hour. She had nothing else better to do. Time had become her enemy.

"Oh, Mrs. Smith, I want to thank you for the gift you gave my son. Right now they're in Hawaii for their honeymoon, compliments of Sonya's parents. So maybe you can tell me what it was, unless it's to remain a mystery until they return."

"No cause for a mystery Sadie Mae, I purchased a set of crystal lead goblets from their bridal registry, and I included a small monetary gift, something that can always be appreciated."

"How thoughtful Mrs. Smith. That was so kind of you. Well, I'm giving you a special thanks and I'm sure soon you will receive an official thank you in the mail."

"You're welcome. It was my pleasure."

When Sadie Mae walked away, she thought about how fortunate Mrs. Smith was to have wealth. Although she understood money did not make anyone happy, it had to be nice not to have to worry about it all the time. Mrs. Smith and her husband had traveled all over the world, and they did not have just one beautiful home, they had two. Whatever amount she gave to Roc and Sonya, it did not put a dent in the Smiths' checking account, Sadie Mae thought. What a life her boss had—truly blessed.

Sadie Mae had hoped when she gave Joey and Chloe permission to visit their friends it would give her an opportunity to be alone with Rockey. She didn't want the kids to hear the horrible things she had to get off her chest. Their heated exchanges always led to yelling and screaming, and most of the times it resulted in ugly name calling. Sadie Mae hated for the kids to see them argue. The last time Rockey called her a name, she had to hold Roc back, he was so angry with his father.

Before she even opened the door, Sadie Mae imagined Rockey's face. As usual, he'd begin with all his pathetic excuses to justify his behavior. She'd heard them all before, starting with his mother's untimely death, when his father became a womanizer. As a young child, he felt deprived because he never experienced the tenderness of a mother's love. Different women were always coming and going out of his life and he'd never bonded with any of them. His father was a hard worker and a good provider but awkward with his feelings, so a relationship never developed between them. His cold and lonely childhood was always at fault—unchangeable circumstances Rockey used over and over as a weak excuse for his shortcomings. Just his inherent nature.

When Rockey first met Sadie Mae, he instantly fell for her. He'd said she was the first person he'd ever connected with. At sixteen, expressions of fondness came easy, but after the novelty of love wore off, Rockey changed. He became distant. By then the damage was done. Married with five children, Sadie Mae was in too deep to walk away. Like a junkie chasing a high, she kept hoping the utopian romance she and Rockey once possessed would return. Even after all these years, she still had hope.

When she opened the door, the house was dark and silent. At six in the evening, surely Rockey had come home by now. Yet, as Sadie Mae looked around, there was no evidence of his presence, not even the stench of tobacco. When she turned on the living room light, she noticed down the hall their bedroom door was open. Strange, she thought, because earlier before she left for work, she'd cleaned the room and closed the door.

Overwhelmed with curiosity, she walked toward the open door and went into the room. Unsure of what to expect, she quickly turned on the light. The closet door was ajar. When she saw the bed still made, fear crept in her mind—something was wrong. She held her stomach to calm the butterflies. The sinking feeling only worsened when she saw all Rockey's things were missing. His shoes, suits and hats—all were gone. When she opened the drawers, it was no surprise that they were also empty, but she gasped in disbelief just the same. Rockey had left. Before she knew it, her eyes were filled with unwanted tears. Her body protested, but the water freely flowed down her face as she looked around at the emptiness.

At least, she thought, after all these years he could've had the decency to say goodbye face to face. It was in that moment, she felt that same coldness that loomed through the halls at Mrs. Smith's house—that cold dreary presence of loneliness and despair. Quickly, Sadie Mae ran from room to room. She turned on the television, the radio, flicked on all the lights, and in her haste, raced to the phone. She had to summon Chloe and Joey to come home at once. Sadie Mae needed to hear voices and see some type of movement around her to assure her she was not dying, because it felt like the life was seeping out of her. Surprisingly, when she approached the phone, it rang. Her heart sank. She suspected it was Rockey—she'd hoped and prayed it was him. Slowly, she picked up the receiver. "Hello?"

"Hi Mama, we're having a great time. I just wanted to check on you and see how you were doing. Is everything going well...I mean has that man been bothering you?" Roc said.

Sadie Mae wanted to tell him the truth, but she held back the tears and assured him everything was fine. After all, what right did she have to dump all her baggage on him during one of the happiest times in his life?

After a brief conversation, Roc said he had to rush back to his bride to do more sightseeing around Hawaii. He blew her a kiss through the phone, said he loved her, and hung up.

Seconds later, before Sadie Mae could dial out, the phone rang again. By now, tears were falling down her face and she could not disguise her voice to pretend everything was all right even if she wanted to. Perhaps this time it was Rockey. Maybe if he heard her pain, they could talk. Feeling defeated, she was even willing to listen to his pitiful excuses.

"Rockey," she said in tears before the caller had a chance to say anything.

"Sadie Mae, it's me, Betty...Mrs. Smith. I hope you don't mind me calling you...but you're the only person I have to talk to," Mrs. Smith cried into the phone. "Please can we talk? I need someone to talk to."

"Mrs. Smith," Sadie Mae said, sniffing, "are you all right?"

"No...I'm not Sadie Mae. I'm about to fall apart."

It took more than an hour to fill Sadie Mae in on all her problems. Mrs. Smith was crying so hard she never noticed the quiver in Sadie Mae's voice. Even if she'd heard it, it wouldn't have stopped her. The feelings of loneliness and overwhelming stress needed to come out. She hadn't a clue as to what to do with all the investments her husband had that needed immediate attention. She did not know who to trust.

The wrong person would ruin her financially. "Bill had always said an incompetent financial advisor could break you," she said, "so he always did his research before he consulted with anyone, but he was a savvy businessman who knew what to look for I feel so inadequate, Sadie Mae! I never wanted to be independent. I was never the liberated kind. I'm terrified of my future and not just long-term—even the next five minutes I'm not sure of."

By now Sadie Mae could only sigh at Mrs. Smith's troubles and pray with her over the phone. Seemingly, it was the only thing that helped. During their conversation, Joey and Chloe came home, heard all the noise in the house, and saw Sadie Mae on the phone with her head slumped down. Baffled, they moved towards her until she sat up, and then she motioned her hand to acknowledge their presence.

Twenty minutes later, Sadie Mae was still on the phone. When Chloe and Joey complained of hunger, uninterested in the leftover meatloaf in the fridge, Sadie Mae hushed them with a promise to get fast food. She was in no mood to cook, not tonight.

When the time came to hang up the phone, she felt so sorry for Mrs. Smith that she'd forgotten all about Rockey. But the distraction was temporary. Before she could even demand her kids to get into the car, she was thinking about him again.

After she grabbed her coat and keys in a trance-like state, she took off driving, barely listening to her children's typical teen talk. She just pulled into the parking lot beside the golden arches, ignoring whatever they were saying—some gossip about the latest hip-hop superstar.

At the counter, in the same breath that Chloe ordered a double cheeseburger and fries, she turned and asked Sadie Mae what trip her daddy was going on.

Sadie Mae raised her eyebrows. "What trip?"

"Today, when Daddy came home, he packed up all his things and said he was going on a trip—he said you would tell us more about it when you came home."

"Yeah, Mama, why can't we all go on a trip?" Joey said after he told the young girl behind the counter that he didn't want onions or pickles on his cheeseburger.

A trip, Sadie Mae thought, oh he's on a trip all right. So, the coward had truly left her. She was enraged. Suddenly, her head began to pound as the intense pain rushed upward from her heart. She felt faint. Her hand visibly shook as she went into her purse to pull out a ten-dollar bill. After she gave the girl the money, she rushed to the car without waiting for change.

How predictable of Rockey, she thought on the drive home, *to create a mess, punk out, and leave me to clean up his dirty work.* The more she thought, the angrier she got. Even when Joey complained loudly about there being pickles and onions on his burger when he specifically ordered otherwise, Sadie Mae wasn't drawn out of her trance-like state.

"Yuck! Onions and pickles! I told that girl I didn't want any!"

"Take them off cry baby!" Chloe lashed. "Mama's not going back for something like that."

Sadie Mae was glad Chloe handled his complaint. Being a bundle of nerves, she wasn't sure of her possible reaction.

Now if only all her problems were so easily solved. Sadie Mae glanced at the rearview mirror and saw Joey scrape away the unwanted ingredients, and then bite into the sandwich with still a fair amount of satisfaction. She knew she had to tell the children something, but tomorrow would be a better day to explain. Right now she could not form any clever words to cover up Rockey's so-called trip.

After dinner, when the children were in bed and the house was quiet again, Sadie Mae stared at the phone for hours, but it never rang. She cried in the night. She didn't want to live, she didn't want to get up, she didn't want to go on, but she had to. Funny, as bad as things were, she never considered being apart from Rockey. She'd always hoped things would get better. As strange as it was, she'd become comfortable with the pain of his whorish ways, and adjusted her life to the point that their dysfunctional relationship had become the norm. And now that the foundation of her so-called normal life had collapsed, she was totally confused. For years, she'd prayed and believed that God would save her marriage. Now what was she going to do? This was not the way things were supposed to turn out.

Alone in the dark, Sadie Mae asked herself, *"What will I do if he never comes home? Can I make it without him? If I take him back, will he ever change?"* But there were no easy answers.

In the back of Sadie Mae's mind, she knew it was the end of her marriage, and as much as she regretted it, she had to start looking at life without Rockey. He'd made his choice—a decision she had to accept. As the darkness enveloped her, Sadie Mae kept praying to God. This battle was not hers, but His, and by His grace, she would survive...

Chapter Eleven

Answered Prayers

1997

On a cold winter's morning, Mr. Smith passed away. It was not a surprise after many years of suffering, but when he took his last breath, the unexpected grief was a shock to his wife. The sad irony was everyone including Mrs. Smith, thought it would be a relief when the ordeal was finally over. But death did not bring the serenity Mrs. Smith craved as she emptied bedpans, gave sponge baths and endured the endless nights of interrupted sleep when her husband's screams hollowed through the shadowy halls. Instead, it brought loneliness.

She had thought to herself how unfortunate it was that the American dream must end so tragically without dignity, comfort, or control—so contrary to the life he lived. Just when everything, financially and socially, had fallen into place, the golden years welshed on the promise of a good life. Where was the justice?

More than Mrs. Smith cared to admit, during her husband's agony, she wished his days would just end. No dramatic exit. No reciting his undying love or apologizing for his lack of love as he coughed and gagged on his last breath. No. Quick and easy—if possible, in his sleep. The morbid thought came so regularly that she felt guilty for having the only compassion seemingly possible to have for someone in his predicament. Perhaps it was wrong to think that way, but she just wanted him to be out of his misery and suffering.

When she'd convinced herself her role as Florence Nightingale was an act of love, that she didn't hate her husband and would care for him forever if she had to, the haunting guilt vanished. It was as if the ominous presence of death delayed until she'd made peace with her tangled thoughts. The stillness waited—waited until daybreak early one morning after Bill had a rare restful night. Just as the sunlight came bursting through the curtains, death finally staked its claim and showed mercy. In that catastrophic moment, when night turned to day, and life to death, there was another less obvious closure that transpired. The final page of one painful chapter in Mrs. Smith's life was over, but it was the beginning of another one even more horrible to face—loneliness.

As early as the day after the funeral, Mrs. Smith realized how empty her life was. The house was totally vacant. All the guests were gone. The constant flow of well wishers offering their condolences had ceased. The phone stopped ringing and there were no knocks at the door. For the first time in her life, she was alone. She'd spent the last thirty-five years of her life being the wife of a powerful businessman, surrounded by his friends, his clients, and a host of servants. Standing in Bill's shadow, her life was consumed by his image. And while being blissfully ignorant, she never questioned her position until now, when it was too late to reconsider the choices she'd made.

It was her second glass of brandy and still Mrs. Smith could not rest. The silence was deafening. She walked across her bedroom to the cherry wood armoire and opened it. Then in a stupor, she looked at the thirty-two inch television, and turned it on—not for entertainment, although she was bored, but for the company. A weak substitution, but it would have to suffice. At that point, she would've done anything to get rid of the thoughts in her head. If she didn't get a grip on herself, she thought she was going to lose her mind.

After much channel surfing, Mrs. Smith settled on a John Wayne western. If she was lucky, it would require little concentration. During a commercial, she got up from bed, fixed herself another drink (she'd stop counting after three), and quickly downed the brandy before the movie returned. As she crawled into bed, she assumed the fetal position. Seconds later, she sat up and stared aimlessly at the ceiling.

Yawning was the first positive sign of sleepiness she'd had all night. In her efforts to relax she fussed with the sheets, fluffed the pillows, and pulled the covers back and forth, and then with the remote she adjusted the volume on the television to a whisper. But no matter how much she tried, she could not get comfortable. She twisted and turned for what seemed like hours before she finally fell asleep, but not before she'd cried a river of tears.

When Sadie Mae entered the Smith's house, she thought it was odd that Mrs. Smith was not up and about. She was not greeted by the usual aroma of fresh coffee and dusting sprays. Mrs. Smith bizarrely claimed that cleaning was therapeutic. So much so that six months prior, she'd gotten rid of all her staff except for Sadie Mae and took on most of the chores herself. The ones she did not do, she gave to Sadie Mae. To compensate for the extra work, Mrs. Smith gave Sadie Mae a sizable raise, more freedom in the house, and keys to the premises. This morning, however, was the first time Sadie Mae used the keys.

Walking through the house, she repeatedly called Mrs. Smith, but got no answer. With great concern, she rushed straight to her employer's room. Mrs. Smith's eccentric behaviors had worsened after her husband's death—it was obvious she'd been under a lot of strain. Drinking more than usual and constantly crying, she showed signs of deep depression.

Sadie Mae looked in the room. Mrs. Smith was still asleep. As usual, the room was picture perfect—like a scene from an art gallery—all except for the bed, which was unusually disheveled. As Sadie Mae walked into the room, she marveled at the oil painting of Mr. and Mrs. Smith. It almost consumed the entire wall beside her bed. Sadie Mae couldn't help but wonder if the French artist's work would be intimidating to the next man, if any, to come along.

As she continued to walk across the Oriental rug, her footsteps were light and Sadie Mae was careful not to bump anything. The buffed Asian furniture's glossiness and big brass knobs only made the room more untouchable.

Standing over Mrs. Smith in her huge cherry wood bed which looked almost like a coffin with so much lace and satin around it, Sadie Mae noticed that there was not much difference between the white bedding and Mrs. Smith's pale complexion that peeked from the covers. Stress and lack of sun had taken away what little radiance she'd once had.

"Mrs. Smith, are you all right? Mrs. Smith?" Sadie Mae asked as she softly shook her, but when she didn't move, Sadie Mae worried. Then thankfully, after three nudges, Mrs. Smith stirred.

"Sadie Mae, good morning. I'm sorry, I overslept. I had problems falling asleep last night." She paused and massaged her temples. "And to wake up feeling like I've been hit by a truck is just not fair. But I'm beginning to believe life is not fair."

Sadie Mae looked at the shot glass on the nightstand. "Mrs. Smith, would you like me to run you some bath water, or get you something to eat? It might make you feel better."

"Sadie Mae...I don't think you can do anything that will make me feel better. My days are long and lonely and my nights are even worse. I don't know what I'm going to do. I have nothing and no one. I spend my hours cleaning, drinking, and crying in this Godforsaken castle!" Mrs. Smith cried, tossing her head back onto her pillow. "I never thought I could miss Bill like this...the parties, the entertaining, even him...I never thought I loved him this much. I never knew how much my life was connected to his. He was everything to me. Now he's gone. I have, no children, no husband, no career...no life. I have nothing..."

Before Sadie Mae spoke, she prayed and asked God for wisdom. Only He knew Mrs. Smith's heart and what she needed. At first her mind was blank, so she said nothing. She just held Mrs. Smith's hand and allowed her to cry on her shoulder. She cried so hard her body shook with every weak sob. Sadie Mae wanted to say something to comfort her, but still no words came to her mind. The hard cry debilitated Mrs. Smith and she collapsed in Sadie Mae's arms after the tears finally stopped. Her body was so limp Sadie Mae got worried and started to shake Mrs. Smith profusely.

"I'm all right," Mrs. Smith said straightening her feeble body up. "Thank you Sadie Mae, I needed that," she said holding onto Sadie Mae's hand as if her life depended on it.

"What are you thanking me for? I didn't do anything."

"You are here. You're holding my hand and allowing me to let it out. You're not judging me for being weak. Your unselfish support is exactly what I needed. Only God knows how much I needed to be touched, held, and not judged. Truly your presence is an answered prayer."

Sadie Mae sighed and thanked God for His guidance. For ten more minutes, she continued to hold Mrs. Smith's weak shaking hands in silence. Then suddenly Sadie Mae was inspired to tell Mrs. Smith that she'd cried long enough. It was time to think about the future. To Sadie Mae's surprise, Mrs. Smith did not spurn her suggestions. Then with little persuasion, Sadie Mae convinced her boss to take a hot relaxing bath and just rest for the reminder of the day.

A couple of hours later, Mrs. Smith felt refreshed and went downstairs dressed in her nightgown and housecoat. She saw Sadie Mae dusting, even though the house was spotless. It was obvious she kept Sadie Mae around mostly for company. Mrs. Smith interrupted Sadie Mae's cleaning and called her into the kitchen to have coffee with her. Sadie Mae did not put up a fuss. It was hard trying to look busy. She sat down in the kitchen, rested her dust mop on the floor, and gave Mrs. Smith that warm smile she'd come to enjoy.

As an introvert, Mrs. Smith appreciated Sadie Mae's pleasant and outgoing demeanor. Thinking back, she realized Sadie Mae had always been a kind person even when she was not the kindest or friendliest boss in the world. "Sadie Mae, why are you so nice to me?" she asked.

The question took Sadie Mae by surprise. She'd never thought she was doing anything special. Her grandmother had always taught her that kindness could penetrate through the roughness of anyone's soul. And although Mrs. Smith had a rough outer exterior, Sadie Mae knew deep inside she was a tender, loving person.

"Mrs. Smith, I..."

"Betty...please call me Betty."

"Betty," Sadie Mae said slowly, trying to relax into calling her employer by her first name, "I understand what it feels like to be lonely. And you always looked like you were in a world all by yourself. I just wanted you to know that was not true. I also understand what it is like to be depressed. And if you don't fight back, that darkness, it will overtake you. And before you know it, you can drown in a sea of sorrow."

"I'm sorry Sadie Mae, I forgot about what you're going through with your husband."

Sadie Mae looked at Betty. She'd hadn't told her the whole story about Rockey—only that they'd separated, and the decision was mutual. Even now, almost three years later, Sadie Mae still could not believe they were still apart. And it didn't look like they would ever reconcile. At this point, Rockey refused to see her, and rumors had it, he was shacked up with some Kelly woman half his age.

"Mrs. Smith...I mean Betty...a separation is nothing like the hopeless situation of death."

Sadie Mae was careful not to say divorce. Subconsciously, she still believed they would get back together as soon as Rockey came to his senses; although, he hadn't given her any positive sign of change. Rockey openly flaunted his women around town, and the only thing that overshadowed Sadie Mae's embarrassment was her loneliness and financial wreckage. The burning desire she had to salvage her marriage was even too complicated for her to understand, so she dared not try to explain it to anyone else.

During the conversation, both women realized they had something in common. Suddenly, they were both single. Betty was the first to suggest that Sadie Mae come and live with her. Sadie Mae considered the invitation with an open mind. After all, it was not uncommon to be a live-in maid and, financially, it could be the answer to her prayers. But she looked around at all the priceless possessions Betty owned and realized that it would not be a good arrangement.

"I still have two children at home, teenagers, young, and noisy. I would hate if something was broken or tampered with," Sadie Mae said.

"I understand...children need to feel comfortable," Betty said. Then she paused and looked up as if a light bulb had gone off in her head. "I got it...I got it!" she said glowing. "I'll just sell you the Palmer Hills estate. It's right down the street and whenever I feel lonely I can just get in my car and come to visit you. Or on hot summer days, I can take a stroll and be there within minutes," she said just as plainly as saying "Pass the sugar."

Sadie Mae looked at Mrs. Smith. *Is she serious? I wonder if she...Is she losing her mind?* Sadie Mae pulled the long bangs from her forehead and tucked them behind her ears. She wanted to make sure nothing was obstructing her view of Betty. As she watched her, Sadie Mae felt perspiration stream past her temples and down the sides of her face. She twisted about in the seat as the leather stuck to her body. Suddenly, she was soaked with perspiration.

"Are you all right Sadie Mae? You look as if you'd seen a ghost..." Betty paused and snapped her fingers until the color came back to Sadie Mae's face. "Well don't just sit there and keep me in suspense, say something."

"Are you serious?" Sadie Mae could barely get the words to come out of her mouth. If it was a joke, she didn't know how she would react. For that matter, she wasn't even sure how she would react if it wasn't.

"Why yes! I'm serious!"

"Mrs. Smith...I'm sorry...Betty, I can't afford a house in this neighborhood. With everything that I'm going through and my children in college and being a single mother, all my savings are depleted."

"If I wanted to sell it to you for a profit, then you would have a problem. But my husband has left me financially secure for the rest of my life. I'm a fifty-eight year old woman with nothing to live for, and suddenly, every day, I feel like I'm dying. The house is just sitting there doing nothing. You'll be doing me a favor if you take it off my hands! One less thing to be concerned with."

"But the cost," Sadie Mae said.

"I will make it affordable." Then, Betty looked Sadie Mae dead in the eyes. "Please tell me those are tears of joy, Sadie Mae."

Speechless, all Sadie Mae could do was mumble expressions of happiness. Again she wanted to doubt Betty's proposal, but something inside assured her it was real. And as a sense of gratitude came over her, a flood of tears fell down her face.

Seeing Sadie Mae so overwhelmed made Betty feel a

sense of joy she hadn't experienced in a long time. She felt alive, as if her life had meaning again.

"Are you sure? Do you need more time to think about this? I mean, I will understand if you change your mind and reconsider."

"Reconsider? No way! It's final. Tomorrow I will have the attorney come over and draw up the necessary papers and it will be official."

When the doorbell rang, Sadie Mae escorted John, the Smith's attorney, to the study and took his coat. It was early, but Sadie Mae noticed that the clean-cut attorney smelled like he'd already had a few cocktails—not enough, however, to encumber his thoughts or cause him to stagger, but still, she was surprised.

The middle-aged man was wearing a navy blue suit with a clean, starched, pale-blue shirt and a multi-colored blue tie. Everything was neat and in place all the way down to his stylish black shoes.

"Nice to see you again, John," Sadie Mae said, gesturing him to have a seat.

The attorney popped a handful of tick-tacks into his mouth. "It's good to see you again also, Sadie Mae. How has our friend Betty been holding up since the funeral?" he asked, crossing his legs.

"Fair, but you know how Mrs. Smith is. It's hard to tell

what's on her mind."

Just then, Mrs. Smith came through the doorway with a smile. "Good morning, John," she said cheerfully, reaching out to embrace her attorney.

John quickly extended his hand, afraid to breathe too closely on his client. "Not too close," he blurted. "Coming down with something."

"Oh dear," she replied. "Do you have the contracts?"

"Yes. All I need is your signature and Sadie Mae's, and it will be final," he said, reaching into his leather briefcase.

Sadie Mae was so excited she could not stop smiling. Betty had refused to disclose the selling price. She just assured Sadie Mae she would be able to afford it. However, even with her sizable raise, Sadie Mae was still concerned. Betty and Sadie Mae were sitting side by side. Betty picked up the contract, looked it over, agreed everything was in order, and signed.

Afterwards, she pushed the paper to Sadie Mae. Picking it up as if it were an ancient relic, Sadie Mae scanned the words, but quickly got lost in all the legal language.

"I'm sorry, I don't see the price."

"Right here, at the bottom, ma'am," the attorney pointed out with the tip of his pen.

Sadie Mae looked at it once, then she looked at it again, and then she looked at Betty.

"One dollar?" Sadie Mae said. "One dollar? You're going to sell me a baby mansion on a hill for one dollar?"

Sadie Mae was shaking so hard she could hardly write

her name on the contract. With tears, she thanked God and finally hugged Betty so hard she was afraid she might break her in two.

"Don't get too excited, Sadie Mae, you've got to give me the money to close the deal," John said smiling.

Sadie Mae went into her pocket and pulled out a few bills. Trembling, she searched for one dollar among the fives and tens. When she found it, she gave it to the attorney, still crying and shaking. He took it, signed his name as a witness, shook Sadie Mae's hand, and gave her the keys.

Sadie Mae pulled up in the long spiral driveway that stretched a mile from the street. She got out of the car slowly. It was a moment in time she did not want to rush. She took out her keys, unlocked the door, and walked in the house in total silence. Then she screamed—loud, listening to it echo as it resonated through the hallways. Her dream was no longer a far-fetched figment of her imagination, but a tangible reality. As she continued to look around, the tears poured down her face. Of course there was a lot to be refurbished, but the beauty was not hidden. In the midst of her tears, she praised God for His blessing for she knew it was only by His grace that she'd received such a gift. It was strange, she thought. Just when she'd given up on ever owning her own home, and all her money was gone, He came and gave her the desires of her heart. Truthfully, it was always something she thought would come to pass. But never in her wildest imagination did she ever dream it would be like this, a 5,000 square foot Cape Cod with two master bedrooms, six bathrooms, five bedrooms, two formal dining rooms and luxurious outdoor swimming pool.

For now, Sadie Mae would have to just picture her family in the house. There was just too much work that needed to be done. But she walked to the kitchen and imagined her growing family sitting at a huge solid oak dining room table sharing big Sunday dinners and holiday feasts. Now, when her children flew in from out of town, they'd have plenty of room to stay with her, especially now that Raymond was married and Regina was engaged.

Returning to the expansive front porch, Sadie Mae soaked in the beautiful sunset. She felt Jesus tell her that everything was going to be all right. With outstretched arms, she closed her eyes, lifted her head, and thanked the Lord for answered prayers.

Chapter Twelve

Secrets Surface

July 1997

Six months after Sadie Mae had signed the deed to her new house, she still hadn't been able to come up with enough money for all the repairs needed to move in. It was just too much of a mess to live there with teenagers and other family coming and going.

But meanwhile, Roc was being courted by the Detroit Pistons. At 6'10, he was a phenomenon with speed and finesse. His jump shots, dunking and overall aggressiveness on the floor made management take notice. Although there was nothing official, no contracts or agreements, Roc's future with the team looked secure.

But he still had to wait until after the NBA draft. It was just after the "Bad Boys" era, and the Pistons had one of the worst records in the league, allowing them first draft pick, but Roc didn't care about their stats.

He just wanted to play on the team. It had been his dream since the first time he'd seen them play at the Silverdome, in Pontiac, when he was eight years old. Roc was so confident in his game, he even believed he had what it took to put the team back on the top.

The night of the draft, Sadie Mae's house was filled with people, food, and excitement. All Roc's family and friends were waiting patiently to hear his fate. Sadie Mae had expected a large crowd. She'd been on her feet all day cooking, but she enjoyed the reward. Swollen feet, sore hands, and an aching back earned a huge turnout, and the house was buzzing with liveliness.

During the draft's preliminaries, the house was filled with loud laughter and talking. But when the intense moment came to announce the first draft pick, you could've heard a pin drop until the first name was announced. And sure enough, as they'd hoped, it was Rockwell James. It was official, Roc was a Detroit Piston.

At once, the house resounded with even greater shouts and screams than there had been all night. Unfortunately, Sadie Mae was standing next to her daughter-in-law when she let out an excited shriek that was so loud Sadie Mae thought her eardrums would burst. But instead of getting upset, she turned and hugged Sonya and the two of them jumped up and down like schoolgirls.

When the phone rang, Sadie Mae weaved her way through the crowd to answer it. With all the shouts and congrats going on, she could hardly hear the caller, but could recognize the voice. It was Rockey. Just as Sadie Mae expected, he wanted to be a part of the celebration, but he was not welcome. Up until three months ago, he'd flaunted his affairs in her face. Even some of her church members had seen him around town with different women. Some of the folk's gossiped about it, while others just stared and prayed. It didn't matter what they did, it made Sadie Mae's Sundays uncomfortable and embarrassing to have had her dirty laundry aired in public.

"No, you cannot come over, Rockey," she said emphatically. Then, Rockey slammed the phone down. Strangely, the bang in her ear was a pleasant sound. She'd rather hear that than hear his begging and sobbing which he'd been doing plenty of lately.

Sadie Mae hung up the phone and looked at her son in the next room. He was having such a good time shaking everyone's hand, and just eating up the moment. She pondered over the call because she never wanted to stand between her son and his father. Whatever opinion he had of his father would not be poisoned by her bitterness. So, even though she didn't want to spoil his excitement, she decided to ask Roc what he thought.

"Roc," she said, "that was your father on phone. He wanted to know if he could come over..."

"I hope you said no," Roc interrupted. "I told him the last time he tried to talk to me! I don't want to have anything to do with him. As far as I'm concerned, I don't have a father, and I want him to stay away from me forever!"

Forever estranged was exactly what Roc had hoped for after he ran into Rockey sporting Kelly on his arm at a bar and grill in Lansing last year. The image came to mind like it was last night...

Roc and a couple of his frat brothers were sitting around a table at the bar having a few beers to celebrate the Spartans' victory over Ohio State. Then, Roc saw them. They exchanged glances and once they'd acknowledged each other in the dimly lit smoke-filled lounge, Rockey had the audacity to come over and try to make conversation about the long drive from Detroit. But the attempt was brief. Roc cut him off after he said, "Son I've been keeping up with your career..."

Once Roc heard son, he became visually uncomfortable and did not care to hear what else followed. Did Rockey think his actions could be so easily forgotten?

When the two men acknowledged their relationship, Roc's boys looked at each other in amazement. The family resemblance was apparent—same height, body structure and facial features. But it was the first time they had ever seen or heard mention of Rockey. In college, Roc had always shied away from anything that had to do with fathers.

In an instant, Roc slammed his mug down on the table and lunged up out of his chair. His fraternity brothers watched with dropped jaws as the usually cool Roc became a vessel of hatred.

"Fellas, excuse me. Gotta take care of something," Roc said through clenched teeth. Then, he grabbed Rockey at the shoulder and gave him a forceful nudge toward the back door. Once outside, without an audience to overhear their conversation, Roc did not bite his tongue. He spewed out things he'd held back since childhood.

"How can you even show your face to me? All your women...you've always been a disgusting embarrassment... the kids at school...you should've heard what they said to us when we were little. 'Your mama's a fool and your daddy has more women than a pimp!' Seriously, you're sick. You look so ridiculous parading around town with a tramp young enough to be my sister! Everyone knows you left your own family, your own wife..."

Roc's mouth was moving by itself. He didn't even have to think of what to say, because all of these thoughts had been swirling in his head for years. Rockey just stood there with a "so what" stare as his son's feelings were spilling out into the night air, but Roc didn't care. He wanted to get it all out before his father left his sight.

"In all the years I've known you, there's only one thing you've done...one thing...that warrants respect," Roc said, waiting on his father's reaction.

"Oh, so now you respect me?" his father said.

"Yeah, sure, I respect you...for having the decency to leave my mother alone!"

Roc thought about that night. He had bared his soul and let it all out to his father's face, but strangely, the anger did not cease. Seeing Rockey go back inside, take the woman's hand, and leave the bar unaffected only deepened Roc's hurt. Even as a grown man, at his own celebration party, Roc felt like that wounded nine-year-old who stood at the door and overheard too much.

"No Mama. Don't you let him come. No."

When Roc said no again, Sadie Mae could see the pain in his eyes. His muscles were flinched and he clenched his fists tight at his sides until Sonya came up and kissed him.

"Hey baby, what's wrong? You look like you want to kill somebody," she said.

Roc looked at Sonya and immediately his persona changed. "What could be wrong? I got the woman of my dreams, a pro basketball contract and I'm in the presence of all my family and friends. There's nothing wrong...everything is right. Life couldn't be better."

Hours after Roc's celebration was over, the phone line was jumping. Excited to brag about her son's accomplishment, Sadie Mae made a phone call to Raymond and his wife in Atlanta, only to find out that there was more exciting news! Raymond's wife had given birth to twins, a boy and a girl, earlier that day! She was a grandmother! For a moment she felt old, but it soon passed when she realized how blessed she was to be a grandparent—of twins at that!

She talked to Raymond for hours and then she called her beautiful daughter, Regina. Her conversation with Regina was just as long, catching up on all the different things going on in Texas, talking about Roc, Raymond, and the new babies.

But Sadie Mae's nosey mothering sense was going off. It was quite late at night and her daughter's fiancé, Kevin, was still over. "*Are they living together? Oh no, she thought, I can't let my daughter sell herself cheap and shack up!*" And with that thought, Sadie Mae spoke up.

"Honey, I love you, and I want the best for you. Everything is going so well for the whole family..."

"Mom, what's wrong? You're acting funny," Regina interrupted nervously.

"It's just...the Bible says God blesses a man that finds a wife, not a girlfriend pretending to be a wife...Do you know what I'm getting at? Kevin's there every time I call lately..."

"It is time to celebrate Momma," Regina insisted. "I'm fine. We're getting married very soon!"

"Oh, Regina, just save yourself the pain and heartache of doing things contrary to God's way. Learn from my mistakes. Don't try and grow up so quick..."

"I know, Mama. I'll call you tomorrow, okay?"

And with a loving goodbye, Sadie Mae hung up the phone with a smile. Bottom line, Sadie Mae loved her children and wanted what was best for them. She'd prayed over them all their lives and so far, God was faithful in keeping watch over them. They were all in college, except for Chloe and Joey, but they'd be attending soon. Truly she'd been blessed. All she had invested was not done in vain. Finally, she could see the prolific outpouring of all her labor.

Of course, Roc's good fortune was seeping through the airwaves and the entire nation was listening. On the other side of the world in California, Sherri got a call.

After three rings, she stumbled her way to the phone.

"Hello?"

"Hey, it's me. Turn on the TV. Right now. You gotta see this."

Sherri turned on the television as directed by the caller. Once she'd adjusted the reception, the dingy thirteen-inch screen showed a replay of Roc grinning during his televised interview.

"Your boy made the big time. Pro basketball," the caller said.

Sherri focused her hazy vision. She looked at Roc. He still looked good, even better than he did the last time she saw him over a year ago when she'd come home for a visit and bumped into him at the corner store near his house. The day came to Sherri's mind and she remembered how emotional she felt when, just before she could say hello, some girl had come up, hanging all over Roc. Seeing him with another woman was nothing to trip about, but the feelings remained just the same. Because of the awkwardness and to dodge any questions about the pregnancy or what happened after she left town, Sherri had turned and left the store that day.

But here, in her apartment, when the TV showed a close up on Sonya smiling next to Roc, Sherri recognized her. She was the girl with him in the store, and she also remembered her from school.

Remembering was hard for Sherri after last night—too much partying. But still she tried to challenge her brain. As she sorted through the scattered imagines in her head, she looked around at her surroundings. It was a mess—a hodgepodge of old furniture, clutter, and drug paraphernalia. The tiny studio apartment had reached its capacity in junk. There were stacks of classified sections with big red circles, reminding Sherri that she still didn't have a job. Also, the many sports pages made it known that a sports fan, especially a basketball geek, lived there.

As Sherri listened to the caller, she reclined upon the sofa bed—a piece of used furniture that never converted into a sofa because of a malfunction. She then propped her heavy head upon some dirty laundry nearby. Still absorbing the information, she continued to listen and look.

She'd become acclimated to the jumbled sight and was not bothered by the trail of filth that trickled from the living room to the kitchen. Even as she pierced at the pale yellow wooden cabinets, her eyes were not fixated on the dirty dishes below that spilled over from the sink and covered the table, but instead upon the colorful birthday trinkets that looked out of place amongst the disorder.

When Sherri sighed and looked at the ceiling, the view was no better. In fact it was worst. The structure was practically dilapidated. The slumlord she'd had for the last three years had yet to do anything about her complaints: faulty plumbing and the need for fumigation. Peeling paint and a cracked window were serious housing violations, but you would never know it, because he'd yet to fix them. And the disheveled blinds he'd put up to conceal the spider-cracked window allowed just enough sunlight in to expose what the night had hid so well. The coffee table was covered with drugs.

The birthday boy, Sherri's boyfriend, shared the sofa with her and his friend was lying on an old chaise lounge across the room. One of them grunted and, simultaneously, the other yawned, showing life in their otherwise dead-like bodies.

"What time is it?" Sherri finally asked the caller rubbing her eyes and then scratching her arms.

The caller replied, "Time to get paid!"

After all the times Roc and Sonya had shared their love, intimacy had never been sweeter than tonight. Roc thought about how special the whole night had been as he looked down at his wife, resting in his arms. He had taken the time to express himself and he held back on nothing. It was the first time in their relationship he did not feel inferior or inadequate because of lack of money. Sonya deserved the world, and now finally he could give it to her. Tonight he made her a promise to always take care of her, and to always love and respect her.

The mood was perfect—surreal. They sipped wine and listened to the mellow sounds of George Benson. After sharing their bodies, they shared their dreams. Then they cuddled in silence as their starlit eyes gazed toward the heavens. The view from their tiny campus apartment window wasn't always the best, but tonight, the stars looked reachable. Roc had never considered himself a religious man even though he was raised in the church, but tonight he felt connected with God and thanked Him for everything.

Intoxicated by the scintillating moment, they began to whisper their plans for the future. Sonya decided to discontinue her studies. She would be happy with an associate's degree in liberal arts. Roc was the brains in the family. She never liked school and they were going to be rich, so who needed education? Besides, she was a princess, and her dream was to care for her castle and take care of her king, like her mother did. Roc agreed that Sonya would stay at home. He'd watched his mother work all her life, and now that he was in a position to do better than his parents, his wife wouldn't work.

As Roc fell asleep, Sonya continued to dream Like Roc, she too was obviously excited by the prospects of prosperity. In her mind, she escaped from the plebian lifestyle she knew to the rich and famous lifestyle. Sonya pictured the big house, nice cars and shopping trips to Italy, Paris, and Europe. But more than that, the ease of having money would probably relieve some stress and she could finally have a baby—for her greatest desire was to fill a huge house with lots of children. As an only child, she longed to have a big family, maybe three girls and three boys. Perhaps having half a dozen children could eclipse the miscarriage she had last spring. It was a tragic thing to happen, and even worse, there was no medical reason to explain it. No physical complication and no family history to suggest potential problems—just three months into the pregnancy, the baby aborted itself.

"You're still young, and before you know it, you'll be expecting again," Sonya remembered her doctor saying with a comforting smile. That was over a year ago, and still nothing had happened. However, she and Roc were enjoying the process of trying...

Chapter Thirteen

Face-Off

Deeply aggrieved, Rockey felt spurned by his family. Tonight was a milestone in his son's life and he was not invited. It was late, way after midnight. He wanted to rest, but his ever-present guilt wouldn't allow his mind to shut down. Too many ghosts from his past chased away sleep.

After fighting with the covers, he got up from bed, walked to the window, and stared out. The moon was full. He lit a cigarette, and then immediately put it out. He opened a can of beer, and then poured it out. He wanted something—he needed something. Company would be nice, he thought as he looked around his studio apartment.

It wasn't much, but it was where he called home since his bad streak with women. At least now, no one else could put him out like Kelly had. Right after she met some small time gangster with deep pockets, her attitude got funky. At first the dude just gave her a few dollars here and there. But then, when the man started showing some real interest and giving up some serious cash, the stuff hit the fan. Kelly began dressing like her teenage daughter, got a platinum blonde weave, and started going out night after night.

Then one morning she got up and told Rockey to get out. She gave no particular reason why, she just told him to leave. When Rockey insisted he deserved an explanation, Kelly looked at him with her fake green eyes, batted her false lashes and said, “I want you to leave because my new man needs a place to stay. Besides, I never asked you to leave your family!”

Rockey was speechless. What could he say?

Without keys or any official ties to Kelly, Rockey had no choice but to leave. But before he could worry about being lonely or homeless, he hooked up with Della. Unlike Kelly, Della was faithful, calm, and laid-back. But soon Rockey discovered she had other issues. She was dense, one of those sistas that had a pretty face, but an empty head. What Rockey could never understand, was how Della could be so good in bed, and so bad at everything else—namely housework. The chick did not even have the common decency to make up a bed or wash dishes before mold grew on them. She did not even use bleach and water to clean the bathroom. Instead, she burned potpourri and scented candles all day. Needless to say, his stay with her was brief. After that chick, he was glad to get his own place.

Having given up on sleep, Rockey was dressed and walking out the door. When he took off in his car, his plans were to go to a club. Maybe one of his favorite watering holes could prove to be lucky tonight, and he'd run into an old friend—or meet someone new.

But the strangest thing happened in route to the club. His vehicle made a detour. It was as if it had a mind of its own and before he knew anything, he was at his old house beating at the door. His bizarre actions even surprised him and he dared to imagine what Sadie Mae would think.

When she came to the door, Sadie Mae's icy stare sent chills up and down his spine and immediately, Rockey second-guessed his impromptu decision.

"What are you doing here?" she said angrily. "You have no right coming here like this in the middle of the night! What do you want?"

"We need to talk."

"For the last time, Rockey, we have nothing to talk about," Sadie Mae said. "You left me without so much as goodbye, remember? And then you kept silent for three years! Now you're harassing me because you're finally ready to talk!?" Taking a step into the doorway, she pointed her finger in Rockey's face. "Like I've told you a thousand times...I don't want to hear what you got to say...it's too late."

After an uneasy moment of silence, Rockey said, "Please just give me twenty minutes and I'm gone."

Sadie Mae could not believe it. For years she wanted desperately for this day to come, to hear what words he had to explain his cruel actions. But now that the moment had arrived, she was no longer interested in why he left.

"Twenty minutes? I'll tell you what Rockey...I'll give you two seconds to get off my porch or I'll call the police!"

"Sadie Mae...please...I'm begging you! I need you back! I'm sorry—"

Sadie Mae tried to slam the door in Rockey's face, but he stopped the speeding door with his body. In the midst of the commotion, Sadie Mae saw her neighbor's porch light come on across the street, and she reconsidered talking to Rockey. If she left him outside banging on the door, it would cause a scene. The neighbors already knew enough about her business and she didn't want to give them anything else to gossip about.

"You got five minutes. Start talking," she said, leading him inside.

Rockey stepped into his old house. He had not been there in over three years. He looked around and took it all in as if it was the first time he'd been there. It was quiet, peaceful, clean, and in order. He searched quickly to see if there was anything left around that represented him, and there was nothing—no sign of his presence anywhere.

"So what is it you need to say?"

Rockey wanted to confess his love, but he knew it was not the right time. He looked at Sadie Mae. Her eyes were ablaze. "I'm sorry for the things I've done. I need you. You got to give me another chance. I know how I made you feel, and like I said, I'm sorry." He paused and lowered his head, "I can't take this anymore."

In the still of night, Rockey pleaded with Sadie Mae. He

knew deep inside she could not resist his persuasive charm. Like incantations, he repeated his regrets and apologies over and over. Then finally what he was saying provoked a reaction in Sadie Mae he was not prepared for.

"What right have you got to come into my house and talk to me about being sorry?" she huffed. "You're sorry all right, the sorriest person I've ever known. You're not only sorry, but you're also selfish and pathetic!" she said through clenched teeth, glaring. "When you paraded your women in front of me, you didn't care about me or my feelings, but now you're hurting, it's time for us to get back together? The heck with you and your feelings! What you're feeling is nothing compared to what you've put me through. All your lies, women and years of heartache! Ha!" she yelled, throwing up her hands in disgust. "You say you can't sleep? It's your conscience beating you. And as long as you're the same low down, dirty, selfish person, you will never have a decent night's sleep. God gives rest to the weary, not the wicked and He is whipping your behind for all the low down things you've done to people! And furthermore, Rockey, nothing pleases me more than to know you actually have a heart and it is hurting!"

From that point on, the conversation became a heated face-to-face confrontation. Rockey accused Sadie Mae of giving more attention to the kids than to him. He said she was always too tired and worn out to attend to his needs.

"A man and a woman—they supposed to love it up. You know, a man's body got needs! How am I supposed to act when my wife doesn't want to show any interest? Any love?"

"Oh, come on! How could I possibly show any love when you were always gone prowlin' around like some sewer rat? You want me to follow you around and throw myself at your feet?"

"Some women know how to be attentive. How to dress, how to wear their hair, their nails..."

That did it. Sadie Mae had more sense than to listen to Rockey's degrading tactics. She knew that Rockey's infidelity had, at one time, taken a toll on her looks.

"I never lost it, and you know it. I may have stopped wearing the make-up and the high heels for a while, but I'm still the same package! I still got it!" she glared. "Look at me! I look better now, without you, than I ever have!"

Rockey had no clever comeback because, it was a fact, Sadie Mae looked good. She was radiant and it even appeared to him that she had slimmed down and toned up. She looked at peace.

Silence fell on the house for a brief moment. Sadie Mae was convinced she'd gotten her point across. Even if Rockey spoke, she was no longer willing to listen.

"It's time for you to go," she said. "I want you to leave... now."

Rockey looked at Sadie Mae, and realized she was serious. She meant he had to leave, so he left. Afterwards, he stood outside the house and cried for hours. He could not believe Sadie Mae did not love him anymore. He wondered where he'd go from here. What would he do?

From her kitchen window, Sadie Mae stared emotionless at Rockey. She'd given him all of herself and he never appreciated her. Even now she believed he was only feeling sorry for himself. She knew the tears he was crying had nothing to do with her. It was still all about him. He wanted something, and he couldn't have it. It was a shame, Sadie Mae thought. The Bible says a man that finds a wife finds a good thing. Rockey had a good thing and he was too filled with selfishness to see God's blessing.

Chapter Fourteen

Stardom

A New Beginning
2 Years Later

It was Ladies' Day at First Bethel Assembly. Dressed in a chic black suit, Sadie Mae stepped to the podium and took the microphone. It was time for testimonies. She'd waited patiently through Mother Harris's solo, the children's skit of famous women of the Bible, and recognition of visitors and friends. All were beautiful, but now it was her time to shine. Sadie Mae was not modest when it came down to talking about God's goodness. Some may have mistaken it for bragging or boasting when she shared all her blessings, but Sadie Mae didn't care, she just wanted to give God His praise.

She'd been that way since she was a little child back when her grandmother would take her to church. Even then, she understood prayer changed things. Her grandmother was the one who taught her how to pray. She said age did not mean anything—David was a child when he defeated Goliath.

Like David, as a young child, Sadie Mae took on the

giant of alcoholism that held her mother in bondage. She prayed that her mother would stop drinking and disappearing for days at a time. Every night, Sadie Mae talked to God about her problems, and after some time He delivered her mother from her addiction. Not only did her mother stop causing chaos in their household, but she eventually started to go to church. And right before the final stages of dementia had stolen her mind, she became a devout Christian. So no one could tell Sadie Mae about God. She'd known Him all her life. And after what He'd done for her lately, she wanted the world to know He was worthy of her praise.

She didn't have the time to tell her life story, but what God had done in just two years was enough to marvel the folks. She'd been taken from Brewster Avenue's crime infested streets to the suburbs of Palmer Hills with one dollar. She would've been happy anywhere as a homeowner, she said, but she'd learned when God does things, He always does them in grand style.

Over the years, if nothing else, she'd also learned the most important thing she had was her faith. It kept her going during unpredictable times, like when the cost of renovating her dream-house was too expensive and the bank had one hundred reasons to deny her loan. Her faith never faltered. She had so much faith that even when Betty offered to step up with the money, Sadie Mae declined the offer. She knew her friend had done enough. It was time to be still and let God be God. She knew He would come through as He always did.

So when Roc's career finally took off and he gave her

a blank check to finish all the repairs, all Sadie Mae could do was say, "What an awesome God I serve, only He can make a way out of no way!"

After Sadie Mae talked about her house, she gave God glory for her health, her strength, and her children, then she stepped down. The people were probably waiting for her to say something about her husband, but she never did. In the past two years, Rockey had been attending church faithfully. His new found religion had the church people talking. It was mainly because they knew of his history and womanizing ways.

Since he'd been attending church, his relationship with Sadie Mae was a mystery the congregation pondered about. The women wondered because he was a good looking, seemingly unattached man. The men were wondering because Sadie Mae looked good and she was living in that big beautiful house alone. Although neither wore a ring, they never announced if their divorce was official.

After Sadie Mae took her seat, Rockey came in. As usual, he sat next to her. Every Sunday it was the same thing. They glanced at each other, barely smiling.

Rockey had never wanted anything as much as he wanted Sadie Mae back. Recently, since he'd been coming to church, she'd stopped being hostile to him. He didn't know what was worse, her being distant and silent, or being so close and cordial, but untouchable.

"Beautiful testimony," a woman in the pew in front of them said. She turned around and shook Sadie Mae's hand.

"God has truly been good to you. I just want you to know He ain't finished with you yet. He's gonna bless your marriage child, so you won't be ashamed to talk about your husband no more. I just want you to know I'm praying for you."

Rockey smiled when he heard someone else was praying for them besides him. When the woman turned back around to face the pulpit, her funny green hat obscured his vision, and he had to scoot closer to Sadie Mae. He was surprised when she didn't move away.

Meanwhile, as Rockey prayed for Sadie Mae's affection, his son was praying the same prayer as he tried to make conversation with Sonya. She wouldn't respond. Roc knew she was still angry about the earring she found in his gym bag, but he felt that five days of the silent treatment was enough.

Since his success, Roc felt that his wife's insecurities were overwhelming, and at times Roc found it almost impossible to come home. It was true that on the road he'd fallen into temptation and had some indiscretions, but that never stopped him from loving Sonya. If anything, he actually believed the affairs made him appreciate her even more.

The very first time a young girl came to him, he adamantly refused her generous offer. But on the road the madness never stopped. Girls built like top ten models wearing practically nothing kept showing up at his every turn, begging for some attention and eager to do whatever they had to do to get it. They kept coming, and coming, until one weak moment Roc gave in and slept with a groupie who found her way into his hotel room. The encounter was incredible, and after that, the guilt lessened with each rendezvous. While the faceless, nameless girls meant nothing, sleeping with them had become a part of who he was and he wasn't about to stop.

For a while, his secret was safe. Sonya trusted him until a young lady who wanted to be more than a one night stand decided to make herself known. After Roc had too much to drink and passed out, the girl got his cell phone. She called Sonya and gave her an ear full of information. After she gave Sonya play-by-play details, she woke Roc up and gave him the phone. When he came to himself, the girl was gone and Sonya was infuriated on the phone. It took Roc months to get Sonya to speak to him. But their love prevailed and she learned to trust him again.

After that incident, Roc promised to be faithful. But his idea of faithfulness was to be more careful. From that point on, when he entertained on the road, he never left personal items around. He never had anything to drink and absolutely no chick was ever allowed to fall asleep in his room—when it was over, she had to get her stuff and go. So far, the arrangement was successful. Most groupies were just thrilled to spend some time with a superstar.

Believing he had the best of both worlds, Roc was able to have all his wild fantasies fulfilled and still come home to have Sonya. Life couldn't get any better. At times it was stressful, but Roc felt he was man enough to handle it, in fact, he loved the double life. Because of his speed on the court, he'd acquired the nickname Rocket, but the name was also symbolic of his personality—explosive and fast. But at home, whenever he was there, he was still just Roc.

Sonya let out a loud sigh and changed her position on the couch, keeping her back toward Roc. If it wasn't for the sound, Roc couldn't tell whether or not she was awake. Even though he lavished her with expensive gifts and gave her everything her heart desired, there was still a sadness about her. She'd been obviously trying to buy herself into a better mood, and that concerned Roc too. She seemed to be turning into a shop-o-holic as the talk show hosts called it. She'd go shopping three to four times a day, but Roc never complained about her spending because at first it seemed to be keeping her happy. But now, it didn't even seem to help. Was her sadness mainly because they hadn't had kids yet? He knew Sonya wanted kids, but he was not keen on the idea. He wasn't sure if he could be a good father. After all, it wasn't like he had such a good example of how to be one.

Roc looked at Sonya watching the shopping network, purposely tuning him out. When she picked up the remote, he cleared his throat to get her attention.

"I'm going over to my mother's, do you want to go?" Roc asked. He waited to hear Sonya's response, but heard nothing. When he left out the door, he looked at her and she turned away.

Roc's mother was only a few minutes away. He'd purchased a hilltop mansion just a couple of blocks from her the day after he signed on with the Pistons. It was great, a two million dollar mansion that was close to family and close to his mother's irresistible cooking.

Normally it was always good to attend Sunday dinners at Sadie Mae's house, but today Roc didn't feel much like being around people, even family. He just wanted some time to himself. Before he knew it he was in his old neighborhood, at the same old basketball court where his love for the game began. It was a dreary autumn day and the pavement was empty, except for one young boy. Roc got out of his black Bentley, walked over to the boy, and started to play some one-on-one with the kid.

"You're good," Roc said, as he watched the young boy stretch his long body toward the net.

"Thank you," the boy said.

"How old are you?"

"I'm eight years old."

"You're like I was, tall for your age. Well, like my mama used to tell me, if you keep it up, you will one day become a strong player. So keep it up young blood."

When the boy took a good look at the stranger towering over him like a skyscraper, he recognized it was Rockwell James, the Rocket. He got overwhelmingly excited and ran to his mother and asked for a pen.

"Mama...it's the Rocket, from the Detroit Pistons! Please, can I have a pen so I can get his autograph?"

The boy's mother walked over to Roc with her son, and extended her hand.

"I'm so pleased to meet you...Rockwell, is it?"

"My friends call me Roc."

"Can I please have your autograph Roc?" the boy pleaded. "My friends won't believe this. I can't believe it!"

Because Roc had a weakness for women, he could not help but check out the kid's mother. She had a pretty face, but she was heavy and the weight took something away from her beauty.

"What is your name?" Roc asked the boy.

"Cordell."

"And your name?" Roc asked his mother.

"Justine," she answered.

Roc wrote some encouraging words and signed his name on the boy's jacket where the kid insisted he should write it. Then he rubbed the boy's head and walked off the court.

When Sadie Mae hung up the phone, she could only shake her head. Over the last two years, Rockey's conversations had gone from apologetic to intense begging. Now he wanted to know if they could go to church together next Sunday, but she knew it was just another ploy to get back in her good graces. Suddenly Rockey claimed he had sowed all his wild oats and he was ready to be a good husband, but now Sadie Mae didn't want to hear it. She did, however, agree to go with him to church before she hung up. Secretly, she didn't mind seeing him suffer as he continued to realize the pain he caused.

When Sadie Mae heard a key jiggling the lock, she was not surprised to see it was her son coming in the front door. He had promised to come by, but it had become so late—the company had all left, and she thought Roc had changed his mind.

Roc sat down at the long kitchen table, and as usual, Sadie Mae prepared to fix him a plate.

"What did you cook today, Mama?"

"Chicken and dressing, yams, macaroni and cheese, collard greens and for dessert, I baked your favorite..."

"Peach cobbler?" Roc said with a smile.

"Yes...I thought Sonya was coming with you," Sadie Mae said as she piled the food on his plate.

"She changed her mind."

"Did she change her mind, or did you do something to make her change her mind?"

"Have you been talking to her, Mama?"

"Well, as a matter of fact I have. She didn't say you two had had an argument, but I could tell in her voice something was wrong."

"Something is always wrong with Sonya. Lately she's always upset."

"Son, I know what it is like to be in a marriage when you feel unloved. And that is what Sonya is feeling. I can see it in her face. I can detect it in her conversation. The problem is you're not making your wife feel loved."

"Mama, any and everything Sonya wants, she gets."

"Roc, she needs more than material things to make her happy. Remember, you just got rich...that girl was in love with you when you didn't have a dime. I recall she married you when you didn't even have a job, only a dream. I know marriage is hard, but it takes two people to make it work. You don't need to be here up under me. I know how you feel about me...go home and tell your wife how you feel about her," Sadie Mae said lovingly to her son. "I just got off the phone with your father who's all sad and lonely. If nothing else, learn from his mistakes and treat your wife with respect. Show her how you feel."

"Mama please don't insult me and compare my marriage to yours. I'm nothing like he was."

"True, you don't curse at your wife and you can afford to give her what your father couldn't give me, but you cheated on her and you constantly neglect her, and those are definitely traits of your father's."

"Mama, I've made some mistakes, but I'm not messing around on her anymore. Sonya's got some problems too. She shops incessantly. She barely ever speaks to me and hardly lets me touch her in any kind of way, and she's obsessed with having a baby, but I don't know how that's gonna happen when she treats me like a stranger. I think deep down inside she blames me for the miscarriage. She hasn't said it, but I can see it in her eyes. And then she has this notion that our marriage is supposed to be like her perfect parents' marriage. I swear Mama, I get so tired of her comparing me to her old man, like he's some kind of god or something."

"Roc, marriage is as hard as you make it, or as easy as you make it. When you bring outside interference into your marriage, like addictions, women, and unrealistic expectations, it is a formula for destruction. You're the man of the house. Many times Sonya follows your lead. Be a man. Sit her down and try to talk out your problems. It's the only way they will be resolved. That was a big problem with your father. He didn't know how to talk about things. And the thing is, you detest him so much, yet you're following in his footsteps. When was the last time you went to church and thanked God for your blessed life and your beautiful wife?"

"No disrespect Mama, but I've sacrificed and practiced long hours to get what I have."

"Roc, who do you think gave you the strong legs to run up and down that court, the long arms to reach those impossible shots, and above all the good mind to do something with them? You think you're the only one who ever had ambition and a dream? Every day, millions dream and hope at a chance of stardom, and they're good too, even extraordinary in their craft, but they don't get the necessary breaks." Sadie Mae paused, and then she took her son's hand. "Your father was good in football and he had a promising career, but it just didn't happen. It wasn't because he wasn't the best of the best, it just didn't work out."

Roc was silent.

"Roc, don't get too high and mighty and think for one second you came this far on your own. God is watching over you. The Bible says, 'Pride comes before the fall.' If you want to stand strong and long, give God His praise," Sadie Mae instructed. "Honey, all I'm saying is, don't give up on God. Keep Him in your life. And don't give up on your marriage either."

"Mama, I love Sonya."

"Don't tell me. I know how you feel. Tell your wife and make her believe it."

Roc took Sadie Mae's advice. After dinner, he went home with flowers and candy he'd purchased on the way home. To make the mood sweeter, he even took home a double portion of Sadie Mae's peach cobbler. He knew how much Sonya loved it.

When Sonya saw he was the bearer of gifts, she smiled. Again, Roc apologized for the earrings and kissed Sonya so passionately and sweetly that she forgot why she was angry.

Chapter Fifteen

Baby Blues

Seven weeks later…

Sonya was only a few weeks along in her pregnancy when she found herself browsing in the nursery section of the department store. She glanced at the other pregnant women around and didn't feel excluded for once. Having this baby meant everything to her—the epitome of womanhood. Less than fifty feet away was the children's department. All the bright and bold colors sent Sonya back in time to her childhood when she was shopping with her mother. She smiled to herself as she pictured doing the same thing with her child in the future.

The wonderful vision was interrupted by a whining little girl tugging at her mother's flowery cotton dress Sonya looked as the two interacted. All it took was a little attention to pacify the discontented child—one kiss and she was happily off on her way. Sonya smiled with anticipated joy. She had a million stored up kisses waiting for her child.

Although the sex of the baby was not important, Sonya gravitated to the girl's section. She picked up the cutest pink booties and lavender bedding. But before she got too carried away, she grabbed a few neutral colored items and a blue sleeper.

When Sonya left the store, she had two huge bags. She hated shopping alone and wondered about Roc. He was scarcely around and his whereabouts were always a mystery. Having so much free time on her hands only confirmed what her mother had said: that the more money they had, the more they had to spend on self indulgent things to occupy their minds; ultimately spending less time together. It was true, Sonya spent most of her time in the shopping malls buying whatever her heart desired, while Roc was busy buying boy toys like his Maybach Bentley Coupe and his Ferrari that he cruised around town in, alone. Even confirming the pregnancy was a solo trip to the doctor, and then Sonya had to track him down to tell him the good news. Lately, they hardly did anything together except argue and maybe occasionally go out and eat. Well, at least they used to dine out, but that came to a streaking halt when Roc commented Sonya's hips were spreading. Immediately she cut back on the greasy foods and started working out four times a week, the last thing she wanted to be was a sloppy fat housewife. But even having a size six body was not enough to keep Roc home. Maybe the baby would have the power to pull them back together. If nothing else, it would definitely eliminate her having too much idle time, she thought.

When Sonya came home that evening, the house was quiet. Sometimes she hated how big it was, and when she was lonely it seemed to double in size. She kicked off her shoes and plopped down on the couch. She couldn't believe how tired she was. She'd shopped most of the day, although that was nothing unusual. Just normal fatigue from the pregnancy, she thought, reclining into the soft leather. Although she was tired, her mind was wired, and she could not relax. She remembered there was some wine in the refrigerator. Without a second thought she got up, went into the kitchen and grabbed a wine goblet from the cabinet. As she poured, she found there was only enough chardonnay to fill the glass half way, which was fine, that was all she needed. She sipped away at the wine slowly, and then tilted her head back to gulp down the last drops.

It was hardly a buzz, but she did feel a little rush as she walked up the stairs to her room. There she turned on the television and cuddled in bed. When she heard the door open, she knew it was Roc, but she was too sleepy to get up. Even when he kissed her on the forehead she could only smile and continue to rest.

Late in the night when Sonya woke up cramping, she didn't want to believe what was happening, though the pain was familiar. She wiped her eyes and looked at Roc. She was glad to see he'd stayed home and then she looked at the clock. It was only nine thirty. She'd thought it was later. She wondered why Roc hadn't made her get up and change into her nightclothes. Getting out of bed to change, she decided the first thing she would do was take a shower in hopes that perhaps it would soothe her cramps. Roc was sleeping so peacefully, she didn't want to wake him and alarm him about her pain. Besides, she really didn't want to admit something was wrong. Finally after her shower, the hurting subsided. And when she checked herself she was not bleeding like before. Perhaps it was nothing. Sonya slipped into her gown, laid beside Roc and fell back asleep.

Hours later, Sonya woke up again in pain. This time when she checked herself, she was spotting. What had she done so badly that God would not allow her to have a child? When the pain became unbearable, finally she woke Roc up in tears and asked him to take her to the hospital.

With the exception of the impersonal doctor, the emergency room experience was déjà vu.

"Miss..." said the doctor. "Oh excuse me, Mrs. James," he corrected himself as he looked at Sonya's chart. "You've had a miscarriage." At times Sonya felt invisible without Roc, who was somewhere on the phone. She knew the doctor probably would've treated her better if he knew she was the wife of the famous Rocket, everyone else did. "The nurse will assist you in cleaning up, and tomorrow, I recommend that you follow up with your family physician," he said, handing the nurse Sonya's chart. And then he asked if there were any questions before he disappeared, just missing Roc.

Sonya sat on the bed broken in disbelief. The only thing she ever wanted more than Roc was to have his baby. Roc pulled the curtains back and helped his wife get dressed.

He understood her strong desire to have a baby, but the last time this happened, she shut him out and didn't want to talk about it. He didn't think he could go through that with her again. If only he knew what to say.

He took in a deep breath and said with caution, "We can try again, Sonya. I love you." They embraced, but Sonya said nothing. She grabbed her coat, eased off the gurney, and headed down the hall. The ride home was extremely long. Roc didn't want to leave Sonya alone, but tomorrow he had to go back on the road. They were playing the Chicago Bulls. Roc knew Sonya was aware that he had to leave, but he was not sure how she would handle being alone in her condition. After Sonya fell asleep, Roc got up and began to pack. When Sonya woke up, she saw the light seeping from the walk-in closet.

"Roc," she called lightly.

When Roc came out, the closet door was open and Sonya could see he was packing.

"You're still going to Chicago?"

"Sonya, you know I have a game tomorrow."

"Roc, I'm sure you can stand to miss one game. Your wife is ill. Someone from the bench can take your place. You think you're so important to that team that you can't miss one game?"

"Baby, I held you through the night, but what else can I do?"

"I didn't expect you to understand. You're probably thinking about the next groupie you're going to get in bed."

"Okay, you're hurting so you're going to try to say or do something to make me hurt also, but I'm not falling for it, not today Sonya. I have a game tomorrow, you know that. I'm leaving and that's final."

Sonya looked at him in tears. Even when he took off down the driveway, she could not believe he'd left.

Even though Roc's head was not in the game, the Pistons won, 96 to 93. After he showered and dressed, the press was waiting. The news reporter reminded him of every bad move he'd made. When you're a key player, it's almost a crime to have an off game.

In the lobby of the hotel, Roc sat at the end of the bar. He'd had three shots of vodka and was feeling quite mellow when a young blonde approached him.

"You're Rockwell James, aren't you?"

Roc gave her an admirable stare. She looked to be about twenty-three and her low cut top revealed her well-built shape. When she talked, she kept tossing her hair back in a flirtatious manner. When she asked if he was staying at the hotel and she would like to see his room, Roc knew what the deal was. He was interested. He ordered her another drink, excused himself, and swaggered to the restroom as if he owned the world.

Afterwards, when he walked out, a lady was standing across the hall with her back turned. As Roc approached her, she turned around. When Roc saw her face, his heart skipped a beat—it was Sherri. She was heavier and older, but it was her.

"Sherri...is that you?" Roc said bewildered.

"Rockwell James, you remembered me. I must admit I wasn't sure if you would," she said.

Roc was not sure if he should hug her or just shake her hand. The last time he saw her, she was pregnant with a child she'd claimed was his. He'd hoped that was the last time he'd ever see her.

"Of course I remember you," he said, leaning in to hug her.

After an awkward moment of silence passed, Sherri said, "Well, Roc I needed to talk to you. In fact, if we can go somewhere private, it would be nice."

"What do you need to talk to me about?"

"Like I said, it's a private matter."

Roc looked around. The hotel lobby was crowded and whatever Sherri had to say he didn't want anyone to overhear. "Follow me," he said.

Roc returned to the lady at the bar. She looked at Sherri in a huff and batted her eyes. When Roc told her another time, she jumped up from the bar and angrily walked away.

When he offered Sherri to sit at the bar, she looked around and asked if he had a room. Roc thought about it for a second and took her back to his suite.
After all, what harm could it be?

"Can I offer you a drink?" he said.

"No thank you."

"Okay, Sherri what is the big mystery? Why do we need all the privacy? What is it?"

Sherri took in a deep breath and exhaled. She looked around at the plush penthouse room. "Life has been good to you," she said.

Roc did not respond. He just humped his shoulders and rubbed his hands impatiently. "Well I had son. His name is Rodney R. Brown," she said and then showed Roc a picture of a little boy. "The R is for Rockwell... after his father."

Roc stood in shock for a moment. Automatically, he questioned Sherri's motive as he looked at her, waiting for her to smile, but she never did. In the back of his mind, he'd always believed that the child was his, but he'd hoped she had gotten rid of the problem.

"We both know he is your child," Sherri said.

There was silence.

"Roc, I got a man with two other children now, and as far as my son is concerned, my man is his biological father, and I have no plans of telling him anything different. But..."

"But...what...Sherri?"

"You're this big basketball star, with an unblemished reputation, pretty little wife....I've kept up with your career. You're worth millions."

"So this is about money...that's what your motive is."

"If it was just about money, I would've come two years ago. But I didn't. But I must admit every time I see your face on television living this good life, a part of me becomes jealous, because my son deserves to be taken care of, and you're his father, and I think you owe him something."

Roc just looked at her. It was obvious that Sherri had been experiencing some bad times. She looked a bit unkempt.

"Roc, you have your life and I have mine, and I don't want to interfere with what you got going on, but for eight years I've taken care of your son, and you owe me. My man doesn't know I'm here, and your wife doesn't have to know either... it will be our little secret."

Roc looked at the photograph again. It was fuzzy, but as far as he could make out, the little boy could've been his. In fact, the photo resembled one of his childhood pictures.

"How much help are you talking about?" Roc said, hardly able to believe his own words.

"Two hundred thousand," Sherri said easily, as if she'd been rehearsing it for a while.

Roc thought about it. It was not an unreasonable amount. If the media got a hold of it, it would cost him much more. The last thing he needed was some negative baby mama drama in the news encouraging all the other women he'd slept with to come out the woodwork and tell their stories. And then Sonya would have a fit if she knew he had a baby. It would surely destroy her especially now after having two miscarriages. The cards were stacked in Sherri's favor.

"If I give you this money, will you swear to leave me alone and never darken my doorstep again?"

"I promise," she said in her same rehearsed tone.

"Where can I contact you?"

Sherri gave Roc the necessary information and he promised to deliver her a cashier's check the next day. When she left, Roc pressed himself against the door. He shut his eyes and shook his head in disbelief. Was this really happening? As he realized that his bad choices were coming back to bite him, he silently made a promise to himself. He would stop being so foolish and make better decisions. He didn't need the stress anymore. But the self-conviction was brief, because when there was a knock at his door, he opened it, and on the other side was the woman from the bar. Instead of refusing her company, he allowed her to come in.

When Roc heard from Sherri again, it was a week later. She had some sad story about needing money again, and then she said maybe he could send her money on a monthly basis, just a little bit. But he said he had to think about it.

After sleeping on it for a couple of days, Roc was still clueless, so in a roundabout way he asked his mother for advice, but she had no idea what he was talking about because he used the scenario of Abraham and his two sons from the Bible. Finally, after all those years of Sunday school the information was helping him out.

"So Mama...although Ishmael was not the promised child, Isaac, Abraham was still obligated to care for him," Roc said as he engaged Sadie Mae in a conversation about the Bible.

"Of course, the boy had his blood, so naturally it was his responsibility to provide for him, even though the boy was not by Abraham's wife, Sarah," Sadie Mae said.

"Thanks Mama. It's odd, I was just thinking about that Bible story for some reason."

"Roc...anytime you want to talk about the Bible you know you can come to me. Does this mean you're going to start back going to church?"

"Maybe Mama...maybe," Roc said.

After the conversation, he decided to give Sherri the money on a monthly basis. Besides, he could afford it and Sherri looked like she needed it. Although Roc was feeling generous, he was also curious if Sherri's story was legit. To remove all doubt, he hired an investigator.

Chapter Sixteen

It Don't Hurt Anymore

It took a couple of weeks before Sonya or Roc told anybody about the baby. It was too painful for Sonya to talk about, and too much for Roc to understand. When Sadie Mae got the news, she called Rockey. In less than twenty minutes, he was pulling into her driveway and she was very surprised to see him. She didn't know he knew where she lived, because she'd only been in the new house for about two years. She opened the door before he got out of the car. When he arrived on the porch, Sadie Mae just looked at him speechless. Rockey was the first to speak.

"I have known where you lived for a while now. I just never bothered you," he said addressing that bewildered look on Sadie Mae's face.

"How did you find out?"

"Well, after you refused to tell me, one of the church members assumed I knew and told me."

At this point, the animosity Sadie Mae had for Rockey was gone. In fact when it came to him, she had no emotions at all.

"Come in," she said, and he followed her as she showed him around.

Rockey was so impressed. It was even more beautiful than he'd imagined. It was huge, spacious, and elegant. Sadie Mae was doing well. The two sat in the kitchen overlooking the terrace and acres of beautiful open land. It was the kind of house he'd always dreamt of having. What a twist of fate that Sadie Mae would have such fortune when he'd tried everything to move up in the world. At times, he'd even schemed on people, and when his dirty deals did not pan out, he tried his hand at gambling, but Lady Luck never shined on him. He thought about all the times Sadie Mae said, "If you have the faith, God has the solution." Looking around, it was obvious God had solved her housing problem.

After several minutes of talking about the kids, the conversation shifted and Rockey started apologizing for past mistakes, again. Sadie Mae just listened. Even though he'd begun to attend church regularly and showed signs of genuine remorse, Sadie Mae was not convinced he'd changed. Patiently, she listened and then politely redirected the conversation back on their son. The transition was so smooth she didn't believe Rockey noticed.

Sadie Mae addressed the fact that Roc had become distant. It was obvious his marriage was about to end, and it didn't appear he cared. She did not want to come out and say it, but Roc had become the monster Rockey once was. Sadie Mae begged Rockey to talk to his son. She'd hoped he could persuade him to change his life, and warn him of the pending doom if he did not change his behavior.

Rockey watched Sadie Mae as she spoke. He'd never seen her look so beautiful. Every night he prayed that God would show her his true feelings and how sorry he was for all the heartache he'd caused her. It had been almost six years since they'd separated and in that time, he'd gone through pure hell. But the way Sadie Mae changed the conversation it was painfully obvious that she was not experiencing the same agony. She'd moved on with her life.

"Sadie," he said sweetly. He had not called her that since they're courting days. "If I said I was sorry a thousand times would it make up for all the pain?"

"The pain is gone Rockey. You don't need to apologize anymore. I'm all right. But, like I said, this is not about you and me. As a matter of fact, it stopped being about us a long time ago," Sadie Mae said as she got up from the table and walked to the door. "I think it's time for you to go."

Rockey looked at Sadie Mae, then put on his hat and coat and left in a huff, but not before he tried to explain his feelings one last time, calmly. Still, even with gentle persuading, he got nowhere with her.

Finally when he left, Sadie Mae watched as he drove down the circular driveway and disappeared beyond the trees. It was strange to her how time had brought about a change. She never thought the day would come that she did not love

Rockey, but it had arrived and no one could be happier than her. For years he had a mystical power over her. A strange obsession that she couldn't even explain, that caused her to love him regardless of the pain, humiliation and neglect he put her through. But now the spell was broken. From deep within she rejoiced and a surge of energy caused her to smile. It felt good to be in control. She was free, and Rockey wouldn't hurt her anymore.

When the phone rang, Sadie Mae picked it up. She was pleased to hear it was the man she'd met a few days ago. When he asked her on a date, dinner at Carl's Steakhouse, she gladly accepted the invitation. Perhaps it was time to start thinking outside the box. Her marriage was over and it was time to move on.

Chapter Seventeen

Pride Before the Fall

When Sonya smiled at the young man, it was harmless flirting, she thought. It felt good to get a man's attention—to feel desirable again. But before she knew it, the shoe salesman, Deshaun, who she'd seen only three or four times, had convinced her to go to a hotel with him. He was charming and affectionate. But it wasn't that he did or said the right things, it's just that he did it and said it at the right time—at a time when she was vulnerable and starved for affection. Since the miscarriage, she and Roc had done nothing but fight. To avoid her, he stayed on the road. To avenge him she avoided his calls.

The first time Sonya was intimate with Deshaun was the hardest. She had never been with another man besides Roc. Afterwards, she could hardly face him, but the next time it got easier. It was even peculiar how the guilt intensified the encounters with Deshaun. They met each other just about every other day. The fling seemed to be the answer to her loneliness.

Deshaun was not Sonya's type at all. He was short and stocky. The only thing that drew her to him was his unique hazel green eyes and confident smile. Although her heart and mind was not into him, her body craved his touch. The secret meetings were filled with passion, lust, and excitement. She even justified her actions with Roc's cheating. Even though he never admitted he was with other women, the evidence was alarming. Sonya was no fool and hated that Roc insulted her intelligence with his lies, but she played along with his game and hoped he would change. But now she felt as if her actions leveled the playing field. True, the fact remained they were both guilty, but Sonya knew if Roc found out, his ego could not handle it and he would have a fit. So when Deshaun started to become possessive, Sonya got worried—it was time to call it off. As much as she hated to end it, she had to, because the kind of time Deshuan was demanding to spend with her was impossible. Tonight would be the last time they would meet, Sonya thought, as she agreed to see him when he walked her to her car.

"What time will you be there, baby?" Deshaun said.

"Around seven o'clock...my husband is having company over to watch the big fight. Time won't be an issue tonight," Sonya teased before she pulled off in her blue Mercedes. The dull January sun had nothing on her bright sinister grin.

It was seven thirty when Roc realized Sonya was gone. Then it dawned on him that she'd been missing a lot lately.

She'd even stopped complaining about him being on the road. Her odd behavior made him suspicious until Sonya called and said she was over to her mother's house. It was a cold winter's night and Roc thought nothing wrong when Sonya suggested she spend the night at her parent's house because of weather alerts warning of the possibility of threatening weather. He also knew Sonya did not enjoy being in the house with a bunch of men playing poker, smoking, and watching the fight. So he ended the call with the habitual, "I love you...see you later."

Later on, once Roc's company had arrived, he received another phone call. This time it was a strange caller informing him of Sonya's whereabouts. An unfamiliar female voice told him about Sonya's sordid affair and their secret hideaway. The angry informant cleared her throat and quickly repeated the information.

"Who is this?" Roc demanded.

"Don't worry about who I am. But mister—tell Deshaun the next time he decides to cheat on somebody with a married woman, don't brag about who he's sleeping with...the wife of a superstar," the angry female said before the call abruptly ended.

Suspicions validated, Roc quickly reacted like a mad man. He envisioned wringing Sonya's neck. In a half drunken state, he tried to digest the conversation, but his judgment was off and his perception was fuzzy. Of all nights, he regretted he had company—he tried to hold back his anger but he was out of control and no one would stop him from leaving. Engulfed with fury, he vowed to find Sonya and her lover as he broke free from the restraining arms of his friends. Racing over to his desk, Roc flew open the right-hand drawer to grab his pistol and rushed out of the house, jumped in his car and burned down the driveway speeding fearlessly along the quiet neighborhood on the icy roads. His destination was clear. He was very familiar with Sonya's hideaway. Master Suites was an upscale hotel just off of highway 696.

More than twenty miles away, the normally twenty-five minute ride took Roc less than ten minutes to reach. He pulled into the one-way circular driveway, speeding the wrong way by the valet attendants. He came to a screeching halt when he met oncoming traffic.

Roc backed out slowly and followed the attendant's gesture to the parking lot. Roc circled the parking lot three times before he finally saw Sonya's blue Mercedes. As he checked the license plates to make sure it was hers, his heart was rushing. Sure enough, it was Sonya's car, the personalized license plates read, "My Girl."

He imagined her lover to be an older sugar daddy, because Sonya desired the best and it took money to stay at Master Suites. Also, Roc always felt Sonya had an attraction for older men because of her overbearing love for her father, and he felt like Sonya was disappointed with him and the next man in her life would be more like her father. He figured the old dude was probably just enjoying the company of his young pretty wife. Sonya was only twenty-four—twenty-four and naïve, Roc thought.

Roc cased the parking lot, watching the people come

and go. He'd parked his car two lanes behind Sonya so she wouldn't spot his car. The thought of another man touching Sonya inflamed him and not even the sub-zero temperature could cool him. As far as he knew, Sonya had never been with another man, and the fact that her purity had been tampered with made him crazy with anger.

His plan was to ambush them. He contemplated over and over what he would do. First, he would sneak between the cars and hide there until she got close to him, then he would throw Sonya to the ground and then beat up the no good man she was with.

While plotting and planning, he spotted Sonya—time to execute his plan. In the dark, Roc could not make out the man Sonya was kissing. The site of the two of them almost took his breath away! He jumped out of his car, stretched his long legs and grabbed Sonya from behind before she could even see him coming. Without asking any questions, he threw Sonya to the ground as planned and then collared the mystery man. Roc was so enraged he saw red as he began beating the man in the face.

"Roc! Please don't! Roc, please stop! I'm sorry! Don't do anything crazy!" Sonya screamed from the ground.

When Roc finally looked into the man's face, to his surprise it wasn't an old man but what seemed to be a teenager! He did not know whether to shoot him or whip him Heatedly, Roc continued beating the young man in the face. Blood was flying everywhere. During the commotion, Roc's pistol fell. Sonya saw it and kicked it out of sight. She then jumped on

Roc's back in a failed attempt to stop him. Somehow Deshuan managed to break free and he jumped into his car and got on his cell phone. When Roc reached for his gun to shoot out the windows, he realized it was missing, so he tried to use his bare hands to break the glass. The adrenaline rush his body was experiencing caused him not to feel the intense pain. In the chilling weather, most of Roc's body was exposed, but he didn't care. Even when he got on his hands and knees and crawled around on the snowy pavement looking for his gun, he was not bothered.

When he finally found the gun, he heard sirens and threw it in some nearby brushes and stood up. (It would be weeks later before he could retrieve it.)

All Sonya could do was cry and try to figure out if all the good times were worth the pain she was feeling. When Roc started shaking her, she was sure he would hit her next. But oddly he turned and started beating her car. Finally, before he could kick out all the lights, the police arrived and stopped him from causing anymore damage to the car as they made him put his hands in the air.

"Officer I'm sorry...." Roc said, trying to adjust his eyes to the flashing siren lights. "I'm the victim...I caught my wife cheating on me."

"Keep your hands up, sir, and move slowly from the car," a big burly male officer said, as he walked over to Sonya crying on the ground. Another officer, a female, kept her gun aimed at Roc all the while.

Behind the police car was another car, with a woman in

it. She looked to be in her forties. When the police handcuffed Roc, the woman jumped out of her car and ran to see about Deshaun who was still in his car.

In a frantic scream she cried out, "Lord let my baby be all right, let him be all right!" Shaking like a leaf, she knocked on the window and said, "Open up the door baby, I'm here. Are—are you all right?"

When the car door opened, the woman almost fainted as she began to wipe away all the blood from Deshaun's face. "Who did this to my son!? I said, who did this to my son!? He's only seventeen—who did this!?"

In the midst of all the commotion, she saw Roc in handcuffs. "You did this, mister, to my boy? You did this? As sure as God is my witness you're going to pay for this! I will press charges and sue you for every dime you have! My son's girlfriend told me who you were. Some kind of big shot for the Pistons—well call your lawyer because I'm going to make sure you think before you hit someone else's son!" the woman shouted angrily.

At that point, the police recognized the tall man was Rockwell James, the Rocket, a Detroit Piston superstar. Sonya was also amazed. Deshaun told her he was twenty-one. She could not believe it. She'd committed adultery with a child. She was sick and embarrassed.

Roc was put in jail overnight for a cool down period. The precinct said he must serve this time before he could be released to his lawyer.

No charges were filed against Sonya. It was proven that the

sex was consensual. The young man had a list of criminal violations and considering all the facts involved, his mother decided not to pursue a case against Roc.

Although the case was dropped, the courts ordered Roc to undergo anger management classes. The ordeal was not only costly, but embarrassing once the press got a hold of the story.

Chapter Eighteen

Accident

When Rockey heard the news about a Detroit Piston being involved with domestic violence, he never thought it was his son until his face was flashed across his screen. He could not believe his eyes. Roc was being carried away in handcuffs by the police.

Rockey got on the phone and immediately called Sadie Mae. When he reached her, she was in her car on her way to the police station to find out exactly what'd happened. Sonya's mother had already called her from the precinct, hysterical. Rockey wanted to tag along, but the last time he had an encounter with Roc it was bad. So Sadie Mae convinced him not to go, but promised to call him as soon as she had all the details.

Rockey was sitting by the phone when Sadie Mae called him back. She was crying.

"It was horrible," she said. "I never thought I would

see one of my children behind bars. Sonya has been having an affair with a teenage boy," Sadie Mae said.

"She's in jail too?" Rockey interrupted Sadie Mae's sentence.

"No. Apparently the boy lied about his age. Because the affair was consensual, the boy's mother did not press charges on Sonya," Sadie Mae said, still crying.

"Do you need me to come over?"

Sadie Mae didn't even have to think about it before she said no. She had enough on her mind and she just wanted to be alone. After she hung up the phone, she took a shower, read the Bible, and prayed.

Rockey did not bother with getting in bed. He just sat on the couch looking at the television. Still dressed, he wanted to be ready in case Sadie Mae called back with a changed mind. Totally relaxed, unconsciously, he felt himself drifting into a deep trance as his uninhibited thoughts were consumed by dreams. When he opened his eyes, he was standing in the funeral home where his father was laid to rest. Except for an organ player and a few scattered flowers on the altar, the room was empty. The bronze cardboard-looking coffin represented a pathetic and lonely life. Rockey walked closer to look inside. When he bent down to say his final goodbyes, he saw himself staring back at him. The image spooked him and he woke up in a cold sweat. Rockey remembered his father. He was put away on a cold snowy day and not one person was willing to deal with the inclement weather to come out and wish him farewell—not even the woman he was with when he died. He was mean, distant, and uncaring. He'd lived his whole life not knowing how to do the one thing that could've changed him—love. When he died, no one cared. In sixty-one years he'd never reached out and touched anyone.

To be truthful, Rockey did not believe his father had it in him to emotionally connect with anyone. Rockey had always believed his father's introvert personality came as a result of his mother's untimely death. But in the dark, as his childhood unfolded, he remembered his mother's constant complaints about his father's inability to communicate and his wanton desire to be in the streets. Rockey also remembered her complaints of his father's selfishness and lack of affection. Thinking back, Rockey even remembered the hushed voices and whispers surrounding his mother's death.

The day of her funeral, he heard one aunt say his mother killed herself because she couldn't take the neglect and mental abuse any longer. Rockey could still see the surprised look on the woman's face when she realized he was standing behind her. Suicide was taboo in the black community. Quickly, she changed her story and said his mother died of a broken heart. Although throughout his life, no one could tell him how, exactly, a broken heart could cause death. But now, after all these years, Rockey felt like he finally understood because the pain he was feeling was so intense it felt like he was dying, or worse, willing to take his own life.

In the dark, Rockey's deep thoughts forced him to

face some things he did not want to face. A dark secret he'd locked away in the corner of his mind was now disturbed.

Rockey hopped up from the couch wringing wet and looked in the mirror. He was the spitting image of his father. Not only did he have his looks, but when he looked around at the emptiness, he realized he also had his temperament. Rockey's salty tears, mingled with sweat poured down his face as he sobbed and broke down.

He looked around. He'd lost everything. Immediately, he got on his knees and prayed. He asked God to deliver him and his son who was taking on the same low down characteristics he once had. He did not want his son to live the same destructive life. He pleaded with God to break the curse.

Rockey rose up from his knees on a mission. He had to tell Roc to change before it was too late. He was the fourth man in the James' family to be named Rockwell, and everyone had had the same character. The madness had to stop.

Early the next day, Rockey went to his son's house. Sonya was not there. The two men were alone. Roc only allowed his father in to tell him for the last time to leave him and his family alone and he stopped him from coming any further than the foyer. Then he closed the door. When he looked at his father, he would have struck him in anger if he had not looked so differently. It was not just his wholesome attire that was out of character, but his eyes were a dead giveaway that something about him had changed. They oddly reflected genuine sincerity. It was as if the man that stood before him was a stranger until Roc heard the familiar baritone voice probing into his life about last night's ordeal.

"I'm not here to judge you, I just want to know what is going on in your head. If you're honest with me and tell the truth, I can help. I've been there before, and I don't want you to make the same mistakes I made and destroy your family." Although Rockey tried hard not to sound judgmental, Roc's cold persona made him feel as if he was. Rockey even felt like he was tiptoeing through a minefield.

Roc's stare became colder as he said, "You're trying to give me advice? Man you could not point me to the hospital if I was dying. You need to get this straight. I did not allow you into my house to hear what you had to say...only to say this for the last time: I don't want you to be a part of my life, now or ever. Whatever problems I'm going through, I will solve on my own."

Then Roc opened the door and gestured for his father to leave.

"This was something you were always so good at doing," Roc sucked in his breath. "Only this time when you disappear, make it forever!"

"I deserve this from you, but if you despise me so much, then why live the same foolish way I did? Can't you at least learn from my mistakes? Now, you can take what I'm saying to you as advice, or as an old fool passing on some wisdom—take it any way you want to, but just take it. I—"

"You what?" Roc said, opening the door wider.

"I'm leaving...but not before I say what I came here to

say."

"Oh no...you have said enough! Get out!"

Then aggressively, Roc took his father by the arm and forced him toward the door. Instinctively, Rockey felt surpassed anger rise up within, and then before he could react, a calm feeling overtook him. The strange peacefulness took him by surprise. He exhaled the wind from his lungs and broke free from Roc.

"Listen," he said. "I didn't come here to fight. My father died lonely, miserable and broken. This sad ending appears to be my fate as well. I made my bed and now I have to lay in it. And I'm afraid you're walking in our footsteps. You look so much like me, and now this thing with Sonya—you're starting to act just like me. Don't do it...take control over your sins before it's too late and life is over."

Roc looked at Rockey, he would've considered what he'd said if it wasn't so ridiculous. He examined his father closer. Suddenly, he could see the old familiar Rockey—trying to run game on everyone. This time, instead of using a crooked smile, he was using the Bible.

"Man, I'm nothing like you. If anything, I see right through you. What is this...another little con game you're playing? What? You need money? Is this what this is all about...money?" Roc went into his pocket and brought out a roll of money. "Do I have to pay you to leave me alone? I heard you were doing real bad, living in some rat-hole apartment on Fifth Street," Roc said as he kept on saying humiliating things to his father.

When the insults kept coming, Rockey walked away.

He wasn't sure how long he could hold his peace. But Roc had just gotten started. He followed Rockey to his car shouting obscenities, even after Rockey had taken off.

"Oh, you're in a hurry now? Now, you don't want to listen!" Roc said as he jumped in his Bentley and followed his father. Roc wasn't sure what he was going to do once he caught up with him. Head him off, he supposed, and tell him all the things he'd kept hidden for so long. Remind him again of his embarrassing childhood, all the lies and neglect he'd felt...

When Roc saw his father's brake lights in the snowy haze, he sped up and floored the accelerator from 55 to 80 in just seconds. Blinded by tears and rage, Roc hit an ice patch in the road and lost control. From a distance, Rockey saw his son's car veer off the road. Devastated, Rockey made a sharp u-turn in the street.

The 911 dispatcher could barely understand what Rockey was saying.

"Sir, are you all right?" the woman said.

But Rockey could barely answer. Between fear and sub-below temperatures, his words were scarcely audible. Then finally when he calmed himself down, he confirmed his whereabouts and the accident scene to the woman.

"Your son's car is wrapped around a tree, and your son was thrown from the car," she repeated his words.

"Yes."

"Is he breathing, sir?"

"Barely," Rockey said.

"Sir, please do not move him. The paramedics and ambulance are on the way."

Chapter Nineteen

The Blame Game

When Sadie Mae arrived at the hospital, news reporters were camped out everywhere. It was early on in Roc's career, when his every move became front-page news.

Judging by the crowd, it was no wonder how a false allegation had leaked out accusing him of being under the influence of drugs and alcohol at the time of the accident. It was just a cruel lie created to further tarnish her son's reputation. She was convinced of that, even before she heard the whole story.

Although she'd only parked a few feet away from the entrance, hospital security had to escort her in. As Sadie Mae was ushered through the people, she avoided the numerous microphones shoved in her face and the blinding camera flashes. At this point, her only desire was to escape the media circus and see about her son. The hospital gave little information over the phone—only to come immediately. With each step, Sadie Mae's stress level mounted and the different voices launching accusations and questions at her only worsened the tension.

"Mrs. James, can we have a comment?" she heard in passing as she kept a steady forward momentum. Then suddenly an anxious anchorwoman standing in her path overtook Sadie Mae's view. With a straight face the woman said, "Mrs. James is it true your son will never walk again and his career is over?"

It was the first time Sadie Mae had heard the bad news. Not even Rockey had said anything like that. He'd only said the doctors were not sure of the damage. Horrified, she could not respond as she almost fainted. Rockey was already inside when he saw the commotion from a distance. He rushed through the crowd to comfort Sadie Mae, and when it became obvious that she was too distraught to answer any questions, the attention immediately turned to him. Rockey heard whispers as they referred to him as the estranged father. Up until then, he'd not been known publicly, but the news spread like wild fire when he made the 911 call.

"Sir is it true you were at the scene of the accident? Did your family tension escalate to this tragedy?" one anchorman asked.

Like vultures on the prey for blood, the heartless men and women went after the two of them. Not letting up, they kept scavenging for answers. Even after Sadie Mae and Rockey had reached a quiet hallway, the reporters continued the questioning; only this time, it was aimed at the paramedics who had answered the call.

Finally, Sadie Mae could get some answers as she and Rockey were greeted by Sonya in the trauma ward.

"Sonya, how is Roc?" Sadie Mae said.

"He's in a great deal of pain, but he's alert thank God, and that rules out brain damage. But before the doctors rushed him off to surgery, they talked to me briefly about the seriousness of his legs," Sonya said, covering her face with her hands. She looked at her mother-in-law with hot, heavy tears. "They're crushed. There are multiple fractures in nearly every bone. There is a chance he may not walk again, or if he does, only with the aid of a cane," Sonya said, crying.

"Were you able to talk to him?" Sadie Mae said.

"He was heavily sedated. I couldn't make out everything he was saying, but I did manage to understand one thing." Then Sonya looked at Rockey. "He said the accident was your fault, Rockey. What happened?"

Up until that point, Rockey had been silent, almost invisible. He knew the accident was not his fault.. or was it? Of course he did force his son off an icy road, but he was responsible for the rage and anger that led up to the unfortunate moment. When Sadie Mae and Sonya looked at him for answers, he wanted to take off and start running. Like Roc had said, he was good at running, but the time had come for him to stand his ground and be still. At first he stuttered, and afterwards when he took in a deep breath, the words flowed properly.

"I went to your house to talk to Roc. As usual, we got into a heated argument. I left, and he jumped in his car and followed me. I saw him speeding after me in my rear view mirror. I should've stopped, but I didn't. When I saw his car veer off the road, I turned around.... Maybe if I had turned around sooner this would not have happened."

"Or maybe, if you had never gone to our house, this would not have happened," Sonya said in anger.

Sadie Mae was speechless. Knowing how his son felt about him, Rockey should have never gone to his house. She was just as angry as Sonya, but it was not the time for blame.

"It's time for prayer, not blame. There is a chance Roc may never walk again," Sadie Mae said as she reached inside her purse and pulled out her cell phone.

"Who are you calling?" Sonya asked.

"My prayer partners from church," Sadie Mae replied as she began to dial the numbers.

The next day, after Sadie Mae and over a dozen members from church prayed all night, Roc made it out of a six hour surgery which had gone extremely well. The doctors were thrilled, but still skeptical about his career. When Roc inquired about his future, the doctors could only say time was the determining factor. The possibility that Roc's basketball days were over made him despondent and depressed. He refused all contact from his teammates and refused all interviews to dispel the myths about his drunk driving.

Roc was alert when Sonya walked into his room, but

when he closed his eyes and did not respond to her voice, she assumed he was groggy from all the medication and left. Outside his room, he heard voices engaged in conversation. As each person spoke, he pictured their face one by one: Regina, Raymond, Joey, Chloe, Ms. Betty, Mr. & Mrs. Jones, and then he heard Rockey. Immediately, he became heated. He had even more cause to hate his father now. Because of him, he might be crippled and lose everything.

Fighting the intense pain, Roc reached for the button to buzz the nurse's station and through the intercom, he demanded more pain medication. He was in no mood to deal with Sonya, his family, his friends, and especially Rockey and he wanted to stay in a drug-induced state for as long as possible. Before his second attempt to buzz for help, a nurse came in. Roc was in too much pain to flirt, but under any other circumstances, she would have been someone he would've gotten with. She was a petite, brown skinned cutie. As Roc watched her put a vile of medication in his IV, he checked her out from head to toe. Perhaps his next request would be a sponge bath...

When Sadie Mae could not find Rockey in the cafeteria or the visitor's lounge, she considered the hospital chapel. Two years ago, she would've never thought of it, but now it was worth a try. When she walked inside, it was empty, but the atmosphere was so peaceful that before she knew it, she was sitting down. When it rains, it pours, Sadie Mae thought, thinking of all the recent trouble with Roc—domestic violence, jail, and now an accident. Sadie Mae didn't realize she was crying until she felt the tears run down her cheeks. Deep in her soul she believed Roc would heal physically, but it was his heart she was concerned about. If he could not play basketball again, she knew his life would spiral out of control. The sport was how he identified himself and if it was over, she feared he could not handle it emotionally.

As Sadie Mae prepared to leave, Rockey entered the chapel.

"Betty told me you were here," he said.

"I came here looking for you, but I found such peace, I had to stay."

"I never meant for anything bad to happen to Roc. I went to his house to make him see how he could lose everything, like I did, if he didn't change," Rockey said, lowering his head into his shaking hands.

Sadie Mae did not have it in her to comfort Rockey. Besides she knew at this point only God could give him peace. And while it was an "I told you so" moment, she dared not say it. She'd preached to him for years about his selfish ways and he tuned her out. But God has a way of making Himself heard. It's a shame Rockey had to be broken down to nothing to finally listen.

As Rockey watched Sadie Mae leave, he realized he'd lost the one person in the world who once loved him unconditionally. She finally turned her back on him. Foolishly he'd hoped reconciliation was in the hands of God and time. That is why he prayed and waited. But now, standing alone, he realized they would never transcend their differences and coalesce as one again. So all that wishful thinking he'd done was for the birds. He really thought when he came to the chapel that he and Sadie Mae would cry together, pray together, and the grace of God would cover them and a miracle would take place. A miracle of healing.

But the craziest thing of all was that Rockey thought, even after all these years of strife and division, his son would actually listen to anything he had to say. But, there, standing alone, Rockey's perspective changed. Living right was not all that it was cracked up to be. In fact, it seemed like the more he tried to live right, the more he felt like a fool. At least when he was in the world, he didn't care about what people thought, and he got more respect. It seemed like Sadie Mae loved him when he was hurting her, disrespecting her and neglecting her. Now she barely gives him the time of day. Suddenly Rockey felt like having a drink. He wiped the tears from his face, jumped up and took off. When he burst through the chapel doors, he ran into one of the men from church. Ro ckey recognized him. He was one of the prayer warriors Sadie Mae had called. A godly man was the last person Rockey wanted to see. He was on his way to the bar and he didn't want to hear nothing about Jesus.

"Brother James, praise God! It's good to see you. I just talked to your wife. She said your son is showing some positive progress in his legs. It just goes to show you, it don't matter what the doctors say...God has the last word!" the man said.

"Thank you for praying for my son. I really appreciate that," Rockey said as he looked at his watch. "I've had a long day, and, if you excuse me, I got to be going."

"Sure, I understand. I don't want to keep you, but since we bumped into each other, maybe we can have a quick word of prayer. It won't be long, I promise. It's good when women pray, but I don't think it is nothing like the voice of a godly man in the ear of God. After all, as men, God charges us to cover our family, and we must take our rightful place as head of our households and honor the family God has given us."

Rockey thought about it for a moment and then agreed. What did he have to lose? The bar wasn't going anywhere. It would still be there when they got finished praying.

Rockey had only met the man in passing at church maybe once or twice, but he felt a strange kindred spirit towards him. For no apparent reason before they prayed the man told Rockey a little bit about himself—his family struggles, his addiction to gambling and how he lost everything chasing the luck of chance. The part of his testimony that really blessed Rockey was how God restored his life from ruins. Before Rockey knew it, he'd told the man what he was struggling with and where he was headed. The man smiled and said it was just divine intervention that they'd bumped into each other because he'd gotten lost on his way out of the hospital and ended up in front of the chapel. The man prayed with Rockey and gave him the necessary encouragement to keep the faith. When the prayer was over, so was Rockey's urging to drink. He decided to stay at the hospital with his family.

When Sherri heard about the accident on TV, she immediately got on the phone and called Roc's cell phone, but there was no answer. It went straight to his voicemail, but she didn't leave a message—Roc had made it clear that their affiliation was strictly on the down low.

Chapter Twenty

Hard Times

Finally, after six months of grueling physical therapy, Roc was able to walk without the aid of a cane. Although he was told he was blessed to walk again, in reality, he did not feel blessed—his basketball career was over. He had several pins and plates and his fragile legs could not support the activity of a vigorous sport. At twenty-four he was forced to retire. On the day the Pistons management bought him out of his contract, they threw a big party in his honor. It was the last day he was treated like basketball royalty. Since then, Roc had refused all contact from anyone on the team—being around the players made him feel like a charity case.

It was Sunday, and as usual Sadie Mae had a big dinner at her house after church. When she called her son, he refused her invitation for the second time. It was the third week he'd declined to be around family and friends. Roc had become reticent about his feelings. He was more comfortable nursing a six-pack of beer or a bottle of vodka in front of the television alone watching sports channels. His depressive state even hindered him from seeking solace in reading—as he had always done before. Reading good books was now on the end of his growing to do list.

As usual, Roc sat in the family room of his house, a place of torture, surrounded by his Piston's memoir. This evening, he'd been sitting on the couch for hours staring at the wall filled with certificates and pictures. Most of them dated back to the beginning of his career. The pictures were hung by Sonya and Sadie Mae during his glory days. Back then, he was too busy to be bothered with tedious things like that. Sonya had even made several scrapbooks that were sitting at his fingertips. Now, he'd browse through them daily which only worsened his melancholy mood.

After he'd looked through the scrapbook for the third time, he slammed it down on the table and exhaled deeply. He then went into his housecoat pocket and brought out a pack of cigarettes, and pulled to him a strange object that adorned their house lately, an ashtray. Smoking was a new habit he'd acquired that infuriated Sonya, if for no other reason than the horrible smell. At first he started out just smoking cigars every now and then, but now suddenly he was a chain smoker. He claimed the infatuation for tobacco came from boredom. It was strange because he'd always complained about his father's nasty habit.

After smoking two cigarettes back to back, Roc swallowed the last drop of beer from a can he'd nursed for the last twenty minutes and got up. He then walked toward the kitchen not resisting the urgency to get another. What was the point of watching a good game without a brew?

It was five o'clock when the game finally ended and Roc had yet to get dressed, shower or shave. There were times he went for days without addressing his hygiene. Other than complain about him smoking, Sonya said little about his out of control behavior. The way she doted over him with affection, Roc was convinced she was just glad to have him around full time.

When Roc heard Sonya come downstairs, he knew she would be dressed for dinner. Even though he'd withdrawn himself from everyone, she still participated in all the family functions. It was the third Sunday she'd gone solo.

Roc did not mind that she went. In fact, he'd planned on giving her the cold shoulder just so she would leave him alone. He just felt like being by himself. But when Sonya came down the stairs, she looked so pretty and fresh, she made him feel dirty. As a matter of fact, she looked too good, even overdressed.

Earlier, Sonya had told him she was getting out of the house with or without him, but Roc assumed she meant to dinner with his family. But that was a casual affair, and Sonya's white mini dress was not appropriate. The dress had to be new. He'd never seen it before. He would've noticed as it was sheer with the back open. She was even sporting a new pair of white sandals. While he guessed at whether Sonya had gone to the mall or not, he became convinced when he saw her freshly done pedicure.

"Since when did you start wearing heels and mini dresses

to go over to my mother's house? Roc asked suspiciously.

"Actually, I was not going to your mother's house. Some friends and I were going to Hart Plaza and then Greek Town for dinner," Sonya said.

"What friends?"

"Renee and some of her friends.... Why? Do you have a problem with me leaving?"

"No," Roc said. "I was getting ready to get dressed and go over to my mother's house. I changed my mind. I wasn't going to go, but I think I need to get out. I was hoping you'd go with me."

"But I already made plans."

Roc looked at her suspiciously. He'd never gotten over her cheating on him and he believed Renee encouraged her to do it.

"What—why are you looking at me like that?"

Roc knew if he forced the issue, Sonya would get angry and stay at home, and that was just what he wanted her to do. He didn't trust her anymore. To Roc's surprise, Sonya did not back down. She insisted on leaving and tried to convince him to go with her. But Roc was stubborn and refused. Sonya asked again, but when Roc said no, she left.

Dumbfounded by Sonya's actions, Roc's first instinct was to follow her. He took a shower and got dressed. But after he got cleaned up, he had a change of heart. Instead of Greek Town, he decided to go to Sadie Mae's house. But when he opened the door, he reconsidered everything and didn't feel like doing anything. He went back into the house, put on his pajamas and returned to the family room with a can of beer.

A few weeks later when Roc found himself in his attorney's office filing for bankruptcy, his insolvent state hit him. He was losing everything. Even though he realized bankruptcy was a man's legal right for financial restoration, the clemency of a second chance only made Roc feel more depressed. He'd failed and the world reinforced his failure with the stamp of bankruptcy for the next seven years. Mentally, he visualized the media headlines: "The Rocket finally crashed in bankruptcy court."

His attorney, Gregory Nelson, a fraternity brother, advised Roc of a management position at a small manufacturing plant that made parts for the big three automotive companies. He told Roc with his engineering background he could pull a few strings and get him the job if he wanted it. The job could not compare with his past, but it was decent pay and it could help him get out of the financial slump he was in. It did not take much for Roc to accept the offer.

Before Roc left the his attorney's office, the appropriate phone calls were made. When the company learned about Roc's education profile, the job was a given. They eliminated the red tape and the ordinary protocol and hired Roc based on Ron's word and Roc's name.

Roc was somewhat thrilled he'd gotten the job. He knew Sonya would be happy also. When his cell phone rang, he didn't bother to look at the number before he said, "I got the job baby."

"What job?" a strange voice echoed in his ear.

"I hope that means you can start back paying me child support!" the caller said.

Immediately, Roc recognized it was Sherri.

"What do you want Sherri? You can't squeeze blood from a turnip. I don't have any money. You seem to know everything about me, and how you're getting the information on the other side of the world, I don't know. But I'm surprised your source didn't tell you I've filed for bankruptcy, and legally I'm broke. Now do whatever you want to do, and tell whoever you want to tell. I don't care!" Roc said and hung up the phone.

Chapter Twenty-One

Coping with Consequences

It was the first day on the job and Roc was greeted by some former fans. A few workers were even waiting in the office lobby to get his autograph. It was the latest buzz around the plant. Rockwell James, the Rocket, former NBA superstar, was the new maintenance supervisor. Between completing personnel forms, Roc answered questions and entertained his new colleagues with basketball stories. At first, Roc hid his shame behind a fake smile, but soon after the attention appeared genuine, his tarnished ego came shining through. To his surprise, what he dreaded turned out to be exhilarating.

As he signed autographs, he caught the eye of one young lady. She had that girl-next-door look. The kind of girl you took home to meet the family. Her skin was fair, like she was mixed or something. She looked to be about 5'6, with long legs. She reminded him of a runway model. When she reached out to shake his hand, he could not help but give her an approving smile in hopes that she'd pick up on his subtle flirting.

"Hello," she said. Her voice was soft and sweet. "I know you don't remember me, but my son and I met you about two years ago, in the park in my neighborhood. You signed his jacket and he has never worn it again. He keeps it in the closet hanging up as a keepsake."

Roc looked at her. He was puzzled. How could he forget someone so strikingly beautiful?

"I apologize. I've met so many people, it's hard for me to remember everyone, but I can't imagine forgetting someone like you. What is your name?"

"Justine," she said. "And you're called Rocket."

Roc flashed his seductive smile, and checked her out with his big sexy eyes. It was strange. He couldn't believe he was making the moves on this chick, but it was something about her that made him crazy inside.

"Rocket was just a nickname on the court. Please call me Roc, short for Rockwell."

For the next fifteen minutes, the lobby was filled with people. Then suddenly the crowd disappeared when a loud bell to return to work went off. After the excitement died down, it was time for Roc to get focused. He was given a tour of the plant.

First, he was given safety glasses to protect his eyes from flying welding sparks that escaped the welding guns. Roc saw how most of metal was assembled by huge presses, and then how some required manual labor. And when the loud roar of presses cycling and recycling began to make his head ring, he realized the need for the earplugs he'd been given. That instant, he decided to put them in his ears.

The plant was huge. As Roc walked on, every now and then a hi-lo driver drove past and shook his hand, welcoming him to the job. For a moment he considered all the walking evolved until he was told he would be given an automatic cart to drive around in.

After Roc had seen the plant, he was shown his work crew. He would be over the skilled tradesmen. Then finally, Roc was shown his work area. He shared a small office with another supervisor who looked like a prison warden. Everyone called him by his last name, Oakley. He was not personable, and after eight hours, the only thing Roc knew about him was he was soon to be promoted to General Manager, a position higher than Roc. So far, the fact that Oakley would soon be his boss was the only disappointing news he had gotten

The ride home was uneventful. Rush hour traveling was the worst. As Roc watched red brake lights go on and off in bumper to bumper traffic, he was haunted by Justine's smile. He did not stop thinking about her until Sonya called and they discussed possibilities for dinner. Roc knew it really wasn't about the dinner. Sonya just wanted to know how his day went. Although financially, they were struggling, Roc was determined Sonya would not work. As a man, he was still bothered by the childhood image of his mother working hard and long hours keeping her away from them. He felt that the measure of his manhood was how well he took care of Sonya.

However noble his decent act was, it went deeper than just doing the right thing. It was his duty to be the sole provider.

Having decided on steak and potatoes, Roc was ready to say goodbye when his wife spoke up.

"You haven't said anything about work yet. How was your first day?" she asked.

"Better than I expected," Roc said, changing lanes for the third time. "It's a big plant, and there is a lot of walking involved, but I was told I would have a cart to drive around in."

"How about the pay?" she said.

As unsettling as he found Sonya's question, it was typical of her. She hadn't been shopping in almost six months. He knew she was feigning for some extra cash, like an alcoholic thirsts for a drink. When he told her he was not in the six digits, she sounded displeased until he said he made enough to give her a few dollars to go shopping.

After three weeks on the job, Sadie Mae convinced Roc he had something to be grateful for. God had brought him through a car accident, bankruptcy, and given him a new life after basketball. He'd also blessed him with the ability to keep his house and hold onto his marriage. As Sadie Mae campaigned for Christ, she was determined not to take no for an answer. Roc was coming to church. She reminded him that this Sunday was Family & Friend's Day, and afterwards, dinner was at her house.

Sunday, Sadie Mae arrived at church minutes earlier

than Roc and Sonya. When she got there, she was surprised to see Sherri's mother. She'd never seen her at First Bethel before. Sadie Mae went over and sat behind her. When she overheard Mother Harris introduce her as her niece, Sadie Mae understood why she was there. Sherri's mother took some pictures out of her purse and showed Mother Harris. Sadie Mae tried to get a glimpse of them without looking obvious.

Although it had been years since Sherri had left town, Sadie Mae still believed she never got an abortion and she had a grandchild somewhere in the world she may never know. When Sadie Mae could not get any closer without looking like a snoop, she tapped the woman on her shoulder.

"Excuse me," she said, "but aren't you Sherri's mother?"

"Yes, I have a daughter named Sherri. Do I know you?"

Sadie Mae could not believe she'd forgotten who she was. How easy is it to forget the parents of the boy who supposedly messed up your daughter's life? As the woman talked, Sadie Mae noticed she quickly put the pictures back in her purse.

"I'm Roc's mother. Roc...the young man your daughter said—"

"Oh, well, I'm sorry...now I remember you."

"How is Sherri?"

"Well...we don't hear much from her. I'm really not sure how's she doing."

Sadie Mae was about to ask whether or not Sherri had

the baby, but just as she was about to ask, Roc and Sonya came into the church and sat down next to her. When Sadie Mae asked her son if he remembered the woman, Roc insisted that they move.

Roc had his reasons for moving. Someone was leaking his information to Sherri and he didn't know who it was. As far as anyone knew, Sherri had gotten an abortion, and he wanted to keep it that way. The last thing he wanted to deal with was a lost son after all these years. As a matter of fact, he hadn't heard from Sherri in months, and before she got antsy and called him again, he would send her a check in the mail.

Just when Roc got comfortable and stopped thinking about Sherri, he saw his father's face. What's he doing here? Roc thought as he looked at his mother, bewildered.

"You know your father belongs to this church. I can't stop him from coming," Sadie Mae said.

Rockey came over and spoke to everyone, and then had the common decency to sit on the other side of the church. Roc was relieved. He wasn't sure if he could've stayed if his father was anywhere near him. Not even in the house of God could the two men overcome their differences.

Chapter Twenty-Two

When Love was Sweet

1 Year Later

Roc inhaled deeply, sighed, and looked out his bedroom window. From the hilltop view, his secluded street looked quiet and peaceful. It was midnight and very hot for the fall season. With the central air on the blink again, he was pleased when a sudden mist in the air dropped temperatures down into the fifties. Restlessly, as he lay between consciousness and sleep, he listened to the soft whispering wind hum through the trees, and the singing crickets as they serenaded their lovers. Then reluctantly, he thought of Sonya. God's sweet lullaby was cradling the sleeping city, but the serenity of it all only reminded Roc of his insomnia, and most of all his loneliness.

The room was still and dark, almost lifeless without Sonya. But his thoughts of her were so alive and so vivid that he could only smile at the images that danced in his head. He remembered Sonya kissing him softly and passionately.

Her toned black body glistened with perspiration, like black sparkling coal. Roc recalled when, beneath a romantic moon, their bodies exchanged pleasures to Luther Vandross crooning "A House is Not a Home," soulfully gripping each note...The sensuous memory played on and on in his mind as Roc chain-smoked in the dark.

Meditating, Roc reached for his drink, a glass of expensive vodka sitting on the nearby nightstand to rid his dry hacking cough—just another reminder that his basketball career was a thing of the past. Also just a memory was the money, press, fame, and glory. He cringed at the depressing thought of being average, and downed two big gulps of vodka to numb the pain. His fifth straight shot and still the strong liquor burned going down. He longed for sleep to come. If he could just close his eyes, he wouldn't have to watch the room spin around.

Because sleep would not come, Roc's mind would not shut down. Thinking about his life made him disgusted. Not only had his career ended, he thought his wife was cheating on him. Infidelity was no joke. He had no concrete proof of her unfaithfulness, but intuitively, he sensed her betrayal. Because if anyone knew the game, he knew it, and he knew it well.

Against his will Roc thought about all the years he'd done his dirt. Naively back then, he never knew his cold and callous actions were destructive. He was a man, and that's what men did—cheat! It was all he knew—all he'd ever seen from his father or heard of his grandfather. It was in his blood to be a womanizer, and besides that, the few men he knew that did not cheat were referred to as wimps and henpecked punks. Roc was a lot of things, but a wimp wasn't one of them.

As life would have it, you reap what you sow. Now he's the one played—the one in pain. But the million dollar question was, could he handle it? He reached out to the empty space in bed and caressed Sonya's pillow.

After a few more drinks, Roc passed out. He was dead to the world until the phone rang. Incoherently, he fumbled in the dark to locate the irritating noise. After the fourth ring, he angrily grabbed the receiver to silence what sounded like sirens going off in his head. In a state of confusion, when he finally realized it was the phone he held, he habitually checked the caller ID. It was Sonya's cell phone.

"Yeah?" Roc spoke dryly as he glanced at the clock—half past midnight. Although he'd been asleep for a couple of hours, it felt like he'd just passed out. He batted his heavy eyes, trying to adjust to the darkness.

"Hey Roc," Sonya responded softly, as she pushed her words out with a big yawn. "I'm pulling into the garage. I was just checking to see if you were still up."

"Just barely," he grumbled.

"Okay just barely...get your butt up and come and open the door."

As soon as Roc heard the request, he jumped straight out of bed. The vodka had made him inquisitive. He wanted to know where she'd been, why she was so late and most importantly, who she was with. He raced to his feet to get some answers. However, after so much consumption, he felt goofy and clumsy. He found a simple thing like walking to be almost impossible. When he put one foot in front of the other, he felt like the weakest man in the world as he tried to lift his heavy feet. Not only that, his head was spinning and his knees wobbled so hard he could barely keep his balance. He nearly fell to the floor several times until he just stopped, and concentrated on his next move.

"What the heck?" Roc said, as he caught himself and leaned on the wall for immediate support.

In his stupor, Roc was not aware of time. What seemed to be seconds for him were in fact minutes. And the minutes seemed to be hours for Sonya as she waited impatiently for him to open the door. She became frustrated and could no longer wait. Fussing to herself, she struggled to find the correct house key on an overloaded key chain. One day, she'd get around to color-coding the stupid things or at least get rid of the useless ones, she thought, as she stood on the dimly lit porch. Roc had promised to replace the blown light months ago, and had yet to get around to it. Nothing ever got done unless she made a big fuss.

When she finally entered the house, it was quiet and dark, and there was no sign of Roc. Assuming he never got out of bed, she immediately clicked on the lights, only to find him at the bottom of the stairs passed out. Startled by the sight, she rushed to his side.

Fiercely, she tugged at him, hoping he'd say something, but instead he remained mute and flopped against the black iron rails, completely oblivious of her presence. Sonya did not waiver as she continued to shake him profusely. Back and forth, she wrestled with him, but his limp body just fell back over.

By now, it didn't take a genius to figure out the problem. Roc reeked of alcohol. To Sonya's dread, it was another one of his drunken escapades. The last time it happened, she recalled, he slept on the cold bathroom floor. His body ached so badly the next morning he called in sick for work. He griped and complained a whole week because his check was short, but she was determined that would not be the case this time—money was too tight and she didn't want to hear his mouth. Although he was practically dead to the world, she was determined to get him to bed. She just had to figure out a way to get him on his feet.

Sonya went to the kitchen. A crystal pitcher was the only thing within reach. Quickly she grabbed it, put it beneath the automatic icemaker, pushed the button, and did not let up until she heard the overflowing ice chips hit the floor. For a brief moment, Sonya contemplated the outcome of dousing Roc with ice. Certainly it was a cruel act. But truthfully, she had no other choice. It was the only thing she could think of to jolt some life back into him.

As her arm swooped down and then higher in mid-air she halted when she heard a loud groan—a growling grunt of agony that echoed in the stillness.

"Oh, I'm sick. I feel nauseated. Sonya where are you?" Roc said in a drunken haze.

Sonya let out a sigh of relief. Although she was angry about his condition, she was relieved to hear his voice. She looked at the ice and then at him. It would serve him right if she'd thrown the ice on him anyway, but what thrill would it be? He was too drunk to know. He was even too drunk to form words that made sense.

Sonya put the pitcher on the island, and then looked at the big man sprawled across the floor. He looked like a helpless child instead of a once all American jock. Of all things to think about at that point, she thought of her wedding vows. "For better or for worse..." the words came like a whisper from God's lips reminding her of the covenant she made to love Roc unconditionally as God loves. The problem was, lately the worst days were out-numbering the better ones. She wondered if God was aware of that.

She sighed at the difficult task before her. Relentlessly, she'd given her marriage her all, waiting for the big payback—a perfect husband was the goal, but she'd settle for just plain ole' good. Determined, Sonya mustered all the strength she had, and with amazing power, she graciously took her more than six foot tall husband and wrapped him around her tiny body and ushered him to their bedroom. All the while, Roc was still going on and on, jabbering in a drunken slur. He demanded to know where she'd been, why she was late, and who she was with. He repeatedly asked the same questions, over and over, assuming he sounded coherent. However, in transit from mind to mouth, his words were severely distorted. Bewildered, Sonya did not answer.

Roc attributed her perplexed look and quietness to guilt. He then broke free from Sonya's clutching arms, steadied himself, stood upright, and clearly asked, "You're still cheating? I know you were with that boy!"

Sonya was hurt. She'd apologized a thousand times for the affair, and he wouldn't let her forget it. He threw it in her face practically every day. She wondered when the madness would end. Since his accident, he'd become almost impossible to live with.

Then suddenly, Roc stopped jabbering and started swinging at Sonya. In a fierce drunken rage, he began aimlessly throwing a flurry of punches, but with his tear-filled, bloodshot eyes, his vision was too impaired to make contact possible. However, Sonya didn't want to take any chances of getting hurt by her insanely angry husband. She bolted to the other side of the room and yelled, "What on earth is wrong with you? What is it? I can't understand you! You're jabbering and blubbering like a fool!" Then, seeing that Roc wasn't coming toward her, she added, "Roc, everyday you're becoming more and more like your father." She knew Roc hated to hear that, but it was the truth. He'd become the same unhappy, miserable, mean man his father was, causing havoc in his household.

"Are you seriously trying to hurt me?" she said in disbelief.

Hurt you? Roc thought. Not even drunk did he have any intention of harming Sonya, but it looked like she had no problem causing him pain. He watched her in a maze of confusion as she rattled on and on. Emotionally, the pain was too much to bear and physically, his head pounded, his stomach ached, and his strong body weighed heavily on his weak knees. Roc collapsed to the bed seeking some relief. Rest, his only refuge, came in the blink of an eye.

The night had proven to be a disaster. Sonya was glad to see it come to an end as she realized her negative role in the unfortunate chain of events. Thinking back, she could've called Roc and told him where she was. It's not like hanging with her girls, Kim and Renee, was a just cause for secrecy. Or better still, knowing Roc's jealousy and insecurities, she could've come home after the first glass of wine instead of two hours after the last round.

Accountability! It was times like this Sonya hated being married. It was not always the blissful union it was cracked up to be. When you're single, you're free to do what you want, when you want, and as long as you want to do it—with no questions asked, contrary to being matrimonially shackled (as her single girlfriend Renee says when referring to marriage).

Funny, Sonya thought, how people interpret others' lives. Over the years, she'd heard her mother refer to her in-laws' marriage as "unequally yoked." She said it meant when one spouse was saved and the other one wasn't. Sonya knew her parents didn't think less of Roc's family. It's just that it was obvious they were not happy with each other. True, Rockey had never been a church-going person like Sadie Mae, but in Sonya's opinion, the term "unequally yoked" was too deep and too spiritual to agree with. From the outside looking in, judging their situation, it was just simply two people who were incompatible. And Sonya could relate, because she was beginning to think the same thing about her marriage. Then she wondered if they would end up separated like his parents. The thought made her sad.

Sonya looked over at Roc. It was only after she was sure he was asleep that she went near him. Now that he was settled and the house was quiet, Sonya took an inventory of their bedroom. It was a mess. Roc could be such a slob at times, especially when he drank.

Again she looked around. All of Roc's dirty work clothes were on the floor beside the hamper. But what bothered her more than soiled laundry, dirty dishes, and the Sport Illustrated magazines that littered their room, was the air. It was musty with the stale odor of tobacco. The stench overwhelmed her, but, even more bothersome the sight of an overflowing astray on the nightstand. Sickened, she emptied it immediately. As much as she hated it, tonight the astray was the only thing she would clean. It was too late and she was too tired to do anything else The morning would come soon enough, and if the cleaning fairy didn't come in the night, the work would patiently wait on her until daylight.

Sonya slipped into her gown, climbed gently into bed, and turned off the light. As she settled into bed, she eased under the covers, drew in her pillow, and found her way to Roc, resting beside his body in the oversized bed. The fresh air permeated. She relaxed, snuggled closer against him, and wrapped his muscular arms around her.

In the dark, all their problems disappeared. His strong rhythmic heartbeat throbbed against her. It was soothing. Her body experienced a warm sensation being near him. Sonya immersed herself in the feeling and with tear filled eyes, she wished for the days...when love was sweet.

Chapter Twenty-Three

Good Morning Heartache

Not even Roc's coldhearted look could make Sonya budge as she lay still in the glow of the orange sunrise. Although her body was immobile and her eyes were tightly shut, she could sense Roc's presence. She envisioned him towering over her, still furious—his angry eyes piercing right through her, tearing at her heart.

Sonya knew if she dared to make a move, it was on. Another healthy portion of last night's leftover drama was imminent, and she did not want to go there.

It was not that her life was in jeopardy. Roc's bark was worse than his bite, and no one knew that better than her. But she also understood it was the start of a new day, and nothing could steal the anticipated joy out of it quicker than two people bickering at the crack of dawn. The shadowy thoughts of impending doom kept her still. Even as his glaring eyes nudged at her, and he spewed false accusations at her—even when his escalating tone frightened her and his sobbing hurt her, she did not move.

Roc was convinced that she was mindful of his every move, and his wife's determination to discount his feelings ticked him off. All he wanted to do was talk—they needed to discuss some things, but she kept shutting him out. He hated when Sonya played these silly games.

He stared at her—her face hidden beneath her long hair, the tousled gown exposed most of her body, and her ebony skin was flawless. Roc just stared. As he watched, within an instant, the angry eyes that loathed her looked upon her with admiration. He'd always been enchanted by her beauty, and over the years, not much had changed. She was still beautiful. Mesmerized by her, he longed to kiss her, but pride had hardened his heart and he could not imagine exhibiting any kind of tenderness towards her.

"You're crazy," he said, throwing his arms up in anger. He wanted to say more, but it was the ridiculous sight of his reflection mimicking him in the mirror—fussing at a corpse-like body that hushed him. Heatedly, he grabbed his keys and left, kicking everything in his path and slamming every door behind him.

When Sonya heard the last door slam, her stiff body relaxed. Then she got out of bed and peeked out the window. With delight, she saw the nose of Roc's Jeep disappear as he sped from the driveway. Totally at ease, she lifted her eyes and admired the beautiful sunrise. It was bright and energetic. Even the temperatures were unseasonably warm for autumn, the seventies in late October. Inspired by the strong rays bursting in from beyond the trees, Sonya sighed deeply, kissed at the morning sun, and welcomed the freshness of dawn. Uninhibited by the dark cloud of friction that hung in the room, she smiled intensely.

After Sonya cleaned their room to a sparkling shine, she went downstairs and prepared a pot of coffee. As it brewed, she appreciated the overpowering aroma. Unmistakably, it was better than the stifling stench of nicotine that always loomed about no matter how much she cleaned. It was amazing to Sonya how Roc had complained for years about his father smoking, and out of nowhere he picked up the nasty habit after his accident. He said being confined he got bored, and smoking was just something to do, like drinking—it too had just become something to do while he was in the long months of physical therapy.

Sonya flicked on the television as she cleaned. A talk show was on. She heard clapping, and assumed it was another sad tale of someone airing their dirty laundry for a few minutes of fame. Frankly, she thought, some of the peoples' lives that came across the screen had so much drama, they could've easily been put in the hall of shame. Not that her life was so great. As a matter of fact, just thinking about it, the last thing she needed to hear was more drama. Sonya sighed, looked at the ceiling and didn't even bother to change the channel. It wasn't like she was actually looking at the television anyway. It was just on to keep her company and take the monotony out of cleaning.

Suddenly, spellbound by the repetition of dusting and polishing, Sonya became intrigued by the Dick Shock show on television. The morning show was rated number one because of its controversial guests and extreme topics—gay cross dressers, open marriages, Ku Klux Klan, ex-Black Panthers, Skin Heads and the secret lives of celebrities, if there was such a thing. But every now and then Dick would have some human-interest story about the immoral state and breakdown of families. He claimed he wanted to find out what the weakest link was and strengthen it, but his paneled guests were always the weaklings of society. Today's guests were an irate man and a teary woman. Apparently the mousy looking woman had swindled child support from the man for years, until DNA results proved her baby was not his. Now the woman was being sued by the man for monetary restoration. Sonya agreed with the audience, the woman should pay back the money, every last red cent. When the woman started crying, again, and said she thought it was his baby, Sonya got angry and almost choked on her coffee. Immediately she looked for the remote to change the channel; she'd heard enough. And just as she was about to turn the station, the guests started arguing with each other—screaming to the top of their lungs and throwing punches across Dick Shock. Then from seemingly nowhere, the man's wife came from the audience and started fighting with the lady on stage.

Sonya looked on in disgust. How awful it is that a woman does not even know who fathered her child, she thought. If anybody should know, she should. Sonya felt outraged by the stranger's actions. Hurriedly, with the remote in hand, Sonya whizzed through the channels, stopping on a department store commercial. To her amazement, the store was having a gigantic sale. The news excited her. Shopping was her passion. Although their budget could no longer withstand her wild spending sprees, she indulged in them just the same—secretly of course. However, lately Roc had been watching every dime closely. But a half-off sale would be so great! If she played her cards right, he would never know.

With a burst of energy, Sonya finished cleaning the huge house, room by room. And then quickly ran upstairs, got dressed and took off. On the way to the mall, she felt a little guilty. Maybe she was spending too much money. The familiar feeling that impinged upon her was immediately dealt with for the first time. In the short trip, she reasoned with herself. She didn't smoke, she didn't drink, didn't do drugs or gamble. It was only human nature to have some kind of vice to get a person through the day. What she was doing didn't hurt anyone. So it was as simple as that—shopping was a harmless means of releasing stress. In order to stop herself from climbing the walls and doing something she would regret, she shopped. After she justified her actions, everything looked clear—it was either shopping or divorce.

The mall was crowded. As usual, a big sale brought out a multitude of people. Sonya's first stop was the department store, and to her delight, she found some unbelievable bargains—three designer tops, the cutest jeans, and a to-die-for blue blouse. When she passed by the fragrance counter, she had to stop, and purchase some. Not that she needed any, but because it was fifty percent off.

In the lingerie department, she quickly scurried past the skimpy negligees without any consideration. Although her sculpted body would've complimented any one of the teddies worn by the mannequins, she didn't even stop. Why bother? She and Roc hardly ever made love anymore and when they did, there was nothing romantic about it. They'd settled into each other like an old married couple. In passing, she glanced at a seductive tiger print, but quickly thought otherwise and kept on walking.

Sonya's determined footsteps led her across the hall to a more upscale store. As she browsed around, she didn't see too many bargains she appreciated, but it was the "new arrivals" that caught her eye and made her want to shop until she dropped.

Standing next to the new fall collection, she scanned the tags. Sonya knew the prices were definitely out of her budget. At best she could only get away with the fifty dollar scarf shifting between her fingers that accented the knitted suit on display. Sadly she had to remind herself, it was no longer the good ole days when money was no object.

As she stood and looked, she envied the other shoppers. It wasn't fair how some folks had it and some did not. She was just as good as anybody else. The more she thought about it, the more she realized she deserved something special that did not come off the clearance rack. Besides, she was actually ahead of the game. She'd barely spent two hundred dollars on the usual charge card, and had not even touched the backups. Then suddenly, like a hunter on the prowl, she grabbed a designer purse and matching shoes. When she realized she needed something to wear with them, she eyed two brown suits. Indecisive about which one to buy, she got them both. Although both her hands were full, she was not nearly ready to stop, but when she saw the three hundred and fifty dollar price tag swinging from the jacket, she realized her adventure was over.

At the counter, she paid with her card, and mentally calculated how much was left on the limit. When the transaction went through, she gave a sigh of relief, grabbed her bags and left.

All the shopping had made Sonya tired so she stopped to satisfy her craving for a cup of French vanilla cappuccino with extra whip cream and a blueberry muffin. At the coffee shop, she found herself in line behind the cutest couple. Young love—Sonya could tell. The couple couldn't keep their hands off of each other. They made eye contact, and acted as if they were the only ones around. Hopelessly, Sonya thought of Roc. Out of nowhere, she started to feel bad about what happened earlier. She should've said something to him, but deep inside she knew it wouldn't have made a difference. He was determined to believe that she was cheating, and no matter how many times she said she wasn't, he wouldn't believe her.

But if nothing else, she thought, at least I could've sat up and listened to what he had to say. "God," she whispered silently, "I miss being in love." Sonya watched the couple as they walked away. She did not divert her eyes until they were completely out of sight.

"Next! Miss, can I help you—are you ordering anything?" An impatient young girl said from behind the counter, grabbing Sonya's attention.

"Yes. I'm sorry. Can I please have a cup of French kissing...I mean French vanilla cappuccino...and a blueberry muffin?"

After Sonya received her order, she realized she'd forgotten to ask for the whip cream. She looked back at the girl in her green uniform still not smiling and decided not to ask.

Sonya sat at a quaint table by the window, watching all of the people coming and going—so many different lives, so diverse, yet profoundly the same. She was amused especially by the little children. After two miscarriages, she'd given up on motherhood. Sometimes she felt like God was punishing her for some past sin or something. She'd give anything to have a baby....

Sonya's thoughts were interrupted by her cell phone. She thought it was Roc before she looked at the number displayed and when she saw it was her friend Kim. She ignored the call and let it go straight to her voicemail because even though Kim was cool, Sonya got tired of hearing her talk about how much fun she was having being single.

After having her coffee, Sonya headed for home. She'd done enough spending for one day, but just as she was about to leave, her eyes caught a glimpse of a tan purse. It was one of few she did not own. The purse had C's embroidered all over it and standing right beside it were matching tan boots on display in the window. By now, money had become an issue. If she spent anymore, Roc would surely find out. But Sonya craved the items. She salivated as haunting thoughts that said, Buy it. Buy it. Buy it...You deserve it. You can afford it, overwhelmed her. The thoughts were generated from her selfish needs, and she could not hush them. Suddenly, bombarded with countless emotions, she realized she was experiencing something controlling that she had no power over. The anxious thoughts compelled her to do something, anything—whatever it took to acquire the items. The negative energy caused her heart to race and her palms to sweat. A no matter what feeling overtook her. She could not rationalize anything outside of her strong desires. But just as she was about to give into the temptation, she regained control. She stood back, deeply inhaled, exhaled, and shook off the feeling. Drenched in perspiration, she walked away from the window display and sat down on a nearby bench.

Whoa....what was that? she wondered. Too much spending was making her crazy. For some time now, Sonya had known the outlandish behavior had to stop—but she just did not have the will to do it. After that freak incident, Sonya promised herself she would not charge anything else for a while. Ignoring her thoughts to go home, she continued to window shop. To her surprise, nothing tempted her. She was totally in control, until...she was stopped dead in her tracks by the sight of the sharpest boots in the world in a window. Against her better judgment, she went in to examine the suede boots closer and found they were the perfect match for her new suit. Before Sonya knew it, she was standing in line with the boots in her hand. She reacted so fast she didn't even remember if the salesperson was a man or woman. At the counter, she whipped out her fourth card—the one Roc was very strict about her using. Only in emergency was it acceptable. Well, she'd figure out what to do in thirty days when the bill was due.

On the way home, Sonya's neurotic high declined. She was feeling low—even guilty about spending so much money. She'd experienced the depressing feeling before. It was not anything new, just weird. Even stranger, up until these bizarre occurrences, Sonya never considered herself to be a down person. She wondered where the mood swings were coming from.

By the time Sonya had gotten home, Roc was already there.

He wasn't due home for hours. He must've gotten sent home early. She knew periodically that happened, or, she thought shaking her head in disgust, he was checking up on her which was also not uncommon. Looking at the six shopping bags, she pushed aside the meddling thought of why he didn't call her and let her know he was home. And then she wondered how long he'd been there. The unsolved mystery unfolded as she observed the recent yard work. The severity indicated several hours—all the fallen leaves were gone, the unshapely brushes were in order and like all their neighbors, the grass was meticulously cut. It seem while Roc was trimming the yard, Sonya was doing the same to their bank account.

Still looking at the bags, she wondered where to stash them. Putting the bags in the trunk was not an option. No doubt Roc was probably sitting in the family room watching her every move from the window. Then quickly, she considered the oversized jacket lying on the back seat. It could successfully conceal everything.

When Sonya was sure her secret was safe, she walked in the house virtually happy about her day, in spite of the anxiety, until she met a solemn Roc. He was sitting in the family room, just where she expected him to be, but she did not anticipate the grim face. She'd hoped time and distance would've solved their issues, but apparently they had not. Sonya greeted him and walked into the kitchen. She took out a chicken from the freezer and placed it in the sink. For a man that had so much to say earlier, he barely spoke now.

"How was your day?" she asked.

"Where have you been all day?" he said dryly.

"I haven't been gone all day, only a few hours. I went over to my mother's after I cleaned up. I got bored," she said.

"I bet you got bored."

"Roc, if this conversation is going to lead to more yelling and screaming, just let me know now so I can leave!"

"Do whatever you want to do Sonya. As a matter of fact, why don't you just play dead like you did this morning?"

"Is that my only choice? Play dead or argue with you?" she said. "Can we have one day without being angry with each another, just one? I'm so tired of being mad. Look if you want to talk, we can, but no yelling please." She walked over to him, but he got up from his chair and walked away.

"Okay Roc...you don't want me to touch you. I won't. You don't want me to talk to you...I won't. I'll do whatever it takes to keep the peace. I just don't want to argue another night. Please, not another night."

Roc went back to his chair and turned up the volume on the television and kept flicking the channels with the remote. Sonya just stared at him, accepted his childish behavior as payback, and went into the kitchen.

"Roc," she yelled. "I'm going to fry some chicken! If you want something else, tell me and I will cook that instead."

There was silence until she repeated it once more.

"Don't worry about me," Roc said barely audible. "I'll get something to eat at my mother's house."

Sonya knew Sadie Mae's house was his safe haven. It was where he always ran when things got too hot to handle.

"It's no bother Roc. I really want to."

"I said don't worry about me."

"Okay...whatever! You like your mama's cooking better than mine anyway!" she said as she threw the pink chicken back into the freezer.

Sonya could just about imagine what Roc was thinking

by the baleful look he gave her. It had been over three years since he caught her in the act, but the way he was acting, it was just like it was yesterday's wound, still fresh. Funny, after all the times he'd been unfaithful, she'd expected a little bit more compassion. But it was as if he had forgotten about her forgiving nature.

"How many times do I have to apologize Roc? I'm sorry. I made a mistake, one time, but I'm not cheating anymore. Last night, I was with Kim and some of her friends. I should've called, but I did not, mainly because I knew you wouldn't believe anything I said. And as far as this morning, I just did not feel like facing the drama so early. You got to believe me, I'm not doing anything! I love you and I'm sorry."

Roc walked over to Sonya and looked her straight in the face. "If you did it once, then you'll do it again. I don't trust you and I can't get past that."

After he made the statement, he left, slammed the door, and sped from the driveway. It was his second dramatic exit for the day, but he could care less who was keeping count, or what his nosey neighbors might've thought of him.

Chapter Twenty-Four

Some Woman Named Justine

It was Saturday and Roc avoided Sonya like a plague. She was upset. Maybe it was because he'd come in late or she just liked walking around the house with her lips pouted out. It didn't matter what her problem was, he wasn't going to play her little game. If he asked what was wrong, it would be an open invitation to talk, and the last time he tried to talk to her, she wasn't in the mood. So forget it, he didn't have to ever talk to her again. Talking always led to arguing and that's why last night was so special when he was with Justine.

Justine was his co-worker, but work was not the first time they'd met. It was at the park, when he was still playing for the Pistons, and although he couldn't remember the day, Justine quickly reminded him as she shook his hand the first day on the job. The thing that baffled Roc was how he'd forgotten someone so attractive. Though rumor had it around the plant, she didn't look the same back then. Recently she'd made some major changes, lost weight, got a new haircut, removed the glasses and had laser surgery on her eyes. Roc couldn't picture her the way people said she used to look. All he knew was she was fine now.

Reminiscing, Roc could not believe the luck he had last night when, just out of nowhere, he ran into Justine in his old neighborhood. It was good to see her smiling, just standing there buying a pack of cigarettes.

"Hey Justine," Roc said, checking her out.

"Hey Roc," she replied.

"I thought that was you. But I didn't know you smoked," he said, looking at her hand and noticing her hot body.

"I don't. These are for my mother. What are you doing here?"

"You know, I used to live in this neighborhood and every now and then, I come around and visit some of my old stomping grounds."

"That doesn't surprise me. I've seen you around here before," Justine smiled.

Although the conversation started out about cigarettes, before Roc knew it, he and Justine were in his car talking about everything: kids, sports, parents, the job and finally, relationships. Several hours later, somewhere around daybreak, he asked Justine if he could call her sometime. When she nodded yes, he couldn't believe it.

Ever since they parted last night, Roc couldn't shake Justine out of his mind. The more he tried not to think of her, the more he did. The thought hung around until finally Sonya started talking.

"I'm going to the mall."

"Fine," he grunted. "Who with?"

"Lunch with Renee. Oh yeah, and your agent called," Sonya said, indifferent. "The number's on the counter." Then, she picked up her keys and left.

Roc was glad to hear his agent had called. After the accident, Roc could no longer play, but still he knew the game. His agent was working on getting him a coaching job. He had some wheels spinning, and there was a strong possibility Roc could be the assistant coach for his old team, the Pistons. Roc was excited as he returned the call. When he got kicked over to voicemail, he left a message, hung up, and then he stared at the phone. He thought about calling Justine but then changed his mind. It was still early and he wasn't sure if he should.

As Justine parted the kitchen curtains, her sleepy eyes squinted at the bright autumn sun. She'd only had a couple hours of rest last night. Vaguely, she remembered hitting the snooze alarm three, maybe four times before finally pulling the covers from over her head and slowly crawling out of bed. Still tired, she paced the floor at a snail's pace—stretching and yawning, trying to wake up. Although she'd already finished two cups of strong black coffee, it had not perked her up. But instead, being caffeine intolerant, she was now sleepy and jittery. It was Saturday, and as usual, she had a busy day ahead. Her nine-year-old twins, Cordell and Candice were very active. Cordell had basketball practice and Candice had dance lessons. All she wanted to do was crawl back into bed. But that wasn't going to happen...not today. Her plate was too full. "Oh!" she hollered as she pushed away the worrisome bangs from her face. "I need energy!"

She turned on the radio and heard the last chorus of Anita Baker's "Some Ole Love."

"Good morning sleepy heads. You are listening to the sounds of WHIT oldies but goodies hits on your FM dial. Enjoy the sun people, unlike the hits, it won't be around all day! There is a ninety percent chance the temperatures will fall down to normal today, even a chance of snow. It looks like we're going to have a gray day, so keep it tuned to Rockin' Rog, your smooth DJ and I will chase away those dark clouds with the sounds that make you wanna stay in...and play house. Are ya feelin' me out there? I'm talking to the grown folks now... ha...ha...all the mamas and the daddies out there...I said... can you feel me? Rog...your smooth DJ....yeah."

Justine glanced at the cloudless sky and doubted Rockin' Rog's prediction, but enjoyed his compilation of Anita Baker's greatest hits. The music sounded good to her. In fact, it was one of her favorite Anita Baker cuts, "Sweet Love."

She hummed the melody, and right in the middle of the modest and humble room, Justine began to sway from side to side on the green and white weathered tile. And, out of nowhere, like a lovesick teenager, she thought about Roc.

She saw his piercing eyes—his tall muscular body, and

to her surprise, she was smitten by his creamy caramel skin. It was hopeless, but she tried not to think about all the trouble he was going through at home. Last night, he had poured out his soul to her. While his conversation was vague, his emotions were crystal clear. He was hurting. He did not come right out and say it, but it sounded like his wife had all the issues. She came across like one of those sistas who had a good man in her corner and was too stupid to appreciate him. If Justine could, she would tell the silly woman to wise up and recognize what she's got.

It was a shame, Justine thought, that he was a married man. There was nothing good about dealing with someone's husband. And if anyone knew, Justine knew firsthand. A married man was taboo—a one-way dead end street and she had no intention of ever taking that route again, not even if the scenery was eye-catching. She wasn't worried about what she was feeling because she knew it was just innocent infatuations.

Having heard footsteps come into the kitchen, Justine looked up and saw Cordell rubbing the sleep from his eyes, still yawning. Finally, he looked up at his mother and asked for cereal, even before he said good morning. It was no secret Cordell was not a morning person, but Justine accommodated him anyway with a bowl of Crunchy Crunch.

"Mama, basketball practice is in thirty minutes. The coach says I can't be late anymore. Can you please get me there on time today?" Cordell said without looking up.

"Is it possible, to hear good morning and please?" Justine said.

Cordell looked up and said both things, barely smiling. By the time he finished most of his cereal, he had a bit more personality. Justine was glad to see even a little smile. He'd come a long way since the days they had shouting matches in the morning because of his stubborn and headstrong ways. If it wasn't for her mother helping her with him, she didn't know what she would do.

It seemed like just yesterday, Justine thought, as she watched Cordell down his cereal in cartoon pajamas, since she first held her babies in her arms for the first time. The element of surprise was never so pleasant—two bundles of joy to love. No one thought she would go through with it. She was so young to take on such a huge responsibility. One minute, young and carefree, then instantly a mom, a single mom at that. With little preparation, the first year was the hardest. Caring for Candice had always been a breeze, but Cordell was the type of child that always needed attention, and he would do the things to get it, good or bad. The other day, he made a mess and Justine almost had to spank him to make him pick it up. She hated hitting the kids. But her mother did not tolerate Cordell's behavior and was coaching Justine not to be so lenient. It just looked like a lost cause, as she continued to take orders from her children. Even today, after basketball practice and dance class, Justine had to haul the kids to a Piston's game as tired as she was, because Cordell did not want to go with Justine's friend who'd agreed to take them.

Roc's agent called back and invited him to the Piston's game to talk over the prospects of coaching. When Roc accepted the invitation, his agent insisted that Sonya come along. He hadn't seen her in awhile, and it looked good to have her with him. Because Roc was not the only one campaigning for the position, the strategy sounded good, so he agreed to bring his wife.

When she came back from her trip to the mall, Roc invited Sonya, but she refused to go.

"No way. I don't wanna be seen anywhere with you. Why don't you go with the person you were with last night?"

"Like I told you, I wasn't with anyone. I had too much to drink and I fell asleep. Would you prefer I had tried to drive home drunk?"

Believing Roc's smooth lie, Sonya figured it wasn't like it had never happened before, so she gave in and agreed to go.

When Roc was ready to go, he paced the floor, waiting for Sonya to come downstairs. Impatient, he yelled, "Sonya, you don't have put on make-up and get all dressed up! We're only going to a basketball game. Will you hurry up? I don't want to be late!"

"I'm coming!" she replied.

When she was finally ready to go, they jumped into his car and sped down the driveway. Sonya had spent a lot of time getting ready and really tried her best to look nice to impress her husband, but he never said a word. Even when she fluffed her long hair, he remained distracted and oblivious.

From the box seats, the game looked bad when the Pistons were losing by fifteen points. In his mind, Roc was formulating all kinds of plays that he thought would successfully bring the team back into the game. But he was just a spectator, like thousands of other people watching, with no authority to do anything else but observe.

During halftime, Roc went for refreshments. Sonya was busy talking to the agent's wife. The two had not seen each other since Roc's basketball days, and they had a lot to catch up on. As he left, he overheard the woman compliment Sonya on how good she looked, commenting about how sweet her boots looked with her jeans. Sonya was the only woman Roc knew that wore heels everywhere. It did not matter where she went, she had to dress up for it.

There had to be a million people trying to get refreshments, so Roc went to the restroom in hopes that the crowd would die down after he came out. When he was leaving the restroom, he heard a faint voice calling his full name.

"Mr. Rockwell James...number 29 the Rocket! Mr. Rockwell James!"

Roc turned around and saw a little kid.

"It's me, Cordell, you signed your autograph for me a year ago."

Roc just smiled at the boy, and rubbed his head. He knew it had to be someone he'd seen in the past, but like most of the people he'd met during his basketball days, he'd forgotten. Just too many strangers.

"Yeah, kid I remember you." Roc said as his habitual response came naturally.

"I told my mom you would remember me if you saw me. My mom works with you," Cordell said. "Justine Jones."

When Roc heard the name Justine Jones, his ears perked up.

"You're Cordell. Of course I remember you. Where is your mother?" Roc said, grinning ear to ear.

"She's waiting for me outside."

Roc grabbed the kid's hand, walked through the crowd of men in the restroom, and to his delight, he saw Justine standing outside. She looked even greater than she had the night before. She looked so comfortable wearing gym shoes and jeans.

"Mama!" Cordell yelled. He broke free from Roc and ran to Justine. "I told you he would remember me Mama. I told you."

"What are you talking about?" Justine said.

"Rockwell James, he's here...right there."

When Justine turned around, her heart went into her shoes. Roc looked so good. She could have just melted in his smile. He was so tall he looked like a skyscraper over the other people.

“Roc, I can’t believe this. Two times in two days we’ve ran into each other. We’ve got to stop meeting like this,” Justine said with a smile.

For ten minutes or more Roc, stood talking to his co-worker. When he saw Sonya approaching, he excused himself in a smooth manner and walked away.

Before Sonya made it to Roc, she went into the lady’s room and freshened up. By the time she met up with Roc, he was at the bar. She moved close to him, and after he ordered a beer, she asked for a cola. After she’d gotten her drink, she asked Roc about the lady he was talking to. It wasn’t until he acted forgetful that she thought something about it.

“What do you mean, what lady? The lady you were just talking to,” Sonya said.

“It could’ve been a fan, a co-worker, anybody. There’s a million people here, and people recognize me all the time.”

“Well, Roc it did not look like you were having a conversation with a stranger.”

Roc could tell Sonya was getting upset. He had to say something to calm her down.

“I think it was my co-worker and her son I was talking to. Her husband was in the bathroom.”

“What was her name? If she was a co-worker, you’ve got to know her name.”

Roc knew if he gave her the wrong name, and she ran into the woman on the street or something he would never hear the end of it for lying.

“Justine...why?”

Sonya just looked at him, suspicious. "If it was that innocent, then why couldn't you just say she was some woman named Justine?" Sonya huffed.

The Pistons never did come back. They lost by ten points. When the game was over, Roc went in the locker room and talked with all his old friends, and afterwards he and his agent met with the team owner for about fifteen minutes in his office.

On the way home, Roc and Sonya were silent. Roc did not have much to talk about. His mind was on the meeting—things did not look or sound good. He felt like they were giving him the brush off, although his agent said to stay positive. Roc was not sure why Sonya was quiet. He had a sneaking suspicion it was about Justine, but he dared not ask. Besides, he'd gotten use to the silence.

Chapter Twenty-Five

Financial Woes

It only took two nights for Roc to become acclimated to the spare bedroom before he slept peacefully. However, tonight he was experiencing restlessness, but he was totally convinced that his state had nothing to do with Sonya. It had nothing to do with missing her touch. In fact, the last time they'd slept together was the night of the Piston's game three weeks ago, and they had barely made contact. The tension had been so thick it could've been cut with a knife. The same night Sonya removed all the ashtrays and demanded he stop smoking. At that point, Roc was sure that sleeping in separate rooms was absolutely necessary.

After hours of staring at the ceiling, Roc realized he'd lain in bed long enough. It was time he got up and did something. But what? Mentally, he checked his growing to-do list. The only task small enough to accomplish so late at night was balancing the monthly budget. Already uptight, he was not in the mood for paying bills, but he never was.

The first of the month was only a couple days away, and it was always a stressful time—too many bills and not enough cash. Lately, he'd become a master at manipulating money. He'd often heard Sadie Mae call it, "robbing Peter to pay Paul." Now he knew what she meant.

To avoid the headache that would no doubt come, Roc feebly decided to face reality and pay some bills. He lit a cigarette, gathered all the mail from his nightstand, grabbed his checkbook, and went downstairs to the den. He'd always paid the bills blindly, but tonight he would examine each invoice in the hope that the mystery of their overwhelming debt would unfold.

Roc realized the timing was perfect as he crept down the stairs. The house was quiet and serene—no ringing phone, noisy television, or Sonya to distract him. He was glad she was visiting her mother. Well, at least that was what she said when she left several hours before.

Roc sat at his desk and laid out the numerous statements before him. Like a seasoned private eye, he searched each one for clues. Minutes later, after he'd worked his way through half of the bills, the evidence was conclusive. Sonya's wanton spending was the culprit. Roc was astonished at all the money she was still squandering, even after they'd discussed their financial crisis. Was she nuts, or was she just trying to make him go crazy? He continued to sift through the maze of statements. Both the primary and secondary charge cards were over their limits, which meant extra penalty fees. "More money," Roc said to himself, "that we don't have." By now his bewilderment had turned to anger.

When he examined the dates, he saw his wife was shopping practically every day. Apparently, the talk meant nothing to her because afterwards, she kept spending hundreds of dollars as if it was nothing—like she did in his basketball days.

Roc agonized over the ordeal for at least thirty minutes, but the minutes seemed like hours. He was so mad he could barely concentrate as he wrote check after check, paying only the minimum payment required. At this rate, they were sure to be in debt forever.

As he neared the end of the pile, it occurred to him that he had not seen the emergency-only credit card statement. His stomach started doing somersaults at the thought of the potential balance. Where was it? he wondered, in fear, frantically shuffling through the mail. Suddenly, Roc heard a noise. It was the garage door shutting. Sonya had finally come home. As he peeked out the window, his eyes twitched faster and faster as she neared the house. He quickly lit a cigarette, taking in deep drag to calm his nerves. Through the heavy smoke, he watched her walk up the long driveway.

Upon entering the house, Sonya could see the light from the den spilling into the hallway. That only meant one thing—Roc was still up. The thought made her flinch. She'd hoped to avoid an encounter with him. She foresaw an inquisition as to her whereabouts, and a reminder of how late it was. Or worse, she thought, he'd just stare at her and say nothing. His words caused tension, but his silent treatment was mental abuse.

Thinking of Roc, she sighed, closed the door softly, slipped off her shoes and crept toward the stairs, sinking her feet quietly into the plush carpet. Standing at the foot of the staircase, she paused briefly, resting herself against the railing. If she was lucky, she could make it to her room before there was any sign of Roc. But, before she attempted to conquer the first step, something prompted her to turn. To her dismay, she was standing face to face with Roc, fuming. Spooked by his sudden presence, Sonya stepped back and gasped, clutching her pounding chest. She opened her mouth, but before the words you scared me could fully escape from her lips, Roc's hands flew into the air, followed by a shower of paper falling from above. When she looked down, a mass of letters almost covered the huge vestibule's floor.

Sonya had never seen Roc that upset, at least not when he was sober. He was so angry, it seemed he couldn't speak. He just stood there, huffing and puffing, biting down on his bottom lip. The fire in his eyes silenced her. When she saw all the statements, she knew what had prompted his outrage. Her obsession with shopping, which she'd tried so hard to hide, had come back to bite her.

She wanted to announce that her mother had paid off the emergency card, but she was too afraid. Since Sonya was unsure how much Roc actually knew, to speak on her behalf would've been premature. She did not know if his anger stemmed solely from the monthly statements, or if another overzealous creditor had called, inquiring about recent purchases as to suggest possible credit card fraud. When she'd gotten too carried away with spending in the past, she'd received such fraud alert calls. She'd thank the caller and stop spending for a few days. Unsure of what to say or do, Sonya pondered her thoughts in silence.

"Give me the credit cards," Roc said, grinding his teeth, staring at her. He wanted to ask her if she'd lost her mind, but he was too angry, and feared the possible outcome. He knew Sonya's smart mouth and impudent ways could ignite an explosion, even possibly a physical altercation if she said the wrong thing. As a child, he'd sworn never to hit a woman. However, at that moment, he could not be sure of where his emotions would take him. She knew money was tight, and he was breaking his back just to make ends meet. His pride was crushed. He felt betrayed and taken advantage of.

Roc inhaled deeply and said, "Tomorrow I want you to take back everything. I don't care how you do it...but I want these charges eliminated." He began to walk away, then quickly turned back and said, "Where in the world is the American Express statement?"

Sonya remained silent. She removed the paid-in-full receipt from her purse and handed it to Roc. He snatched it out of her hand and examined it. Void of any facial expression, he did not even bother to ask who paid it. He didn't care.

"The cards...give me the credit cards," Roc said.

Although it was not in Sonya's character to be submissive, she complied with not so much as a whimper.

She stood motionless until Roc disappeared. It wasn't that his demand posed a great problem. Most of the things she'd brought were still in bags with price tags and receipts intact. She had merchandise stashed everywhere. It was just a matter of gathering up everything and returning it.

For some time now, Sonya had had no desire for the purchases once she brought them home. It was the feeling of importance she experienced while making the purchase that she craved. Once the sale was made, the thrill was gone. Practically in tears, Sonya wondered how she would spend her days now.

Chapter Twenty-Six

Questionable Friends

When Roc woke up he felt like he'd fought someone in his sleep because he'd tossed and turned so much, but body aches were the least of his problems. Thoughts of his future took center stage. He'd never considered divorce before, but perhaps it was time to weigh out all options.

Love had been the only common thread that tied Sonya and him together, but now that it was gone, what was there to hang on to? They didn't have the luxury of kids to use as an adhesive to hold their marriage together like some couples sadly did. Although Roc would always love his mother, he believed she only stayed in that abusive situation because of her kids, having the audacity to believe she was doing the right thing. But he was smarter than his mother. He knew when enough was enough.

Although divorce was foreseeable, pondering over it was indeed peculiar. The prospect of living without Sonya had once been unbearable, but things were, without a doubt, changing. Even the simplest things were becoming intolerable. Just this morning, he and Sonya passed each other in the kitchen and there wasn't even a mumbled "Good morning." Even murmuring had proven to be painful.

Roc was stunned that Sonya was even up. It was still early and he knew she was not up to see him off to work. He had scarcely seen her face, as she avoided eye contact, got a glass of water and rushed back to her room.

After Roc finished making his lunch, he went into the den to catch a few minutes of sports before he took off for work. When he sat down, he noticed the cordless phone was on the couch away from the base. No doubt, he thought, Sonya was probably on the phone and hung up when she heard him stirring around. That only meant she was giving her friend Kim the low down about what happened last night. One of the things he hated about Sonya was her eagerness to share their business, but now he could care less who she told or what she said.

On his way to work, Roc observed the cool autumn morning. The sun occasionally made a bashful appearance through the dark roaming clouds and he boldly predicted the season's first snowfall would be soon, maybe even tonight, on Halloween.

When Roc pulled into the parking lot, he sped past the black and orange blinking neon sign, "Blackwell Automotive Manufacturing Company." The eye-catching billboard stretched across the entrance gate. Then like second nature, he lit a cigarette, quickly glanced at the dashboard and checked out the time. It was seven thirty-five. Not quite starting time, he exhaled a sigh of relief. He had a little over twenty minutes to spare before he had to start his long day dealing with cranky hourly personnel and stuffy management.

Sitting in the car, he automatically started thinking about Sonya and all the spending she'd been doing. How could he be so stupid to let things get so out of control? As far as he was concerned, he was drowning in debt and two paychecks from a new residency...the poor house.

His thoughts were depressing him. And then, out of the blue, a familiar yearning came over him—a powerful thirst, but not for water. He needed something stronger—a stiff drink to take the edge off the gloomy morning.

He'd been known to take a drink or two secretly on the job with his colleagues at the bar over lunch to relax, but this would not be for relaxation. Right now a drink was essential to get his day started. He opened the glove compartment and nested among papers was a fifth of Jack Daniels. Some of the friends had given it to him some months back on his birthday, but because he was a vodka man, he had not gotten around to breaking the seal.

Without a second thought, he opened the bottle and downed a gulp.

Roc opened the bottle and raised it to the rearview mirror for a toast. "It's just me and you Jack," he said before he downed a gulp.

Although he was parked in a secluded spot, three lanes from the back of the lot, he cautiously looked around to see if anyone saw him as he tipped the bottle one last time before he got out of the car.

The solace Roc was hoping to find in the whiskey bottle was found. When he walked into the plant, he stepped high and stood tall. Earlier, his problems weighted him down, but now he felt like he had mastered them all and he was standing on top of the world. Thanks to his boy Jack Daniels, Roc was feeling no pain.

Although he was feeling good, he was conscientious of his whereabouts—work. And one of the things Roc had always appreciated about vodka was it was virtually odorless unlike bourbon, which had a distinct aroma. A strong smell, Roc feared, could bring unwanted attention from management.

To mask any detection of alcohol, Roc stopped at the vending machine to buy some breath savers and coffee. As he stood at the machine, he saw the plant manager with Oakley. Quickly, Roc made his selection, got the candy, and put it in his mouth. Of all the people to run into, why Oakley and his boss? he thought. Roc felt a little panicky watching them approach.

"Roc," Oakley said. "You look like you had a rough

night. The clock says eight o'clock and it looks like you need more than coffee to get you going."

Roc did not respond until the refreshing taste of mint exploded in his mouth.

"Oakley, I know what time it is, and my night was just fine," Roc said as he quickly left their presence.

After a few sips of coffee, Roc decided to visit Justine. Right now she was the only person that could make him smile. During the last few weeks, they'd become real close. So close, some people had started talking because it was common knowledge that Roc was married, and Justine had an on and off relationship with someone in management at the plant.

When Roc got to Justine's area, she was not there, but he had an inkling where she would be. Confidently, he walked around the corner into the break area where, instead of hearing the constant sound of machinery cycling and recycling, he heard Justine's joyful laughter. She was sitting at a table, engaged in what looked to be an enjoyable conversation with a male coworker. When the guy saw Roc, he excused himself, got up, and left. Justine was puzzled by the guy's swift exit, but when she turned around to call his name, she saw Roc, and instantly her face lit up.

"Was I interrupting something?" Roc asked as he watched the man leave.

"You're never an interruption," Justine replied, not caring how corny she sounded.

Roc walked over, put his hand on Justine's shoulder and said, "That's good to know," in a low and gratifying way.

"And how is my favorite girl doing today?" he asked, sitting down close to her.

"I'm doing fine. Now that you're here, I'm doing even better," Justine said. She felt like she was digging herself into a deep hole of embarrassment. Everything that came out of her mouth sounded silly and she could not stop blushing like a lovesick teenager.

After twenty minutes of complete isolation, it turned nine o'clock and Roc and Justine were no longer alone. The break area became inundated with people and a woman came over and sat at their table. She started talking about her grandchildren and all the plans she had for them later on that night for Halloween. Justine politely nodded and pretended to be interested, but Roc remained quiet. He felt ostracized from the conversation, too much family and children talk, so he decided it was time to go.

Getting up from the table, he said, "I'll see you for lunch, Justine." Then he smiled, gave the older woman a nod, and left.

Justine was not ready for him to leave but she wasn't sure if she should stop him. When the woman made a remark about Roc's wife being a nice lady, Justine felt a little embarrassed and decided not to go after him. The urgency to go after him scared her though because she felt like she was being taken over with too many strong emotions when it came to Roc.

Chapter Twenty-Seven

Sticky Fingers

Not wanting her mother to know she was upset, Sonya tried to disguise the quiver in her voice when she answered the phone.

"Hi Mama," she said.

"Hi baby. Doesn't anyone ever pick up the phone anymore without looking at the caller ID?" her mother chuckled.

"Mama, I knew it was you before I looked. No one else calls me this early."

"Nine-thirty is not early. Your father and I get up every morning before seven o'clock. But, honey, I didn't call to discuss the time. I was just wondering if you were still coming over later to help me and your dad pack for our cruise."

"Yeah, Mama, I haven't forgotten. But I have a few stops to make before I come over, so I'll be there around lunch time or a little later."

"Honey, is everything all right? You sound a little down."

"I'm okay, Mama. I guess I had a restless night."

"Sonya, I don't mean to pry, but how is it between you and Roc? He's not still upset about your spending, is he?"

Sonya paused. She knew telling her mother about all the drama going on in her household would only worry her. But perhaps it would be all right to ask for a little advice. After all, giving advice is what mothers are supposed to do.

"Mama, everything's going just fine over here, but how is it you and Daddy can keep things going better than just fine. What is your secret?"

"Sonya, as a child growing up, you knew there was always much prayer going on in our house and nothing has changed. Your father and I believe in keeping God in everything we do, especially in our marriage. There's no great secret. Stay on your knees and keep God first."

"Mama, can you just talk to me without making everything a sermon?"

"Child, I'm not preaching to you, I'm just trying to let you know you need God more than you think."

"Okay Mama, I'll see you later on."

Sonya hung up the phone and shook her head. She couldn't believe she asked her mother for advice about love and she started preaching about God. Is that all she did was live and breathe for God?

With heavy dread, Sonya mentally prepared herself for the hard day ahead. A morning of returning all her prized possessions and an afternoon with her mother.... If anyone needed prayer she did.

Sonya had already returned most of the items from her back seat and now she was emptying the trunk, working on returning the things she'd pulled from the basement, the attic, and from under her bed. She had a list of excuses she gave to the merchants as to why she was returning everything. Some were unwanted gifts, some were too small, too big, too tight or too loose, and finally, out of sheer exhaustion, she stopped giving explanations and said it was just because.

When she had gotten down to the last bag, she'd returned over fifteen hundred dollars of merchandise. No small chump change. That should shut Roc up for a while, Sonya said to herself as she walked toward her final destination. But before Sonya went to the department store, she decided to go into her favorite perfume shop and sample some of the testers.

Call it a woman's intuition or just plain common sense, but Sonya realized, before entering the store, that she didn't have any money and going in would be a bad idea. Standing in front of the store window, she debated what would happen if she went in. No doubt, she'd see something she wanted and it would be torture if she couldn't buy it. It was not fair. Roc was controlling her and she truly did not believe their financial problems were as bad as he was making them out to be.

Just as she prepared to walk away, she heard a pleasant and familiar voice.

"Hey girl!" the sales woman said from behind the counter. She recognized Sonya from her frequent visits to the store and beckoned her to come in. It was obvious that Sonya needed some gentle persuasion because she'd been standing out front for several minutes.

"I see you've been doing some more shopping. I heard that store has a gigantic sale," the woman said in reference to the big bag Sonya was carrying. "You must be married to a millionaire, and I ain't hatin'. I just know a true diva when I see one and girl I spotted the diva in you a long time ago. Girlfriend you got it going on—and since you got it like that, why don't you try some of this perfume. It's new and it's on sale—one time promotional price. Half off. Only a hundred and fifty dollars for the gift set. Here, try some. I know a woman of class such as you can appreciate the rich quality," the sales woman said, finishing what sounded like a well-rehearsed sales pitch with a tailor-made grin to match.

Sonya sensed the woman was working on commission, and she wanted to tell her she could can the hype because she was not buying anything, but instead, she politely told her she was just browsing.

"Well just sample some of this, girl, and it will change your mind," the over-zealous woman said, spraying some perfume on Sonya's wrist.

When Sonya smelled the perfume, she knew she had to have it. It smelled so good. But she also knew it was something she could not afford.

The seductive scent lingering in the air was enticing to Sonya, but she resisted the urge to indulge herself, looked at the woman and said, "Another time. Not today."

When the woman walked away, it took all Sonya had inside to hold back the tears. She did not feel victorious, she felt sad and defeated.

In a state of depression, Sonya picked up the gift box to examine it closer. There was nothing unusual about its contents—just lotion, body spray, and perfume. But the soft pink and red gift box was strikingly beautiful covered in lace and bows. She couldn't remember wanting anything so badly. She had to have it.

For the first time in her life, Sonya reasoned the cost in her mind. When she did the math, the bottom line figure said she could not afford it. Still, that intense feeling to acquire what she could not have took dominion over her thoughts. The battle between right and wrong raged within. Again, Sonya cursed her husband, blaming her torment on his selfishness.

In a daze, Sonya walked around the store with the gift set in her hands until it disappeared. When she realized the gift set was in her bag and she'd put it there in a moment of weakness, it freaked her out and she started shaking. What had she done?

As she nervously contemplated her next move, thoughts screamed out in a panic. Leave the store now—get out! Quickly, Sonya scanned the store to see if anyone was watching her. When no one appeared to be concerned with what she was doing, she knew the opportunity to escape had presented itself. She hurried toward the exit. With one more step, she would cross the threshold to freedom. As she prepared to breathe a sigh of relief, she heard someone say, "Miss Sonya!"

Frozen in her steps, Sonya had become imprisoned by fear. Yet, somehow in response to the sound of her name, she managed to turn her head. She hoped her guilt was not transparent. Oh God, she thought, Roc is going to have a fit. His wife has been caught stealing. Mama's going to have a heart attack. Her baby is a kleptomaniac! Then she thought, I'm going to go jail! And her heart started beating so fast she thought it would explode.

Lord, if You get me out of this, I will never do anything like this again! Sonya prayed silently.

"Miss Sonya, girl, did you hear me? I was calling you to see if you wanted to try another scent, maybe something from our Guess collection?" the sales woman asked, still grinning.

Instantly, Sonya recognized the power of prayer. She thanked God for not allowing her any embarrassment. And as normalcy crept back into Sonya's body, she felt the grip of fear loosen its stronghold and she was able to move again.

"No. I'm sorry I didn't hear you. But, like I said, today is not a good day for shopping. I'll try some other scents another time," Sonya replied.

"Okay, girl, I'll see you around."

Sonya walked slowly out the door, but she realized there was still the possibility of the gift set having a hidden censor; a device to trigger the alarm system. As she crossed the entrance, she anticipated hearing the piercing alarm sound off, but nothing happened. She had made it, a clean getaway, and she did not know whether to laugh or cry.

After Sonya left the perfume shop, she kept on walking, faster and faster. Her stride did not break until she was on the other side of the mall—the exact opposite end of the department store where she had unfinished business. Oh well, Sonya said to herself. It'll have to wait until another time. She was not returning anything else today.

Tired out, Sonya sat down to rest. Convinced that no one was watching her, she took the gift set out to admire it once again.

Captured by its beauty, Sonya fought back the emotions that flooded her. She managed to suppress each one except the hollering voice of guilt. No matter how she tried to escape it, like a broken record, it played over and over, you stole...you're a bad person...you're a thief, and Sonya promised herself she would never do anything like that again.

Then suddenly, a different feeling rushed in Sonya's blood rushed with excitement and in the depths of her soul, a devious thrill was ignited.

Chapter Twenty-Eight

Time for Love

When Sonya arrived at her parents' home, her mother was troubled by the undefined look on her daughter's face and wondered why she was wearing dark shades on a cloudy autumn day. "Sonya, is there something wrong? Who are you looking for?" she asked as her daughter glanced nervously over her shoulders. Suddenly Sonya's look became more perceptible. It was guilt.

"I thought I saw one of my old friends walking down the street, that's all," Sonya said walking into the house. "Nothing's wrong."

"Your mouth says nothing, but your expression tells a different story. You look like you did when you were a little girl and I caught you stealing from the cookie jar," her mother said.

"Well, Mama, we both know that's not the case. I'm too old for such juvenile cranks. I just feel a little strange today. I think I'm coming down with something."

If you say so," Mrs. Jones replied, quickly dismissing Sonya's strange behavior. She knew there was something going on in her daughter's life, but in respect for her privacy, she backed off. However the same rule did not apply to curiosity. She had to inquire about the box in Sonya's hand.

"Are you still doing all that ridiculous shopping?"

"No Mama. Believe me, my shopping days are over. This is just something I picked up for you while I was taking care of some business at the mall. It's a going away present."

"We're not leaving for at least two more weeks."

"Well when you leave, I don't have to worry about getting you anything because it will already be taken care of."

"Okay now I'm curious—what is it?"

"It's a gift set of a new fragrance and it smells really good," Sonya said, giving her mother the box.

"You're right honey, this smells heavenly," Mrs. Jones said, sniffing the perfume with excitement. But then, she saw the price tag. "Three hundred dollars?" she said in shock. "Sonya, this cost too much money. I can't accept this."

"Mama, please take it and don't worry about how much it cost. I didn't pay that price for it, it was on sale."

"Well how much did you pay?"

"Not much, Mama, not much. But, like I said, don't worry about it."

"Honey, are you sure?"

"Yes, Mama, I'm very sure, and if you're worried about the money I borrowed for the credit card bill, don't be. I'll pay you back soon. Mama, don't let my debt stand in the way of you accepting my gift. The bargain I got was a steal. Trust me, I did not step outside my means to purchase it, so can you please accept it and be happy?"

Mrs. Jones looked at her daughter suspiciously. Something was wrong, but again, she resisted the urge to pry and accepted the gift.

"Okay honey—I thank you with much love."

"You're welcome," Sonya said as she embraced her mother. "Now where is Daddy?"

"Your father is out back trying to put up Christmas lights. He said he wanted to get it out of the way before our trip and before the snow comes. He's probably up on the ladder."

Sonya left her mother and went to the backyard in search for her father. When she saw him, he was in the garage sorting lights and listening to the radio, his classic eight-track stereo, the one he refused to part with.

Before Sonya made herself known, she just stood and adored her father from a distance. For years, he was her hero. He was a big strong man with a huge heart for her, and an even bigger one for her mother. She'd always dreamed of marrying a man that possessed his qualities. But that's the thing, Sonya thought to herself, dreams are good to have, but they don't always come true.

As Sonya walked closer to the garage, she heard B.B. King singing in the background. Hearing the blues was no surprise. Her father was a connoisseur of music—all kinds. For as long as she could remember, he'd always slipped away to a secret hideaway and listened to his music. He did not discriminate. He appreciated all music—jazz, blues, gospel, rock & roll and even some classical.

"Hey Daddy," Sonya said, going up to her father and kissing him.

"Hey precious. How's my baby girl?" he replied.

"I'm doing so-so Daddy. I just came over to help you and Mama pack for your trip."

"Yeah, your mama told me you were coming over today," he said, turning the radio down to give his daughter his undivided attention. Just one more thing Sonya admired about her dad. He always made her feel like she was special and deserving.

"What's with the shades, precious? There's no sunshine out today. Are you hiding behind them?"

"No Daddy, I'm not hiding," Sonya said as she took off the shades to expose her big brown eyes.

Once the barrier of the shades had been removed, the conversation poured. The dull autumn sun took on a life of its own as Sonya and her father centered their talk on it and the inevitable cold days to come. After the weather, they talked about other trivial things until Sonya was comfortable enough to open up to her father. Over the years, he'd proven to be trustworthy with her secrets.

"Daddy if I tell you something, can you keep it from Mama? I just don't want her to worry about me."

"Honey, what's wrong?"

Sonya looked at her father, deep into his eyes and said, "Daddy, it's not me, it's my marriage. Roc and I—well, divorce is threatening."

"Baby, is that man hitting you or abusing you in any way? I know the kind of environment he was raised in, and the apple doesn't fall too far from the tree. "

"No, Daddy, it's nothing like that. Our problem is bad communication. It has built a wall between us. We never talk to each other. We just yell and argue all the time. Daddy, I don't know what to do. I have loved Roc since I was eight years old and realizing it is almost over hurts so bad."

"Sonya, every married couple has problems. Believe it or not, your mother and I have had our share, but the secret is putting God in the equation."

"Geeze, you sound like Mama."

"That's because God is the answer you need. I can't help it if it's not the one you want to hear."

"Daddy, it's not that. It's just that—well, I'm really not sure what it is. I just don't believe God is what I'm looking for right now."

"But honey, can't you see? Without God, you're already missing the main ingredient. Before you give up on your marriage, seek God. Take your marriage before Him in prayer and believe He can change things and watch His mighty hand at work."

"Sonya!" Mrs. Jones yelled from the house. "When you come in, bring in the suitcases from the garage."

"Okay, Mama, I'll be there in just a moment."

Then Sonya turned back to her father. "Daddy, I guess that's Mama's way of saying come on, so I better go in and help her," she said. But before she went in, she added, "I didn't mean to tell you anything that would upset you, it's just that I never realize how bad my marriage is until I come around and see how good you and Mama act towards each other. I can't believe how much you two still love each other after all these years and still manage to have trust and respect for each other."

"Precious, you can have the same thing. With God all things are possible. Just like He resurrected His Son from the dead, He can resurrect a dead marriage. Trust in Him, and believe anything is possible. It is never too late for change. Never too late."

Sonya received her father's advice and saw a loving and gentle God through her father's eyes.

"Precious, you can always come and cry on my shoulder. That's what I'm here for. And I hope my words were not spoken in vain, and you truly seek God, not just for your marriage but for your life. You know, your mother and I miss you going to church with us. Maybe this Sunday you and Roc can come and join us."

"We'll see, Daddy, we'll see. But right now I better go in and help your wife before we both get in trouble."

The drive home seemed exceptionally long for Sonya. She was forced to do what she hated doing—think things out. Putting her life in perspective had never been one of her strong points.

She reflected on the shoplifting incident. Somehow giving the item away relieved her of the guilt—out of sight, out of mind. After some serious soul searching, Sonya promised herself to put the horrible experience behind her. But she knew her situation with Roc was not that simple. She rehashed the conversation with her father. Somewhere in his words was the answer to her problem. But it was not God, Sonya was convinced of that. Her marriage required more than a spiritual fix. But what? Sonya thought strongly until the word—*change,* echoed in her head. Change, that's it! Sonya said to herself.

Starting right now I have got to do things different if I really want my marriage to work. I'm going to change my attitude, change my spending habits and starting tonight, I'm going to change the separate bedrooms...

Chapter Twenty-Nine

Mysterious Defiance

Sharing a cozy lunch in the break area, Justine and Roc were sitting side by side, talking and laughing together when their errant flirting was interrupted. Oakley came in to inform Justine that she had an emergency phone call.

Hurrying to Oakley's office, Justine worried about the terrible things that could be wrong. But, as soon as she picked up the phone, her children's principal calmed her.

"It's a very serious matter and I think it's best that you come to my office immediately," Mrs. Reddy said.

Justine was happy her children weren't seriously hurt, but she dreaded to hear what they had gotten themselves into. Wanting to leave right away for the school, she opened the office door and approached Oakley.

"I'm sorry, but I have to leave. The school—it's an emergency with the kids—I need to go," she said.

"I can't allow it, sorry," he said expressionless.

"This is very important to me," she urged.

"I hope your job is important to you," Oakley replied sharply.

Justine did not want to petition him on a personal level, but she had no choice. She reached out and gently touched his shoulder. Calling him by his first name (which nobody at work knew) she said, "Bruce, it's about Cordell. He's gotten into some trouble at school. The principal said he attacked some kid during recess."

When Oakley responded to her touch and tried to make eye contact, Justine looked away. Her attention immediately went to his desk. She looked at the clutter of paperwork on the desk hiding the cherry wood finish. Then, she raised her eyes to the ceiling and looked at the dull beige paint. Justine thought to herself. If those walls could talk, what secrets they would tell of her.

"I really need to go Bruce," she said, avoiding closeness.

"We all have needs, Justine. Is your new boyfriend meeting yours?"

"Is that a yes or a no, Oakley?"

Taken by her sudden professionalism, Oakley backed away and said, "Yes, Miss Brown, but I expect to see you first thing in the morning."

They were definitely a sight, the three of them sitting

outside Mrs. Reddy's office. Her daughter, Candice, had one black eye, another student, Anthony, had two black eyes, a busted nose, and a swollen lip, and her son, Cordell, had an attitude. Justine folded her arms and raised an eyebrow. All three children lowered their gaze to the floor. She smoothed her hair, checked her reflection in the office window, and then knocked on the principal's door.

"Please, come in," she heard Mrs. Reddy say.

"There's a hook there for your coat. Go ahead and have a seat."

"The children look awful. Are they okay? Have they seen the nurse?" Justine asked.

"Oh yes, Mrs. Brown—"

"Actually it's Miss. I'm not married," Justine interrupted.

"Oh, I'm sorry, Miss Brown, I thought you were. Cordell is always talking about his father."

Father? He must be talking about his uncle, Justine thought to herself.

Mrs. Reddy continued, "Yes, they've been thoroughly examined and the external wounds will heal. What I need to talk to you about concerns the children's thoughts, actions, and consequences. I told you on the phone that Cordell's violent actions today were very serious. He needs to be punished, not only at home but through the school as well. We also need to discuss the cause of this much rage. He threw punches one after the other, even after Anthony was pinned down and bleeding. What happened next worries us the most.

He actually picked up a stick and was thrusting down, ready to stab Anthony in the neck. Violence of this extreme stems from something internally. He's screaming out for attention."

The two of them talked over the incident and collaborated over what the plan of action should be. Justine could hardly believe the account Mrs. Reddy gave of what had happened. She absolutely did not think that her son was capable of hurting someone like this. She didn't have any answers.

"Miss. Brown, what can we do to help your son control his anger? What do you suggest?"

"Well," Justine said, "I plan on having a long talk with him as soon as we get home, and we'll take it from there."

Not sure if Justine understood the magnitude of the problem, Mrs. Reddy said, "I don't mean to alarm you, but may I humbly suggest you seek professional counseling for your son? I have been in the educational system for some time now and I have seen amazing results from counseling..."

Justine couldn't believe her ears. My son's not crazy. A psychiatrist? But he's so intelligent, she thought.

Reluctantly, Justine ended the conversation by asking the principal for her list of recommended counselors and promised to contact one soon.

Cordell was sent home with his mother while the other two children were sent back to class for what was left of the afternoon. On the car ride home, they were completely silent, but as soon as they got home, Justine asked her son for a complete explanation from his point of view.

"At recess," he began, "Candice was playing some game over by the swings—boys against girls—and they were guessing what the other team was drawing—characters from movies and stuff. Then, it was the girls' turn and when they drew Casper the Friendly Ghost, the boys started in on Candice! They were picking on her so bad about her light skin, Mama! Anthony called her really bad words and said we were nothing but the "n" word trying to be white! They kept yelling the "n" word at her Mama!"

"Oh, honey, I know that's awful, I really do. But violence doesn't fix anything."

"But I didn't start it! Candice was tough and shouted something back at Anthony—something about his Mom—and Anthony punched Candice in the face, hard! That's why I ran over, Mama. He punched my sister!"

Justine heard the sincerity in her son's voice. She knew that he was sticking up for his sister, but it was how far he went, the severity of her son's violence that caused alarm.

"But, Cordell, you might have hurt Anthony very very badly. You could've killed him if Mrs. Reddy hadn't stopped you! How could you do that, honey? I've never been violent, and I've always raised you two against violence," Justine insisted.

"I know Mama. I know. I don't know what came over me," Cordell replied softly.

Justine felt so alone—one of the woes of single parenthood. The mystery of Cordell's defiance was strange to her and strange to Cordell. He couldn't explain it either. He wanted to make his mother happy with him, but he couldn't stay out of trouble. This would be so much easier with two parents, but she had to handle this herself. However, she was out of words for her son.

Chapter Thirty

The Way to a Man's Heart

Later on that day, Sonya had completed her shopping at the market. She only needed a few ingredients for the impromptu romantic dinner she decided to have. The fifty dollars her father slipped her was more than enough to foot the grocery bill. The menu would be tasty but simple—ginger orange salmon over brown rice with sautéed baby spinach and fresh sweet rolls from Dolly's bakery, Roc's favorite bread. She even had enough money to buy a bottle of White Zinfandel.

Hoping a meal could mend torn hearts was a stretch, but in her desperate attempt for change, she franticly acted upon her whirlwind decision. She could only hope the old adage, the way to a man's heart is through his stomach, had some truth to it. Tonight she needed all the help she could get.

Sonya rushed home. There was much to be done.

But before she tidied the place, she marinated the salmon and placed it in the refrigerator, soaked the rice, washed the spinach, and chilled the wine.

When she went upstairs, to her dismay, she saw Roc had been home. His dirty clothes on the spare room floor were evidence he'd showered, changed, and left. She vaguely remembered him mentioning he was going to his mother's house after work, something about taking his niece and nephew trick-or-treating. Raymond and his wife were vacationing in Mexico and Sadie Mae was babysitting. After spending all day with two small children, she had asked her son to help out.

Sonya debated whether to call her husband or not. It had been a long time since she'd phoned his cell. She didn't want him to think she was checking up on him, but her hesitation was blocking their communication and if things were ever going to change, she had to be the initiator, so she made the call.

During the short conversation, Sonya managed to peak Roc's curiosity when she said she had something to give him and she'd be waiting up for him when he got home. In response, Roc anxiously promised to cut his trick-or-treat outing short. He gave no certain time when he would be home, but he said it would be soon.

Sonya was thrilled to hear the excitement in Roc's voice. It motivated her to be even more creative. In no time, she transformed their room into an oasis. The theme was red. For starters, she replaced the drab linens with a set of ruby red satin sheets. And to play into her fantasy of love, she covered the bed with rose petals. And lastly, for a dreamy ambiance, she filled the room with red candles.

Now that her checklist was completed, it was time to address some personal needs. Sonya would indulge herself, but the usual sauna and hot tub ritual for relaxation was out of the question. It was already seventy-thirty and Sonya expected Roc within the hour. Tonight, pampering herself was reduced to basking in a tub of hot water with silky smooth bath oil pearls. It wasn't much, but it sufficed to achieve tranquility.

While toweling dry, it came to her exactly what to wear: the scarlet negligee...

This was a special moment for Sonya, because it had been a long time since she'd felt sexy or even desired to be intimate with Roc. She gleamed with jubilation, and not even momentary doubt could rain on her parade. Although it was a fact, the irritating "what if" factor hung in the balance, but apprehension would not stifle her.

Yes, Sonya was fully aware that there was a chance that all her work was done in vain, because lingerie, roses, and candles were not Roc's thing—he was no romantic. Still, she anticipated his arrival as she checked out her flawless size six body in the mirror. Back in the day, Roc use to call her his chocolate kiss. Tonight, for old time's sake, she hoped he still had a sweet tooth for her.

It was nine-thirty and Sonya felt like a ditched prom date. The salmon was cold, the spinach was soggy, and she was fuming. She wanted to phone Roc again, but pride said no. Instead, she started sipping the flat, warm wine from the crystal goblet.

After three glasses of wine, Sonya's pride was eradicated and she dialed Roc's cell phone only to hear his voice mail prompting her to leave a message. After calling a few times, and still getting his voice mail, she gave in and left a message.

"Hey, Roc...this is your wife. It seems you forgot you had one! That romantic dinner I was going to surprise you with...I gave to the neighbor's dog. But the wine I'm sipping on has me in a forgiving mood, so if you hurry home, we can kiss and make up, and still enjoy dessert...it's on me. Or maybe the surprise is also on me and you're eating off someone else's plate!"

Half asleep and half awake, Sonya found the strength to change the bedroom back to its original state. In her disappointment, she decided to leave one more message for Roc.

"Once again you put your mama before me, I'm sure you confided in her and she gave you some real righteous motherly advice. But now Roc, let me give you some good wifely advice. A good woman..."

Right in the middle of Sonya's thoughts, she shut down. Suddenly all the words she wanted to say were cut off. Perhaps it would be better if she said what she had to say face to face. And then, for the first time, she realized maybe there was nothing else to say. The thought hit her like a ton of bricks—maybe she and Roc had finally run their course and there was nothing left to say.

Chapter Thirty-One

Halloween Night

Roc had received all Sonya's phone calls, but sent them straight to his voice mail. Whatever surprise she'd planned would have to wait until he got home. Knowing Sonya like he did, he figured her surprise was probably some way to swindle him out of some spending money. To be truthful, he was surprised she'd even called him and now that he didn't play by her rules and rush home, it was probably going to be a heated confrontation when he got home. And that was definitely nothing he was in a rush to deal with.

The air was getting cooler and the night sky was darkening. It was late and Roc had played the big uncle to his niece and nephew long enough. They were too young to really appreciate the Halloween outing anyway.

On the way to his mother's house, Roc thought about Justine. He wasn't too far from her neighborhood. Maybe if he circled around a few blocks, he would see her out with her kids. After all, he did remember her mentioning she would be out tonight earlier when they talked at lunch.

Earlier, Justine's mother had complained that she didn't feel well. With her history of high blood pressure, Justine was worried and canceled the kids' Halloween outing. Besides, the way Cordell had performed at school, the last thing she wanted to do was treat him to anything. But Candice didn't deserve to be punished also. So, although it was late, Justine reconsidered taking the kids out, even Cordell.

"Candice, Cordell, get dressed! It's late and we're only going to be out for a few minutes. But a little time out is better than nothing at all," she called out to the kids. Then, she ran next door to get her friend Latoya to go with her.

When there was no answer at Latoya's door, Justine thought she'd spoken too soon. She didn't think it was such a good idea to go out with the children so late alone. Justine knocked at Latoya's door again and again, finally stopping when she realized no one was at home. Disappointed, she decided to go tell the kids the bad news, but just as she opened the door, she heard a voice calling her name.

"Justine! Justine, hey girl...I'm over here."

Delighted, Justine beckoned Latoya and her daughter to come up on the porch.

"I'm so glad to see you, girl," Justine said to Latoya looking at the big bag of candy Latoya's daughter Taylor was carrying.

"Yeah, girl. It's time to call it a night. Did you and the kids go out at all?"

"No...we didn't. My mother wasn't feeling well, but now that she's better, I want to take the kids out for a few minutes. Will you go with me?"

Before Latoya could say no, her daughter Taylor was jumping up and down saying yes. Although Latoya had that, "no way" look on her face, she gave in.

"Only a few minutes. I got to go to work tomorrow," Latoya said.

Latoya and Taylor followed Justine up the stairs. Both mother and daughter were in costume. Taylor was Cinderella, complete with tiara, grown, and glass slippers. And it was obvious, Latoya was the wicked mother. She wore a dingy gray wig, and all the heavy make-up concealed her cuteness and created an ugly aged woman.

"Mama, look at Taylor and Ms. Latoya," Candice said, amused.

"I see. How beautiful she looks as Cinderella," Justine said.

"And what about her wicked step-mother?" Latoya said.

"Yes you're looking quit evil in that black fitted dress girlfriend," Justine said laughing.

"Well, girl I had to camouflage this ugly make-up with something attractive. You know last year the kids had us going everywhere—the police station, fire department, barber shops and every place else brothers might be hanging out. Need I say more?" Latoya said.

"Ms. Latoya, I'm going as Cat girl. My mama brought me a cat mask to cover my black eye and dressed me in all black like you," Candice said.

When Latoya saw Cordell suited down with a briefcase, fake mustache and glasses, she was puzzled. "Cordell, who might you be?"

"Father of the year," Cordell said with pride.

"I told him to be creative," Justine said as she too looked at Cordell in amazement. She felt a little guilty about Cordell's fantasy surrounded a missing element in his life.

"Well, I must say you look handsome. As a matter of fact, Father of the year, you can escort Cinderella," Latoya said, joining his hand with Taylor's. Then she looked at Justine just wearing a pair of jeans and a sweatshirt. "Oh no Justine, you're going to let me look like a fool all by myself, are you?"

"Yes," Justine smiled.

"Ha! We'll see about that..." It took some persuading but Candice, Taylor, and Latoya convinced Justine to dress up.

"Okay, Justine since your son is masquerading as a professional father...whatever that is...and your daughter is Cat Girl, a professional crime fighter...why don't you dress as...Lady J, the oldest profession in the world."

"Are you kiddin' me? A hooker? You want me to dress up as a hooker?"

"Look...if I got to be an evil mama...you can be a sexy mama."

Justine blatantly refused and had a hardy laugh with her friend, but after much playful pressure, she eventually gave in. Within seconds, Justine's simple girl next door persona was converted into a woman of the night complete with spiked heels, blonde wig and a leather mini skirt.

After circling nearly ten blocks, Roc felt foolish and decided to go home and call it a night. After all, his niece and nephew had fallen asleep in the back seat. But Roc dreaded to go home, so he decided to give it one more try.

When Roc turned down Andover Street, to his surprise, he saw a gorgeous woman wearing a sexy leather outfit. As he cruised closer to the woman and realized it was Justine, his jaw dropped. He quickly pulled over to the curb, rolled down the window and called out to her. When she came to the car, he began stuttering as he tried to speak. Justine's face lit up. Although she was embarrassed by her outfit, she was flattered by the obvious effect it had on Roc.

"Who is that?" Cordell asked Justine as he walked toward the shiny black car.

"It's one of my co-workers. Stay right here. I'll be right back," Justine said to her son, giving him the back-away sign.

"Roc, what are you doing here?" Justine asked.

"I...um...um...," Roc stuttered as he stared at her body. Finally, he lifted his eyes and explained he was out because of his niece and nephew.

"I see. They must've had a real nice time. They're asleep," Justine said.

"Just a minute, let me park," Roc said.

"Mama, can we go to the houses now?" Cordell asked impatiently.

"Sure, baby. I'll be right here watching you. But before you go, I want you to meet someone. Cordell, Candice, this is—"

"It's the Rocket!" Cordell said with excitement as he watched Roc get out of his car.

"Oh my goodness," Latoya chimed in, reaching to shake Roc's hand. "I'm pleased to meet you. Justine told me that you work with her."

Then Latoya decided to give her friend a moment. "Come kids, let's go trick-or-treating," she said as she hurried the children away and gave Justine a secret wink.

Roc and Justine stood by his car just laughing and talking. Roc couldn't believe how the conversation flowed—he hadn't talked like that with Sonya in months, maybe even years. All the while Justine was talking, Roc was checking her out. He loved the rush of lust he was getting. He had to find a way to have her, but they were friends...how could he get her to go further? Seeing her like this was so exciting.

Although his niece and nephew remained asleep and he was tired, Roc decided to finish out the evening with Justine and her crew. He hit if right off with Justine's son, talking back and forth about sports practically the whole time. Whenever he could, he cruised behind the kids and talked to Justine, stealing glimpses of her whenever her back was turned.

When the children's bags were too big to carry any longer, it was time to say goodbye. Roc and Justine made plans to see each other after he took his niece and nephew home and Justine had gotten things settled with her kids.

He tried to call home after he dropped off the kids, but there was no answer. Roc was going to tell Sonya he was running late and he was on his way home in an hour or so, but when there was no answer, he assumed she was angry.

No more than an hour later, Roc returned to Justine's house. When he showed up on her doorstep, even though she was wearing blue jeans and a sweatshirt, his heart was still pounding. After they talked for a couple of minutes in his car, they decided to go for a ride.

Chapter Thirty-Two

More than Friends

Roc and Justine were parked beneath a romantic, star-filled sky. The cool night air was an incentive to cuddle. Justine sensed she was in love and, when she looked at Roc, she thought he was experiencing feelings just as sincere.

They kissed for the first time, and Justine knew from the fire and passion that it would not be the last. The car windows steamed up. Roc commented that they were carrying on like two teenagers parked in the woods. But in the cramped quarters, he felt awkward and uncomfortable, so, wanting to keep the momentum going, he suggested checking into a hotel. The invitation took Justine by surprise, but in a moment of weakness, she couldn't do anything but agree. Her head was spinning. She knew what was going on. Hopelessly, she was falling for another married man and just like before, she did not intend for it to happen...but she couldn't stop it.

The feelings were exciting and frightening at the same time.

In an instant, the two of them were in a hotel lobby. Justine started to wonder if she should leave. She knew what would happen if she took another step. She thought about Roc's wife and how hurt she would be if she found out. But, it seemed that Roc didn't love his wife anymore. If it was over between them, then this was okay. She could follow her desire to give herself to Roc and deepen his love for her.

The elevator ride was very quick. Roc breathed heavily into Justine's ear, eager to make her melt and succumb to his slick moves once in the privacy of the room. For a moment, it worked, and Justine dreamily followed Roc down the hall, into the room, and onto the bed.

But, when Justine felt Roc slide his hands down her bare back, she suddenly realized the severity of her decision and desperately wanted to back out.

"Turn the lights off," she said shyly, realizing it was an inopportune moment to second guess her hasty decision to give herself to Roc. But she couldn't help herself. Suddenly she was having doubts about the whole thing. After all, Roc was a married man, and the word around the plant was his wife was beautiful—a chocolate version of Halle Berry. And since she was childless, his wife's statuesque body was probably unblemished, no ugly childbearing scars to hide. The thought made Justine's insecurities become overpowering.

In the dimly lit room, she noticed Roc could still see her, and was studying her body. In silence, he stroked each curve gently and passionately, but his quietness evoked nervousness in Justine. With each touch, she felt herself trembling in uncertainty, trying to read his thoughts.

Justine used her hands to shelter her nakedness. In a room filled with mirrors, she saw herself and felt ashamed. Roc eased her hands away and politely laid them to rest above her head. Justine wanted to give in to his tender touch, but her body was unwilling.

This was new territory for Roc. All the other girls in the past had thrown themselves at him. The way Justine was holding back made Roc have to do some smooth talking. "Relax," he whispered. "You're more beautiful than I imagined," he said seductively, hoping his confession would alter Justine's mood. But it did not—she was still cold.

When Roc felt her slipping away, he cradled Justine in his arms. He had to make her feel safe. He stroked her and flattered her with adoration. "You're beautiful...you're so beautiful," Justine heard him say over and over. Barely audible, the softy spoken words mesmerized her. She felt herself weakening as her desire strengthened.

Roc's magnetic charm was rewarded when Justine's inhibition diminished and she openly yielded the sweetness of her love.

When Roc pulled in his driveway, he just sat there in his parked car, paralyzed with intense guilt. This wasn't just another notch on his belt. He had conned an insecure, trusting woman. And at the same time, he had invited yet another woman into his life, poisoning his marriage.

Chapter Thirty-Three

The Uncertainty of Life

As Sonya entered the kitchen, her stomach turned at the notion of interacting with Roc. Last night's disappearing act resurfaced old wounds she thought time had healed. Crazed with so much disgust and fury, she was actually leery about where her burning emotions would take her. She looked at the scolding hot coffee pot, the simmering grits, and the sharp carving knife set gleaming in the morning sunlight at the end of the counter, just inches from Roc's back, meditating on the possible pain the deadly instruments could inflict. But, noticing how irrational her thoughts were, she prayed for calmness. Only God could stop her from doing something stupid.

Instantly, God blessed her with His peace and composure. Now she could actually look at Roc without having anymore dark and evil thoughts. However, she wasn't about to return Roc's shameless "good morning." She was not having a good morning, and she was not about to wish him one. She was not in the mood to lie or argue. Her cold silence would be the only evidence that she was deeply resentful. She wondered if Roc even cared with the way he hid his face behind the morning paper, occasionally emerging to sip some coffee.

"Havoc in the Home Causes Housewife to Lose It." The bold headline caught Sonya's eye, but she dared not inquire about it. Nothing would make her break her silence...nothing. In fact, if it had not been for the throbbing headache she was experiencing, she would've avoided Roc all together, and the obvious grief-ridden gourmet breakfast he'd prepared—the smell of which only worsened her nausea. From now on, she thought, two glasses of wine was her limit.

As Sonya prepared to nurse the bothersome hangover with a glass of tomato juice, she studied Roc's actions. She loathed his presence. At least, she said to herself, he could try to explain what happened last night. But the coward never revealed his face or even opened his mouth. Even though she was not speaking to him, she would've jumped at the chance to hear what he had to say.

Her intention, once she'd gotten the much needed pain relievers from the kitchen cabinet, was to return to her room, preferably, with absolutely no dealings with Roc. But an urgent phone call interrupted her plans.

"Calm down Mama, what happened to Daddy?" Sonya said, trying to make out what her hysterical mother was saying on the other end.

"Your father fell off the ladder! I called 911...EMS is here. They can't get a pulse...and he's not moving! He's not responding at all!"

"Mama—I'll be right there!"

"No, by the time you get here, we will be at the hospital. Meet me at Maple Ridge Hospital. Hurry."

When she hung up the phone, Sonya's rage subsided. She looked at Roc. He had lowered his paper and was giving her an inquisitive, concerned look and, before she knew it, she collapsed in his arms, burying her tear-filled face in his chest. His strong masculine body was just the pillar of strength she needed.

In a matter of minutes, the fragility of life had snatched all certainty from her and knocked her off her feet. In that awful moment of calamity, Sonya heard herself sobbing in fear.

"Please Roc, it's my father, he's had an accident. Take me to Maple Ridge. We have to hurry."

When Sonya and Roc arrived, the emergency room was unexpectedly crowded for such an early hour. Mrs. Jones was sitting alone, entranced, unaffected by the busy atmosphere. It was obvious she'd been crying. Her eyes were bloodshot and swollen, and her face was sunken in from despair. The sudden terror had wiped away all traces of her captivating beauty.

Sonya trembled as she made her way towards her ghost-white mother to inquire about her father's condition.

"I haven't heard anything since the doctor ordered tests a while ago," she said as she rested in Sonya's arms. "He's still not conscious. The doctors suspect brain damage."

"Brain damage? Oh no! How much?" Sonya asked.

"Right now they don't know. That's why they're running all these tests."

Sonya couldn't believe her ears. Was she dreaming? The accident—falling off a ladder—was it really that serious?

Where were the doctors? Her eyes searched around in amazement. She wanted to grill them until she got some answers. She had a list of questions she'd ask: Will my father be himself? Will he know us? Will he still be able to wrap his arms around me and chase away all my troubles? Will he be able to walk? Talk? As shocked as she was, Sonya knew that more information could bring some sanity to the situation.

But, what if the answers to her questions were ones she didn't want to hear? What if it was just her father's time to go home to God? She feared the prognosis. It was one of those times in life when no news might be good news.

"Honey," Sonya's mother said softly, "we must be strong. This is not the time to give up on God."

Sonya's eyes filled with tears. She wanted to respond, but the lump in her throat got in the way. She resented the arrogant assumption of her mother that she had no faith. It was true, she was not a holy warrior like her mother, but she knew God was their only hope in such a dark hour.

Though she was distraught, Sonya found the power to sit down and chant the Lord's Prayer, word for word—the same familiar prayer she'd come to know years ago in Sunday school. She was glad that it came to her memory so clearly.

Sonya's mother sat beside her and placed her hand on her knee. "Sonya, I've been sitting here worrying myself crazy, and just when I was about to lose my mind, I heard a voice in my spirit saying, Woman, where is your faith? And then the voice very clearly said, Pray and trust in Me. Honey, I know it was the Lord," Mrs. Jones said as she wiped away the salty tears from her lips. "And it came to me that God did not give us the spirit of fear but of love and a sound mind. We must be strong. This is only a test. Now the question is whether our faith can conquer our fears. I believe it can. The Bible says God is Jehovah-Rapha, our Healer, and we must not allow fear to make us forget that. Everything is going to be all right.

God has already answered our prayers and there is a miracle in the making," she proclaimed

And then as the tears continued to flow from Mrs. Jones' face, she stretched her hands, bowed her head and prayed. "Lord, yea though I walk through the valley of the shadow of death, I will fear no evil—I will fear no evil for You are with me. Father God, I have faith and I believe there is healing in the hem of Your garment, and in Jesus' name I know, I know my faith is not in vain!" Her outcry turned a few heads and raised a few brows as she stood up boldly making her confession.

From across the waiting room, another believer raised

her hand in the air and gave her affirmation. "Hallelujah to you my sista!" she proclaimed.

Then, Mrs. Jones heard her daughter's sweet voice, now much more calm, say, "Mama, I too believe."

It was a defining moment as they squeezed each other. Sonya found hope in her mother's warm embrace, and together, their faith was twice as strong.

Although the comforting moment was relieving, Sonya was still compelled to find answers to the questions lingering in her mind. Wearily, she posed a myriad of questions about the dreadful morning. Then, she prayed God's grace upon her mother so she could answer them all with a fair amount of clarity.

"As I remember," Mrs. Jones spoke in a whisper, "your father went outside. He said what he had to do would only take a few minutes. He just had to move the Christmas lights around a little. I didn't think anything about it, but after he'd been outside for so long, I called him and I called him, but there was no answer. And then, when I finally went outside, I saw your father stretched out on the ground with the ladder beside him. God! Oh, oh God! Why didn't I go out sooner? I can't believe—I was reading these cruise brochures, and I should've put them down! Why didn't I go out sooner? I should've gone out sooner!"

"Mama, you can't blame yourself."

"But honey, you don't understand, there is no telling how long he could've been out there calling for me while I didn't hear him. Lord, I did not hear him."

"Mama, don't cry."

"Lord, please!" Mrs. Jones pleaded. "My husband has to be all right! I can't live without him! He's my life!" She felt her faith slipping, but immediately realized it was not her will but God's will that must come to pass.

Like a warrior in combat, Mrs. Jones straightened her shoulders and regained her strength and her faith soared from within, until she saw the man who had greeted her when she first walked into the emergency room. His face was still grim and his demeanor suggested he was even more exhausted and overworked than he was the last time she saw him, some several hours ago. As he drew near, his footsteps resonated in her ears like beating drums, and the closer he got, the louder her heart pounded. As she met the doctor's droopy eyes, she clung even closer to her daughter.

"Mrs. Jones, the test results are back," the unshaved, frail man stated in a heavy Middle Eastern accent. "Your husband is resting and he will be just fine."

The news made Sonya and her mother smile with relief. Sonya saw the blood reenter her mother's face. Every tense muscle in her body relaxed, and her beauty was restored. Triumphant victory filled Mrs. Jones as she swept away a tear rolling down her glowing cheek.

"Mrs. Jones, you need to know, as an emergency physician, I see many things in the course of a day, but today I witnessed a miracle." He paused. "Let me explain. What was initially believed to be brain damage resulting in a cerebral injury that would cause severe paralysis turned out to be a mild concussion. I must reiterate and stress that it was a miracle because there is absolutely no other explanation. All the evidence—his initial coma, the severity of the fall—your husband's accident was life threatening." The doctor's face lit up and the fatigued little man began to smile for the first time in their presence. "Mrs. Jones, your husband was near death and right now he's doing fine. None of our tests show negative findings. Mr. Jones is showing no signs of head trauma. He's very much alert and he's requesting to see you, but it will be a few more minutes before that is possible. At this time, he is being fitted for a temporary cast because he does have a broken ankle, but it's minor. He has been given pain medication for his discomfort. When everything is completed, the nurses will take you to him. Just for precautionary reasons, we'd like him to spend the night for observation. He will be released tomorrow. Are there any questions?"

"Doctor," Sonya's mother said, "did you say miracle?"

"Yes, Mrs. Jones. A miracle. A divine intervention. It has to be."

In the busy corridor, Mrs. Jones started shouting and praising God. "Thank You Jesus! Thank You Lord! I knew You were going to save him! Thank You Jesus!"

Before the doctor walked away, he extended his hand. "If there are no more questions, I have other runs to make. It has been a pleasure meeting you. I'm always thrilled to be the bearer of good news when I speak to family members. Thank you for your patience, and Mrs. Jones, you take care of your husband, my new friend," the doctor said, displaying a genuine smile.

"Thank you doctor," Sonya said, elated, squeezing and shaking the doctor's hands. Then, she turned to look for Roc. He had been quietly sitting off to the side, but now he was gone. Sonya wondered where he was for a moment, but when her mother suggested they go freshen up, her attention was diverted.

Roc, on the other hand, had other concerns. After they all got the good news, he made a fast break out the door. He needed a cigarette and in the cool autumn air, he found a stone sand-filled ashtray to be a common interest among strangers. As fellow smokers hovered around, an occasional "good morning" or "how do you do" gave way to idle conversation. In fact, it was small talk that Roc found himself engaged in when a troubled young lady revealed her brother and his girlfriend were patients at the hospital. In a silent cry for sympathy, she openly expressed their critical condition. Both were near death, she said, at the hands of a jealous and mad woman, her sister-in-law.

Roc looked at the tears streaming down the woman's face, and searched for comforting words, but his compassion reservoir was practically depleted. Whatever he had left, he had to conserve. He had his own problems.

It was six cigarettes later when Roc returned to the emergency room. "There you are," Sonya said. "I was beginning to wonder."

"Any more news?" Roc asked.

"Well," Sonya replied, "not about Dad, but there is a bunch of buzz about a crazy wife who tried to chop up her husband and his mistress with an ax. It seems the wife walked in and found her husband and some woman in their bed and just went ballistic. The two victims are patients here. In fact," Sonya eluded, "most of the people in the lobby are family members of the victims. See, over there? All the news reporters? No doubt, they're gonna put this on the evening news."

When Roc realized he'd spoken to the husband's sister, he marveled to share the news with Sonya. Perhaps he would suggest that Sonya ask her mother to pray for the young lady and her family. But he quickly changed his mind when Sonya blurted out, "They got just what they deserved. The cheating dog! I hope she chopped off his goods!"

Sonya's insensitivity shocked Roc. Alarmed, he shifted his eyes back and forth. In a room filled to capacity, he hoped no one else overheard her statement. But when his gaze came back to Sonya, he froze, caught in his wife's burning glare which was fixed on him. It was the last kind of look he wanted to see. It made him shiver. He thought about Justine and his infidelity. He knew Sonya did not have a clue about her, but her eyes suggested she had an inkling about something. He hated that suspicious gaze. He felt transparent, vulnerable, and above all, guilty. Turning away, he thought, Why can't I stop cheating? Why do I keep bringing other women into our lives?

When Roc saw the nurse gesture for his mother-in-law, he thanked God. The timing could not have been better. "Mrs. Jones, you and your family can come and see your husband now. Please follow me."

The nurse seemed to move slower than molasses. Sonya wanted to run to her father so badly. "Right here folks," the nurse gestured to the opening in the curtain.

There was her father, finally. He was sitting up in bed. His head was partially bandaged and he had a cast on his leg, but he was smiling and stretching out his arms. Mrs. Jones rushed to his side and embraced him gently, whispering her expressions of love in his ear.

Watching them carry on was a beautiful sight to Sonya. As she observed her parents kissing, praying, and crying together, she broke down and cried. Her tears were not all joyous, though. They were mostly tears of frustration. Sonya knew how deep her parents' love was, true soul mates, and she envied them. She desperately wished for what they had. Sonya wanted to connect with her husband at that moment, to reach out and clench his hand, but Roc was staring out the window, seemingly unmoved by her parents' heartfelt reunion. Nothing short of another miracle could make her marriage as blissful.

Although they were not ready to leave, the visit was cut short when the nurse reminded them of Mr. Jones' necessary rest. She said it would only be a matter of time until he would fall asleep from the effects of the pain medication.

"Honey," Mr. Jones said, "before you go, I want to discuss something important. It was the last thing I thought about before the fall and first thing I thought about when I came to myself."

The nurse cleared her throat.

"It'll only take a moment," he assured her.

"Five minutes, Mr. Jones," the nurse said as she left the room.

"What is it sweetheart?"

Mr. Jones took his wife's hand. "Baby, we need a spiritual vacation—just you and me and God. We need to spend some time alone with God—time to renew our love for the Father as well as our love for each other. Our priorities are out of order. Right before the fall, I promised God I would consider an appropriate time to re-group my life after the cruise. I realize now, I was putting God on hold and telling Him to wait on me and my terms. Honey, that thought was the last thing I remember. When I came to, I felt like the Lord was saying to me now is the time. I hate to disappoint you, but aside from my broken ankle, I just don't believe this is the time for us to take a cruise."

"Robert, whatever you want to do is all right with me."

"Truthfully, I feel we should bless another couple that needs a refreshing get-away—a chance to fall back in love with each other. And what better couple to give it to than Roc and Sonya?"

"Daddy, that's a bad idea. Give it to some of your church members. I'm sure they would love to go."

"Come here, baby girl. Take the trip, and put all your troubles behind you. Just like your mother and I need some quality time to spend with the Lord, you and Roc need some quality time to find the Lord. What better place to search for

Him than on a paradise cruise ship? Baby, accept the gift, and pray for God's guidance."

Sonya looked at her father. She could never say no to him. Although she was not thrilled with Roc at the time, she had to admit that the idea of getting away was thrilling.

"If Roc can get the time off I guess we can go," she said.

Roc had hoped Sonya would pass on the generous gift, but she did not, and now the pressure was on him. What would he and Sonya do for seven days except argue? But if he did not give in, there would probably be arguing anyway. It was a catch-22 situation that he had to play by ear.

"Well," he said with a tiresome sigh, "tomorrow when I go to work, I'll see if I can get the time off."

Roc looked at Mr. Jones doze in and out and wondered what his true intentions were. He and his father-in-law never had a good relationship. Roc had always felt Mr. Jones didn't think he was good enough for his daughter. Even when he was financially secure, there was always a question of inadequacy hanging.

When the ladies left, Roc walked over to Mr. Jones and looked at him. His eyes were barely opened, but he spoke. "My daughter told me all about the problems you two are having. Because I love my daughter and hate seeing her sad, I've been holding back my true feelings about you. I haven't wanted to tell her. But I'm sure we both know where we stand with each other. I've heard about all your whorish ways. I guess the apple don't fall too far from the tree. But I'm a man of God and I believe anything is possible, even hope for your marriage. God put it on my heart to give you the trip, and in this instance, I must trust God more than I trust my own opinion. So if you're standing here to thank me, don't. Thank God, because I had nothing to do with it."

When Roc got ready to respond, Mr. Jones' eyes were completely closed, which was a relief. He was going to say all the right things—that he loved Sonya and he knew he'd made mistakes but that he'd do better and truly make things work, but perhaps it was for the best his father-in-law was asleep. Now he didn't have to tell those lies to him. Or were they really lies? Roc pondered. As crazy as it seemed, he wasn't convinced that he didn't love Sonya anymore and he wasn't sure if he could live without her. In all the madness between them, would it be too foolish to believe there was really a chance for their love?

Chapter Thirty-Four

Careful Conversation

The day after their licentious night in the hotel, Justine picked up the phone at least a dozen times to phone Roc. He'd missed work and she was worried about him. Rumor had it he had some kind of family emergency, but what it was, Oakley would not say. Although she wanted to contact Roc, she decided against it.

With her heart yearning for Roc, and her desire still lingering from their encounter, Justine could hardly stand not seeing him. Then, when she got to work on the second day, Roc's smiling face was present at last. As she approached him, her mind was filled with questions and even some anxiety.

"Hey stranger, I missed you yesterday. Is everything all right?" Justine asked, hoping he would validate her curiosity with an explanation.

"Yeah, I'm sorry. I should've called, but I had a family emergency—a close relative got seriously ill unexpectedly," Roc said.

"A close relative?" Justine asked, waiting to hear who it was.

"Yea," Roc quickly replied, but he said no more on the subject. For the first time, he was quiet about his personal life.

"I don't mean to pry Roc, but it's not nice to keep a girl hanging, especially the morning after a romantic evening."

"Look, don't worry about it. I'm here for you. If you feel ignored at all or like I'm not calling for too long, you can call me...on my cell phone."

When he said that, Justine felt better and, instantly, her face lit up.

"So who got ill suddenly?" Justine asked.

"That's not important. But what is important is I missed you, and I want to know how you're doing."

When Roc said he missed Justine, that was all she needed to hear to calm her fears and insecurities. "I'm doing okay," she said, perky. "I hate to admit it, but I kinda missed you yesterday." As Justine spoke, she moved closer to Roc, and then she stood on her tiptoes, and whispered in his ear. "I can't help it, but I cannot stop thinking about the other night. Mister, you know how to make a woman feel," she said.

Then slowly, Justine relaxed her feet and came back down to earth. She smiled, looked at Roc innocently, and gave him a flirtatious wink.

Roc tried to hide it, but he started to blush. His ego inflated and took flight. I still got it, Roc thought as he grinned to himself. This extremely attractive woman was smitten with him, and she was not ashamed to admit it. Caught up in the game, Roc heard himself respond to her tease. "Baby, the best is yet to come," he said as he bent down and kissed Justine softly on her lips. "I'll see you later," he said and walked away.

Justine stared at him until he disappeared.

It was nine o'clock when Roc opened his office door. Oakley was sitting at his desk talking on the phone. It was an irritating conversation judging by his nervous pencil tapping and flustered look. After a heated debate about quality versus quantity was exchanged, Oakley ended the conversation in a "do it or else" tone. Then he abruptly disconnected himself from the caller, but not the problem. It was apparent the frustrating phone call was still eating at him as his dishwater pale complexion suddenly reddened. While the fluorescent light glared down upon his thinning red hair, he barely raised his head to eye level to acknowledge Roc's presence before he returned to the mountain of paperwork before him.

"You're late," he grunted.

Oakley's bad mood was a great contrast to Roc's jovial state. He was floating. It had only been seconds since he'd left Justine's area and her fragrance was still fresh in his nostrils.

Her lingering, sensuous scent enticed naughty thoughts even as he petitioned Oakley for time off and it was not until his request was denied that Roc began to think about Sonya. Almost immediately, her frowning face and nagging voice began crowding out the erotic fantasies that had taken up residency in his head.

The trip meant nothing to Sonya, but Roc knew if she could not go because of him, she'd capitalize on the opportunity to raise the roof with accusation, so the pressure was on. Roc continued to plead his case, even begging a little. But Oakley was strict with his position.

"Look man," Roc said, now angry, "I need this time off and I have some available vacation days. If you don't approve it, I'll have to go over your head."

"If you go over my head, then it is only fair to let you know I will be forced to talk about your little drinking problem."

"What are you talking about?"

"I've been getting some complaints about you drinking on the job!"

"Oakley, I'm not moved by threats. I'm not one of your foremen that you can push around. If you think I got a problem—prove it!"

"Look man, you're not the big man on campus anymore, your superstar days are over with, and contrary to what you believe, you must answer to me. I have the last say around here! So do what you gotta do, and I'll do what I gotta do."

When Roc left Oakley's office, he cursed him and swore he'd take off the time if for no other reason but to tick Oakley off. In less than two hours, Roc had done just that. He took the necessary steps to get his vacation time approved, fully willing to accept the consequences.

Chapter Thirty-Five

Stolen Moments

When Sonya got the news that the trip was on, she asked for some money to go shopping. Roc told her it was not in their budget and she had to make do with what she had. Sonya was furious. For two days, she tried to change Roc's mind, but nothing she said or did worked.

After sulking awhile, Sonya decided to take matters into her own hands. She'd been having an overwhelming urge to try her hand at shoplifting again, but she never did because shame and conviction would always change her mind. But that would not be the case today. Sonya did not even bother to deal with her conscience. In a split second decision she went to the mall, penniless.

Sonya window-shopped until she found the store that best suited her needs. She waltzed into the upscale designer store and went straight to the counter and made small talk with the sales woman as she checked out the store's security.

It was moderate at best. The clothing didn't even have security tags.

They talked for a few minutes, and then Sonya asked to see the little black dress on display in a size six. When the woman turned her back, Sonya quickly grabbed two dresses off the rack and stuffed them into her oversized purse. When the woman returned with the dress in her hands, Sonya looked at the price tag.

"Oh," Sonya said, "I received a couple of dresses from your store as a gift, but I really don't care for them that much. If I bring them back tomorrow, can I exchange them for this one?"

"Sure you can....just as long as you have the receipts. But, even if you do not have the receipt, the policy is to give the customer store credit in the amount of the merchandise."

"Well, store credit is all I want, because I do not have a receipt. Like I said, the dresses were a gift. My husband bought them for me for my birthday. He's such a sweetheart, but his taste is lousy."

Sonya thanked the woman for her help, and then browsed around the store until the sales woman's attention was on other customers. When Sonya left the store, her heart was beating wild and crazy, but it was not from fear. It was excitement.

There were a few more stores Sonya had in mind, and in a mad frenzy, she visited them all. By the time Sonya made it home, she had confiscated a week's worth of clothing with the same con game. It did not matter what the outfits looked like. She'd return them all the next day and get what she really wanted. What a shame, Sonya thought, as she laid out an array of clothing across her bed, look what Roc had reduced her to...

Meanwhile, Justine was delighted. Roc proved to be a man of his word, as he promptly responded to every phone call she made. And the numerous calls became a prelude to romantic rendezvous. Being with him had become intensely passionate and relaxing all at the same time. And with every encounter, Justine fell deeper and deeper into Roc's allure. At times, her feelings scared her—everything was moving so fast.

But her heart was in the driver's seat, and it was as if she was just along for the ride.

Whenever Justine thought about Roc being married, she pushed the menacing thought aside and justified the things he said. She assumed his words were truths, trusting that he'd never lie to her. He told her he had never been unfaithful in his marriage until her, and he had never known how happy he could be until she came into his life. He said Justine was a breath of fresh air. He degraded his wife and said she was lazy and neglected him and their home. She didn't know it was a lie when Roc expressed how selfish his wife was—how she refused to have children out of fear of ruining her precious body. He shared intimate truths with Justine—how he and Sonya never slept together anymore. This line, especially, gave Justine the hope that Roc's marriage would end soon and the justification she needed to give herself permission to open up her heart all the way.

It was mid-day when Justine escaped reality. Daydreaming, from her bedroom window, she cuddled in her favorite chair, and became one with nature. It was a picture perfect early winter day, as the barren trees blew freely in the whispering wind. The tranquil moment ushered in thoughts of Roc. Lately such reverie consumed her every waking moment.

She took in long, deep breaths, and exhaled slowly thinking of last night with him, and what a pleasurable time they'd had. It was their first trip to Canada together. Going just across the Ambassador Bridge from Detroit to Windsor had never been such a big deal before. Justine, who'd practically hit every bingo hall in Windsor with her mother years ago, had acted as if the city's sights were brand new to her. But then, everything she did with Roc was like experiencing it for the first time.

They had gone to dinner, then dancing, and afterwards to the casinos. Roc played his hand at poker and won. He said it was all because he had his lucky charm on his arm.

The night ended too soon and the morning came with the usual sad goodbyes. But Justine knew this farewell was different. It would be a week before she would see him again. A couple of days ago, Roc had told her he was going out of town, but he was being very secretive about the trip.

Over dinner they talked about everything except his trip, and although Justine wanted to pry, she would not upset him on the eve of his departure.

Sitting in her cozy chair, Justine remembered his last words before their parting kiss, "I'll miss you," he said. "I love—," immediately followed. Justine had hoped he would say "you," but he did not. In fact, he stuttered and quickly came back with, "I love being with you." Justine was not stupid—she knew professing love was forbidden in an adulterous affair.

The risks were too high. But even though she knew he could not speak it, his actions made it clear, he was falling for her, and they both knew it. And for now, if she could not have Roc's love, Justine was willing to settle for the next best thing, his body. And this resemblance of love comforted her.

After hours of lying around, Justine became restless. To overcome boredom, she thought of going shopping with her mother, but she was not really enthused with the idea. Perhaps she'd rent some movies and watch them with the twins, but still she was not thrilled. Nothing sounded as good to her as doing just what she was doing, cuddling up in a chair and missing the love of her life.

When the phone rang, Justine jumped to the floor, ran quickly across the room and answered it before the second ring. She was pleased to hear Roc's voice.

"I was just thinking about you and I had to call and let you know," Roc said.

"What a coincidence. I was thinking about you. How is the packing going?" Justine said.

"I haven't even started yet, but it won't take me long. I'm traveling light."

"So, for seven days I won't see you?"

"Yeah, I'll be leaving tonight and I won't be back until next Sunday. I'll probably be too busy to call you, so keep yourself occupied. I don't want you sitting around doing nothing until I get back."

"I promise to keep myself busy, if you promise to keep me on your mind."

"You're always on my mind, but for the record, I'll think about you even more."

When the conversation ended, Justine felt like doing something, but still shopping and watching a movie wasn't it. She felt like writing. It had been months since Justine had written anything in her dairy, but today she had to put her feelings down on paper.

Dear Diary,

The last entry I wrote I was satisfied being alone. My children, job and friends were enough to fulfill me, but oh how things have changed. My whole world is new now, and in the center of it is Roc. Suddenly, he has become my first thought in the morning and my last thought at night, and I love being in love. Yet as happy as I am, I'm equally as sad, because he's not totally mine. He's married, but miserable and although he has not said it, soon he will be leaving her.

Secretly, I dream of being Roc's wife and having his children. It seems so natural when we're together, as if it's the way that things should be. How strange is life...I finally found the man of my dreams and he belongs to someone else. But I must admit, at the expense of someone else's happiness I will follow my heart's desires, and by whatever means necessary, I will pursue this chance at real love.

Chapter Thirty-Six

Lover's Paradise

Sonya never liked flying. Some flights were better than others, but it was never an enjoyable experience being above the clouds. It was just too far from earth for her. The first plane from Detroit to Atlanta was short and sweet in comparison to the long turbulent ride they were having from Atlanta to San Juan, Puerto Rico.

Instead of looking out the window at endless white nothing, Sonya looked at Roc. He was fidgety. After three hours, he'd complained he needed a cigarette. And the movie about Ray Charles was doing nothing to suppress his nicotine craving. But Sonya gloated in his discomfort. Gladly, she took pleasure in the nonsmoking environment.

"Where is the itinerary?" Roc asked, tapping on his armrest.

Sonya went into her purse and pulled out the schedule, placing it on his fold-down table. Leaning over Roc, they perused it together. The interesting islands struck up conversation between them.

"You know, I was talking to my co-worker, and he told me he took the same cruise last year with his friends and they had a ball," Roc said.

"Four islands in seven days sounds like it can be a lot of fun. I didn't think I would like it, but I'm looking forward to it," Sonya said.

"Are you all right with the flight?" Roc asked.

"It's okay. Are you all right with not smoking?"

"It's okay. Soon we'll be landing," Roc replied. Then he looked at Sonya, but habitually, they quickly looked away.

Finally, when Sonya and Roc arrived in tropical Puerto Rico, they boarded a magnificent cruise liner. And instantly, the rough flight became a hazy memory as it was replaced by an image of perfection.

The ship, a huge white fantasy, was bigger and more beautiful than Sonya had ever imagined. As she stood on deck, she looked out at the deep blue waves shimmer as if the ocean was encrusted with crystals. And then she lifted her gaze to take in the clear sky kissed gently by the golden sun. It was paradise. The ocean, the sun, the palm trees, and perfect weather overjoyed her. Sonya had traveled around the world with Roc, but she could not get enough tropical beauty.

After the couple took a quick tour of the ship, they went

to their room. The tiny single bed was no surprise, but it was something they had not thought about until now. It had been months since they'd slept together, and for the next seven nights, it could pose a problem. They looked at each other, threw their bags on the floor, and said nothing.

The first night was the welcome orientation from the ship's personnel, a briefing of all the ship's activities, and an itinerary of all the different islands they were going to visit. Afterwards, Sonya and Roc had dinner with three other couples who went on and on about how great the cruise ship was and how God was using the Christian Cruise Club to mend marriages. One of the things Mr. Jones neglected to tell Roc and Sonya about the cruise was that it was sponsored by their church which was affiliated with the Christian Cruise Club—a Christian traveling club created by a group of Christian family therapists on a crusade to reconcile broken families, strengthen marriages and renew loveless couples. To Sonya and Roc's dismay, everything about the cruise was geared towards the enrichment of marriage.

At dinner, Calvin and Carol did most of the talking. Calvin was a short round guy and Carol was tall and slim. She was talkative and he was quiet, but somehow their differences complimented each other because they seemed like a couple made in heaven. Carol said it was their third trip on the Christian Cruise Club. The first time they went to Mexico and the last time they went to the Bahamas, and they already had plans to go to Hawaii next year. The seven day cruise is perfect for keeping the spice in their marriage. Carol shared that four years ago, they were on their way to divorce court, but through divine intervention, they were lead to get involved in the traveling club. The classes, seminars, and workshops gave them the spiritual, mental and emotional help they needed to force them to reevaluate their relationship and the true essence of love and the plan God has for a man and his wife.

Both Roc and Sonya were disinterested in what Carol and Calvin were talking about, but before Roc could change the subject, another woman at the end of the table chimed in. "Tonight Dr. Paul D. Wright, one of the founders will be lecturing on the true joy of intimacy. His book is flying off the shelves," the woman said. "Oh, excuse my rudeness. I'm Sally Wells," she said, vigorously shaking hands.

"What is the book about, Sally?" Sonya asked before she knew it.

"It's about all the mind games couples play and how they use sex, money, and power to manipulate each other."

When Roc heard sex, he quickly stuffed some glazed chicken in his mouth. The last thing he wanted to think about was sex on this trip with Sonya. But on the other hand, Sonya entertained the idea as she gazed at the magnificent ice sculptures. It had been months since Roc had come near her. The thought of a romantic night was enticing.

Roger, Sally's husband, excused himself to go out for a smoke and Roc immediately got up to join him. As Roc stood up, his long lanky physique and familiar face made Roger recognize him, and immediately, the table was informed that they were in the presence of a mega star, the Rocket, a former Detroit Pistons basketball player. At once, everyone at the table and the surrounding area greeted him with handshakes and smiles. Sally was the only one to apologize for her ignorance. She still had no idea who he was. She hated sports.

Roc and Roger's need to smoke was ignored when the attention was diverted. All the men at the table started talking about sports. The room began to take notice and even some fans came over for an autograph. The men had monopolized the conversation with sports, but gradually one by one, the ladies found their place in the discussion, even Sally. As everyone continued to chat, Roc and Sonya loosened up and even started sharing personal stories with the table about Roc's illustrious basketball career. The grand stories gave their audience a false illusion of Roc and Sonya's happiness as they projected the perfect couple laughing together and even touching each other on occasion.

Sonya went to bed first. She tried to wait up for Roc who'd stayed on deck with his newfound friends, but exhausted, Sonya finally fell asleep waiting. The next morning, she saw Roc asleep in the chair next to the bed. He looked so uncomfortable with his long body all stretched out in that little chair. Sonya felt rejected and foolish for believing a romantic atmosphere and one pleasant dinner could change things. With serious doubts about their marriage, Sonya got up, showered, dressed, and left for breakfast.

When she went out on the ship, Sonya was thrilled to see the huge, beautiful breakfast buffet that was laid out. She embraced the blue skies and golden sunrise and, at that point, she made up her mind that she was going to enjoy the trip regardless of Roc's attitude.

Although it was still early, the temperatures were well into the eighties. Sonya eased out of her robe, pulled back her hair and put on her shades to block out the sun. Again she looked at the enormous spread, grabbed a plate, and prepared herself to indulge. But as she made her way around the buffet table, she felt uncomfortable stares. She wasn't sure if it was because her skimpy swimsuit was revealing or because she was the only visible single woman on the deck surrounded by married couples. As Sonya decided to slip back into her terry robe, she heard someone call her name. She was delighted when she turned around to see it was Sally from last night.

"Good morning," Sally said with a smile.

"Yes, it is a good morning," Sonya replied.

"Come over here and have breakfast with us," Sally said as she pointed out their table.

Sonya agreed, piled some fruit and a muffin on her plate, and hurried over to join everyone. Sally smiled, and commented on Sonya's healthy food choices as she moved over to make room for her. Sonya was greeted by the same group of people from last night. Carol and Sally did not seem to be jealous by her appearance, but instead complimented her.

"Now girl, keep on eating like that and you will be thin forever, but even though you got it going on in that bikini, it's not enough to keep your marriage on fire. I'm a size...well let's just say I'm not your size any longer, but Roger treats me better than he did when I was size six, because through Christ we have discovered the real meaning of love. The seminar they do here is one of the things that helped us to discover real love.

Like I said, it helps couples know how to have real intimacy in their marriage through God Almighty. It's centered on the Songs of Solomon from the Bible and it's today at eleven. Will you and your husband the Rocket be attending?" Sally asked.

"Oh yes, girl, you just got to come! Guaranteed to show couples how to keep the fire burning in their marriage," Carol said, giving her husband a kiss.

"I'm not sure what my husband and I have planned for today," Sonya said.

"Well, looks like he's coming," Roger said, beaconing Roc to their table. "Maybe if I invite him he just might come. Sometimes men can be shy about things like this. I know it took the prayers of my wife and the persuasive power of my male friends to usher me into the right direction."

When Roc got to the table, Roger asked him to attend the seminar. Roc started to refuse, but for some strange reason, he agreed to go.

In the seminar workshop, Roc and Sonya did role reversals, touching exercises and then the workshop ended with the couples kissing. Roc and Sonya had not kissed or hugged in months and the kiss was powerful and emotional. Roc could not believe how good it felt holding Sonya in his arms again. He felt something deep inside his soul connecting with her. The two were kissing long after everyone else had stopped. Sonya tried to control herself, but before she knew it, she was crying, and the two of them held each other as if they were holding on for dear life.

Roger cleared his throat and announced that the class was being let out. Undisturbed, Roc and Sonya continued to stay in the empty room just holding each other.

"I'm sorry," Roc said. "I miss holding you. I miss loving you. I need you."

"I don't know what to do to make it work. All I know is that I need you. We got to make it work. I don't ever want to live without you," Sonya said softly.

The passionate kiss was just the beginning. Sonya and Roc returned to their room and shared new depths of intimacy until sleep enveloped them. For the next six days they participated in every workshop, seminar, and lecture that went on.

At the end of each day the couples were encouraged to attend church service on deck. Roc was against church at first. He'd had enough of church as a child and it was something he felt he'd outgrown. But the leader of the workshop said in order to truly love others, you had to first love God, because only the love of God can make you reach out to others when you're hurt and confused.

The couples were also encouraged to read the Bible together. Something inside Roc made him want to become a student and he did everything he was told to do.

It was the last night on the cruise, and it was custom that the couples renew their vows. Sonya and Roc eagerly took part in the ceremony, bringing an incredible sense of oneness to their hearts.

Afterwards, Sonya and Roc returned to their room hand and hand. The next day, they would return to the reality of their problems and, secretly, both of them feared the days to come.

"So what happens tomorrow?" Sonya asked.

"We return to our roots at church, find a good marriage counselor, and take it day by day," Roc said with conviction. Then he asked, "Are you afraid?"

"Yes, but the only thing that frightens me more than facing our problems is facing my life without you."

"I agree baby, I agree," Roc said, embracing his wife.

Chapter Thirty-Seven

Harvest Time

On Fifth Street, Rockey sat up in bed. The room was empty, of course, but Rockey did not feel alone. The eerie presence of his nightmare still hung about. He'd had bad dreams in the past, but never one that haunted him so strongly. It was reoccurring nightly. Staring out into the darkness, he promised himself to consult with his pastor the next day. If God was trying to tell him something, he needed the man of God to interpret his dreams.

To calm himself down, Rockey reached for his cigarettes, lit one up, and then got out of bed. When he rose, his mind immediately thought about a cold beer. In truth, he was really trying to stop smoking and drinking. He had acquired so many bad habits over the years, but he didn't have the strength to break free from them. It would take a miracle for him to leave the cigarettes and beer alone.

Early the next day, Rockey skipped his Saturday

morning ritual: the car wash, breakfast at Joe's, and pool with the fellas. Instead, he made his way to church. When he arrived, Pastor Mosley greeted him with a warm smile. Rockey had received nothing but compassion and guidance from the men in church on his Christian journey, and this was especially true about his spiritual leader, Pastor Mosley. Although the pastor was a young man of God, he was a spiritual giant in his field and he had a wall of distinguished awards and plaques to validate his prestigious position. In awe, Rockey checked out each one.

"Good morning," Pastor Mosley said as he entered the room.

"Good morning," Rockey responded, sitting down as gestured by the pastor.

"Well brother James—what can I do for you? You sounded frantic on the phone."

Rockey took in a deep breath and spoke slowly. "Pastor Mosley, I need some clarity and perhaps you're the only person that can give it to me."

"I'm listening."

Thankfully, Rockey's concerns poured out easily. He explained how he'd had the same terrible dream for months. The dream started out with him in a huge forest surrounded by endless wilderness. He said he'd run through this maze for hours. Then suddenly, as he stumbled through the trees, he'd end up in an open field with rows of fruit that resembled some type of melon. There among the groves, he'd see Sonya from a distant eating the fruit. Soon after she digested it, though, she'd become ill and throw up. He would try to run to her aid, but a giant figure would capture him and then take him to a nearby guillotine. The execution was witnessed by four men wearing black suits that all looked like him. Once he was placed and secured at the chopping block, the blade was released and just as the razor was within inches of his neck, he would wake up from the dream in a cold sweat.

Pastor Mosley was not sure what Rockey's dream meant at first, but as he prayed for the Holy Spirit to reveal the hidden meaning of it all, everything became clear. He was not sure how Rockey would accept what God had shown him, so he prayed that God would allow Rockey to be receptive.

"Brother James, are you prepared for what the Lord has to tell you?"

"Yes," Rockey said without hesitation.

"The endless wilderness represents the endless darkness that you were in while you were in the world. The repeated sin in your life is the maze of sorrow. The Holy Spirit revealed to me that your daughter-in-law has conceived twice, yet she's miscarried both times. The melon in the dream represents the fruit of life. Her illness is the miscarriages she's experienced. The gigantic figure represents God cutting off the generational curse of the male whoremongers in your family, which are the four men...your forefathers. God has placed the responsibly on your head to end the curse."

"Are you trying to tell me that, because of me, Sonya and Roc cannot have a baby?"

"Brother James, I'm only telling you what the Lord has shown me."

"My son Roc carries my name, and he's the fourth generation to have it. As far back as I can remember, the men named Rockwell have lusted after women and been pitiful fathers. A generational curse is kind of heavy, don't you think?"

"Generational curses still exist in the twenty-first century. Alcoholism, mental illness, and other sickness are passed on. It's just that we've become too intelligent to label them as curses, so we say they're inherited. But the bottom line, Brother James, is all of us have some skeletons in our closets and if we don't address them, we can pass them on to our children. The Father states in Exodus 20:5 that He will visit the iniquity of the fathers upon the children unto the third and fourth generation of them that hate Him."

"I don't hate the Lord."

"God made this reference to idol worshippers, and anytime we blatantly sin before God and bow down to our selfish desires instead of serving God, in essence, we're denouncing Him and serving our own needs. And He says He is a jealous God. You say you don't hate God, but when you willfully go against His Word, that is what you're doing—exhibiting hatred. Let me ask you a question Brother James, do you believe your actions hurt anyone?"

"To be truthful, I never thought there was something wrong with having outside women. As long as no one knew, what was the harm?"

"The harm was, God always knew what you were doing. Satan, your enemy lied to you and made you believe that your sins were safe and they were your little secrets. But God keeps a record of all our sins. Brother James, the good thing is, you can repent and receive forgiveness."

"My foolish behavior has broke up my family and caused me to disrespect my wife and even my children. I'm truly sorry, and I want God's forgiveness," Rockey said with tears in his eyes. "Pastor Mosley, I don't know how to say this and it's embarrassing to admit, but for the longest time, I've never felt like I had the will to overcome the urge to abandon my family."

Pastor Mosley set back in his chair and looked at Rockey. He wanted to share with him his theory about why Rockey felt the way he did, but he had to make sure Rockey understood it was his opinion and not biblical. As a man of God, it was important to make his personal views known.

"Brother James, I want to share something with you, but what I'm telling you cannot be found in the Bible. It is what I have observed through my counseling background and my study of our culture...black heritage."

With those words, the pastor had Rockey's attention. He'd always been moved by black history.

"Well Brother James," Pastor Mosley said as he rubbed his hands together and then removed his glasses, just before he immediately put them back on, "I believe when blacks were enslaved, the eminent threat of being separated from their families caused them to become emotionally detached from their love ones. It was a mental escape from the diabolical act of slavery. I feel this behavior has played itself out throughout successive generations. When a man's pride is ripped from him, the manifestation is deeper than the flesh from whips and chains. I find it not strange that the curse that grips your family line dates back to your forefathers during the time of their bondage."

Rockey just looked at Pastor Mosley. "That is deep," Rockey said. "And you know just thinking about it, the elements that fostered the ominous threat of separation were ignorance and fear. That is why I always made sure my kids had a good education. Knowledge is our only way of escape."

"Knowledge is truly power Brother James. That is why God's desire is for us to first know about Him and then open up our minds to our environment, because only then can we truly overcome our past. And right now, I'm going to pray for you and place all your concerns, your past and your future, in God's hands."

After the prayer, Rockey left the church in a hurry. He didn't want anyone to see him break down. When he got home, the tears fell down before he could even get in his apartment. In shame, Rockey cried out before the Lord like a baby. He even prayed about the sins of his forefathers.

He realized what he'd done, not only to his family but to his unborn grandchildren. Sin had him so blinded that he never thought about the consequences—only the selfish pleasure he got from it. Again Rockey asked God for forgiveness and prayed that He would release his family of any generational curses that were upon them. Then he prayed God's blessing on his family.

Hours had passed and Rockey was still crying and praying when suddenly the tears stopped and he felt peace. It was like the weight of the world was lifted off his shoulders and the burden and heaviness of all the mistakes he'd made was gone. At that point, he knew he'd been forgiven and the curse of whorishness was gone, so he asked God to clean up his life and restore his family.

The following Sunday in church, Rockey stood up and gave a praise report. He told the congregation how he'd been free of cigarettes and beer for one week. Deep inside, Rockey knew if God had answered one part of his prayer that He would answer the rest and restore his family.

Too many times Roc had heard Sadie Mae say "You reap what you sow," but it never meant anything to him until Justine. The bad seeds he'd sown with her had harvested, and the situation was getting out of control. Since he'd been back from his trip, she'd been blowing up his cell phone, and she was showing up in his office, when he wasn't there, leaving notes on his desk. Somehow Justine had found out about the cruise and she was furious.

It had been a long day. Roc was tired and grateful Justine had not tried to contact him. He looked at the clock. It was five thirty. By now Justine's shift was over and she was probably on her way home. Relieved, Roc assumed it was safe to leave his office. He knew he had to talk to Justine, but he just did not know what to say. When Roc stepped out of his office, the coast looked clear. But just as he grabbed his briefcase to leave, he heard Justine's voice. When he looked at her, she was in tears.

"Roc, you can't keep avoiding me. You owe me an explanation. A cruise? You were planning on going on a cruise with your wife the next day when you made love to me and took me to Canada, and filled my head up with all your lies! Why...why did you do that to me?" Justine cried. "You hunted me down like an animal! Everywhere I turned, you were there! How cruel of you to drag me into your life and then leave me. I've called you and called you, and you never returned my calls. You didn't even have the decency to tell me what was going on. Were you lying when you said you were sleeping in separate bedrooms and you didn't love her anymore? You made it so easy to fall in love with you. How could you do that, how could you? Why would you?"

Roc was speechless. He had no idea what to do or say.

"Say something, anything—you owe me that."

"Justine, I never meant to hurt you. I didn't realize I was using you, because I never meant to do that."

"Were you lying to me about how you felt?"

"Justine, don't do this. I avoided you because I didn't want to hurt you."

"Well, Roc, guess what. You hurt me anyway. Were you crazy enough to believe that I would just disappear and you would never have to face me? Oakley told me about the cruise and he also told me that you've had many affairs on your precious wife. I wasn't the first, you liar! You liar! You liar!" Justine shouted over and over until she slapped Roc across the face. Then, she ran off.

Roc was relieved that the meeting with Justine was finally over. He hoped it was the last time he would see her, but it wasn't. Over the next few weeks, Justine left messages on his phone and waited for him at his office pleading for his love.

"Roc, when I love someone, I love hard," Justine said. "I'll be the other woman, just don't stop loving me," she said, wiping back the tears.

Roc looked around. They were in the parking lot, the salary parking lot that was off limits to hourly personnel. By now he knew Oakley was helping Justine to gain access to him. He knew Oakley had a grudge against him for whatever reason, but he did not know it went that deep. As he watched people coming and going to their cars, he felt their stares.

He was angry, but not at Justine or Oakley. He was angry at himself for leading Justine on. If he could turn back the hands of time, he would.

"Yes, Roc, I've been the other woman before. It's not something I enjoyed, but for you I will do it again," Justine said.

"Justine—I don't want you to be the other woman."

"What you mean is...you don't want me, you never wanted me...you just wanted to use me. I'm tired of being used by men, Roc. I'm tired, and finally someone is going to pay for using me! You Roc, you're going to pay for this!" Justine yelled just before she stomped away.

Chapter Thirty-Eight

Regrets

When the drug store test showed positive, Sonya was still leery about the results, so she said nothing to Roc. Things were going so well between them and she didn't want any false hope about a baby to create unnecessary tension. To validate the result, she made a doctor's appointment. Patiently waiting in an examination room, surrounded by soft green walls, she felt anxious. The room was soothing, but even the pastel décor, could not calm her. More than anything, she wanted a baby. She tossed and turned all last night thinking and praying about it.

Over the last eight weeks, she'd become just like her mother—praying about everything. The funny thing was, it was working. All those wasted years of worrying and trying to change Roc, when all she had to do was trust and believe in God.

Sonya pulled open the blinds and stared at the clouds above her. God, she said to herself, I know You heard all my prayers last night, but for my sake I need to say it all again. In Your sweet mercy, let there be life inside of me. Please allow my womb to fulfill its purpose, and not continue the emptiness its known. I know You can Lord, because You did it for Sarah, Hannah, Elizabeth and other blessed women in the Bible who were scorned and mocked because of bareness. Well, You did it for them Lord, so do it for me. I'm Your child too. Lord, I'm not coming to you begging. You're my Father, and according to Your Word, I should come boldly to Your throne of grace, asking for a miracle in Jesus' name. Lord hear me in Jesus' name and answer my prayer...amen.

Sonya looked down and rubbed her belly. Then strangely before she could say another word, her thoughts changed. For the first time in her life, she entertained the thought she'd never considered before, adoption. What if she wasn't pregnant after all? Would adoption be the answer?

She'd always felt, in order to be a real mother she had to carry the baby, but in an instant it was as if God told her, that was not so.

Well Lord, she said to herself with a smile, I want a child, and You can use my body as a vessel to carry it, or perhaps You've allowed another woman to endure the labor of bearing my child. If this is the case Lord, I pray for Your divine intervention to allow me and my child be united.

In that moment, Sonya knew her prayers had made it through, and God was going to bless her with a child one way or another. When she looked back at the walls, she felt peace. Even after she heard a knock, and soft voice asking for permission to enter, she remained at ease.

Sonya looked at Dr. Allen, trying to read his face. He'd been her physician for years and still, it was hard to know what was on his mind.

"Hello, Sonya," he said.

"Hi, Dr. Allen. I'm sorry, I can hardly wait to hear the news. Please don't keep me in suspense any longer. Am I pregnant?"

When Dr. Allen started to smile, Sonya started to cry. She knew what the answer was.

"Yes, my child, you're very pregnant," he said.

Sonya jumped up from the bed, hugged Dr. Allen, and whispered a thank you to God.

"But because of your history, Sonya, there is good and bad news," he said. "The good news is you're having a baby. The bad news is you must take it easy—very, very easy. That means, as much as possible, you must try to live stress-free for the next seven months. Don't let anyone upset you, young lady. If you keep all your scheduled appointments, do as I suggest, get plenty of bed rest, and maintain a healthy diet, even with your history I believe you'll carry the baby full term," he said as he handed her a prescription. "This is for vitamins. Make sure you take them once a day. And if you experience any bleeding or cramping, contact my office and go to the nearest hospital immediately."

Sonya was excited and she could hardly wait to get

home and call Roc to tell him the good news. The closer she got to her home, the further away it seemed. When her joyful tears obstructed her vision, she pulled over into a pizza shop parking lot. She composed herself, reached into her purse and grabbed her cell phone. She could wait no longer. She had to call Roc right away.

When he heard the news, Roc was elated and scared. What if she had another miscarriage? Could their fragile relationship handle it? He kept asking Sonya question after question, wondering everything the doctor said. He asked her if their chances were good this time.

Sonya sensed his strong doubts and told him, "It doesn't matter what the doctor says. God said we're going to have a baby. Now all we got to do is trust and believe in Him."

After Roc heard what she had to say, his faith was reinforced, and his heart gave him the green light to be happy. After all, in just a short time, God had taken their marriage beyond all their expectations.

"A baby," Roc finally said with joy, knowing he was ready to be a good father and friend to his child.

When he reclined in his chair, Roc saw Oakley standing outside the office door. He had a smug look on his face. It was no doubt Oakley had heard his entire conversation and he would tell Justine everything, like he did about the cruise. Of all the bad things Roc had done, hurting Justine was one of the things he regretted the most. She was definitely a scorned woman and Roc was a bit concerned about her threats to pay him back. The only good thing was she worked on the other side of the plant which made it almost impossible for them to see each other. But now, as much as he hated to do it, he had to see Justine. It would be better if he told her about the baby rather than to hear it from Oakley. But, when he got closer to her work area, just past the stock room, on the other side of the cafeteria, Roc realized he was too late. Oakley was already there. There was nothing to do but walk away.

Justine tried to brush Oakley off, but he would not leave. Whatever he wanted to tell her, she didn't want to hear. "What goes on between me and Roc is between us, so please get out of my business," she said.

"You are my business. His wife is pregnant!" Oakley said.

Justine just looked at him. She hoped the factory noise had interfered with her hearing. When he repeated himself, she realized, in fact, she'd heard correctly.

"A baby?" she said and quickly put her hands to her face to hide the tears. "How do you know that?"

"I overheard his conversation with his wife when he was on the phone just now. He was laughing and grinning—the proud papa-to-be was talking so loud, I couldn't help but hear it."

"I'll be back," Justine said before she steamed away.

Oakley went after her down the hallway. When he

caught up with her, he ducked her into a corner for privacy so they could talk.

"I told you he was no good. At least when you were with me, you knew where you stood," Oakley said.

"Where I stood was nowhere. What we had can't be compared to this. I love him! I can't believe I've allowed myself to get in this deep, but I have," she cried.

When Oakley took her in his arms, she quickly broke free and wiped her eyes.

"And since when have you become so interested in my feelings? I've dated other guys since we broke up and you never cared. Why the sudden interest in Roc? You've hated him from the first time you met him."

"Why?"

"I've got my reasons."

"What reasons?"

"Let's just say it goes back to high school, when he did some foul stuff to my sister. It was the beginning of all her problems. I believe because of him she ended up on drugs and everything."

"Your sister—what has Sherri got to do with this?"

"Don't worry about it," Oakley said. "Bottom line—it's time for justice. He's gonna pay for hurting my sister, and he's gonna pay for hurting the kids. Yes, he's gonna pay."

Chapter Thirty-Nine

The Choice is Yours

They say confession is good for the soul, Rockey thought as he rambled on and on to Sadie Mae. He talked about everything from his past sins to his new conversion, excited about the change God had brought about in his life.

He'd been attending Bible study now for about a year trying to get his life back together. When he first invited Sadie Mae to go to the classes with him on Wednesday nights, it was just another ploy to get her back. He knew the one thing she loved was God. He'd even gone as far as buying his own Bible. At first he only read it when Sadie Mae was around, and sometimes in class. However, one day, about nine months ago, he was alone in his apartment, and just out of boredom, he read a few passages. It was weird, for some reason from that day on, he couldn't stop reading it. The first couple of times he read only a few verses, but as time progressed, so did his interest, and the verses became pages, then chapters, and finally, whole books of the Bible. He was amazed at how intriguing it had become. The words seemed to leap off the pages and come to life and he began to thirst for them.

As Rockey became a student of the Bible, his attention shifted from Sadie Mae to God, and no one was more pleased than Sadie Mae. More than anything, Rockey feared she thought he was still full of games, so he stopped talking about reconciling with her and discussed it solely with God—for God knew his heart and his true intentions. But he discussed everything else with Sadie Mae, especially how God had delivered him from many of the strongholds he'd had.

"It's been quite a while since I've had a cigarette, and even longer since I've had a drink. God is good. I'm so grateful for what He has done in my life," Rockey said looking at Sadie Mae sitting across from him in the car.

"I'm so proud of you," Sadie Mae said.

"It wasn't me girl, it was the Lord."

The conversation did not end after Rockey's confessions. It went on and on. In the moonlight, under the stars, sitting in front of Sadie Mae's house just laughing and talking reminded Rockey of their courting days when they were teenagers in love—intoxicated with one another.

"I put Roc and Sonya on the prayer list. I really hope she will be able to carry this one," Sadie Mae said.

"I believe she'll make it this time. You know, maybe I can be a better grandfather to Roc's child than I was a father to him," Rockey said.

"You will."

Again, Rockey looked at Sadie Mae. He'd promised God that he wouldn't say anything to her about getting back together until he felt the time was right. But instead of telling her of his feelings, he asked her how she felt. He put the decision in her hands.

"Sadie Mae, I know our history together is overshadowed with pain and tears that I've caused you, but if you give me a chance, I will spend the rest of our future making it up to you," Rockey said.

When Sadie Mae looked surprised by the statement, Rockey eased her fears.

"I don't want to put any pressure on you. I understand your fears, but before you answer, pray about it."

The next morning, Sadie Mae was on the phone calling Betty. She'd become her confidant and it was second nature to discuss everything with her.

"Oh, I'm glad you haven't left to go to the market yet," Sadie Mae said when Betty answered the phone. Wednesday was her market day.

"Yes, I'm still here. I was just about to get in my car and take off."

"Can you cancel your trip for a while? I'm taking a walk over to see you."

"It is cold outside," Betty said.

"I know it's winter, but I feel like walking. I need to talk to you about something."

"Well, that's strange. I feel like walking too, so why don't we both bundle up and meet each other half way. I have something I need to share with you also," Betty said.

When the two women met each other, they embraced as they always did. Over the years they'd become the best of friends. Betty had become godmother to Chloe and Joey and, when they weren't away at college, they considered her house their second home.

"And where were you last night? I called several times and never got an answer," Betty said.

"That's what I need to talk to you about," she paused.

"I was with Rockey. Last night was the first time he didn't ride me about getting back together. He let the decision rest on me, and it felt good not to be pressured. I prayed about it, and I truly feel we have a chance again. I never stopped loving him. I've just been afraid he hadn't changed, but now I see God's light in him. He can't fake that."

"How can you be so sure?" Betty asked.

"Because a long time ago, I asked God to save my marriage, but God has gone a step further and saved Rockey. That's why I know our marriage can be salvaged," Sadie Mae said.

"You once told me Rockey could not see God because of you. Do you think by stepping out of the picture for all these years, he finally saw God?" Betty said.

"It's been years since we've been separated. And a lot

of things have changed, but changes have been for the better. Even though it didn't seem like that when we were going through them...all things have truly come together for the good," Sadie Mae smiled. But then she noticed her friend's obvious glow.

"Enough about me, Betty, you're glowing! What's up with that?"

"I met a man...well I've known him for a couple of years now, but we just started getting to know each other a few months ago. I didn't want to say anything to you about it, because I wasn't sure of where it was all going." She paused. "But it's serious and he asked me to marry him, and I said yes!"

At first, Sadie Mae was not keen about the idea. Betty had proven to make some bad choices about men since Mr. Smith passed away, but when she heard all about this new man's character and Betty said he was five years older, Sadie Mae came around.

"There is only one thing," Betty said. "He lives in Florida and I'll be moving there after we're married."

"Florida? What I'm I going to do without you, especially now that Joey and Chloe are in college?"

"It's God's timing. You and Rockey need this time alone to start a new life, a chance to fall in love again. Besides, we can visit each other every opportunity we get," Betty said, hugging her dear friend.

When Sadie Mae opened the door, Rockey was surprised to hear soft music and see the house lit up with candles. The aroma of Sadie Mae's cooking filled the entryway. "Come in," Sadie Mae said. She took his coat and hung it up.

Rockey got lost in her scent as she came back closer to him.

"You called me over to talk," Rockey said looking around at the romantic atmosphere.

"Well, we don't have to talk on an empty stomach, do we?"

Rockey looked at her and smiled. "Of course not."

When Sadie Mae gently took his hand and led him toward the dining room, Rockey silently thanked God for his wife's forgiving heart.

Chapter Forty

A Hardened Heart

The next morning when Sadie heard the phone, she picked it up on the third ring. It was so early, she wondered if something was wrong. When she heard Roc's voice, her heart started to pound.

"Roc, is something wrong?" she asked.

She said it so loud that she woke Rockey up and he asked her if everything was okay.

"Is something wrong with Sonya?" Sadie Mae asked her son.

"No, Mama everything is all right. Who's that in the background? You got company?"

Sadie Mae was not ready to tell Roc about the situation. She put her hand to her lip to shush Rockey, and then she continued to talk.

"Honey, we can talk about it later. Why are you calling so early in the morning?"

"Well," Roc explained, "I got the phone call last night, but it wasn't official at that time, but Ross just called to confirm it...I got the job! And guess what Mama! It's not for assistant coach it is for head coach. Larry Black was bought out of his contract and he's going to coach for Chicago. So, because of my experience, they're offering me the head coach position and another guy named Jimmy Bills the assistant position. Today at noon, they're having a big press conference and I want all my family there." Roc paused, trying to decide whether or not to pry further. "Was that my father's voice I heard?"

Sadie Mae waited a few seconds and said yes. Instantly, the excitement left Roc's voice as he gave the time, location, and other details about the press conference. When he hung up, he barely said goodbye.

Roc shared his disappointment about his parents with Sonya, but she gently reminded him of all the changes God had made with him. After talking to her, he felt better about the situation. He still was not comfortable with it, but he'd learned how to put things he had no control of in God's hands. As a matter of fact, that's exactly where he'd put Justine and Oakley—in God's hands.

At the press conference, Roc was prepared to see his mother and father together, but he wasn't sure how he'd respond. When he saw his mother alone, he was relieved.

When the cameras started flashing, Roc felt strange being in the spotlight again. God had restored him, and this time, he would not let pride interfere.

A pushy newscaster came over to the bench and asked

Roc if it was the happiest day of his life.

"No," Roc answered. "Sonya, come here for a second, honey." Sonya came and stood at Roc's side, and Roc said to the newscaster, "The happiest day of my life was when I accepted Jesus Christ as my Savior and the next happiest was when this woman said she would marry me, and now she's carrying my child. Being out of the spotlight, I've learned to appreciate what is important and how to put my life in perspective. I love the game and I will give it all I got, but God and my family will always come first."

Meanwhile, Oakley made a phone call to his mother's house. Sherri answered the phone.

"Mama said you would be there," he said. "Turn on channel four."

Sherri got up and turned on the television, and saw Roc and his family.

"Well I'll be...so he made it back to the top," Sherri said.

"Don't you think you've stayed in hiding long enough? It's time for the world to see the real Rockwell James, Jr." Oakley said. "The real low-life that abandoned you and went off and made a name for himself and never thought about you and your children, Sherri!"

"You're right, but I don't have custody of the twins. There's really nothing I can do."

"The world doesn't have to know all the details—just the facts, and the fact is he's their father and he deserted you in a time of need. The world looks at him as if he's some kind of hero, especially since he's on this new push for Christianity. Well now is the right time to expose all the skeletons hidden in his closet and show the world who he really is!"

Sherri scratched her head. No one knew about the money she'd received from Roc, the lies she'd told him about being married and having other kids, and even the photograph she'd stolen years ago from his house, of him, when he was a kid. But those lies she'd told was a long time ago, in his basketball days. She made up her mind that she didn't care if he told everyone about the money, just as long as he got hurt in the process—it really didn't matter if the world knew what a low-life she was. Sherri remembered the last time she tried to get in touch with Roc. He'd changed his number, but not before he cussed her out and told her to do what she had to do.

Well Roc, she thought, the time has come for me to do what I got to do.

Finally, Sherri agreed to go through with the plan to destroy Roc on national television. Oakley had some connections—an old college friend who worked for Dick Shock. There was an opening the next day on the hit show for a paneled guest. With little persuasion, Sherri agreed to be on the show.

Chapter Forty-One

Payday Is Coming

After Sherri hung up the phone, she called Justine. She could tell Justine was upset about something, but she didn't bother to ask what the problem was—she just asked if she could see the kids the next day. Justine agreed, hung up the phone, and continued to cry for hours. She could not believe the man she fell in love with was the monster Oakley made him out to be, but deep inside she knew it was true. After all, he'd lied about his relationship with his wife and now they were expecting a child. And on top of everything else, according to Oakley, Roc was the man Sherri had dogged out all these years about getting her pregnant! Then, he had the audacity to deny he was the father!

In tears, Justine reminisced the night that Oakley briefly shared his family's problems with her and how it changed her life. Because of her emotional state, Sherri had shared with her brother that she was very concerned she wouldn't be a good mother. And that's when Sherri's pain became Justine's joy.

It was one night after they'd made love in his office when suddenly, Oakley just started talking. He said his sister had two kids, a set of twins—a girl and a boy. As a single mother, his sister was trying to make it in California alone, but it was too much for her, and she'd decided to put the children up for adoption. His sister really wanted their mother to raise the kids, but their father refused to have anything to do with it and insisted that the children were not welcome in his home.

At the time, there was a strong indication that Sherri was experimenting with drugs. Oakley was unable to help because his wife was firmly against taking in the children.

Listening to Oakley, Justine knew she had to do something to help, and after months of consideration, she felt moved to adopt them.

Justine and Oakley flew out to California and Sherri gave up her parental rights without a fight to Justine, but the two women agreed an open adoption would be best. The twins had already bonded with their grandmother and although Sherri was not the best mother, she had a genuine love for her kids. The fact that she wanted someone more stable than herself to raise them was evidence of how she felt and the greatness of her devotion.

On the day when everything was finalized, Sherri had cried and begged Justine not to shut her out of her children's lives. Justine agreed and the twins grew up thinking Sherri was just an aunt in California who visited them from time to time. It was hard for her to see the babies torn away from their mother in that way, but by the same token, it was the happiest day of Justine's life to instantly become a mother of two of the finest and prettiest bright-eyed babies she'd ever seen.

The more Justine thought about things, the more she became angry and confused. Now even more, she wanted to do something to Roc to make him feel the pain she was going through. Roc was not the nice man she'd thought he was.

In fact, he was a dog. She kept calling his cell phone, but he never answered, which made her furious. When her thoughts became dangerous, in tears, she called the church, but there was no answer. In a state of confusion, she left a message for Pastor Mosley. She briefly told him about all the things that she'd gone through and asked that he pray for her and her children. Although she did not give specifics, the message still came across as urgent. Thirty minutes later, Pastor Mosley was on the phone and Justine reluctantly told him the whole story.

"Sister Justine, it's true you've been given a lot to deal with, but God is still in control and no matter what, He has not forsaken you.

"Pastor, I fell in love with a married man! Will God still have mercy on me, or will He make me pay for my sins and take my children away from me?"

"Sister Justine, I'm not sure how God will work things out, but He is a God of mercy and grace, and He loves you even though you have sinned. So for now my sister, don't try to figure out the consequences of your sin, but instead, continue to pray that God's mercy will cover you," he said. Then, he continued to console her for the next thirty minutes until she stopped crying.

The next day, Justine was awakened by a knock at the door. Bright and early, Sherri was there to pick up the twins. Her appearance was shabbier than usual. Even her hair was covered with a kinky looking wig. She was wearing some outdated clothes that looked like they'd come from a thrift store and Justine attributed the drastic weight loss to drug use.

Justine insisted on coming along wherever Sherri was going. Now that she knew the whole story about Sherri and Roc, she was sure that Sherri's plans would be to contact Roc, and she wanted to be present when everything went down. If nothing else, she would be there to protect the twins.

When Sherri pulled into the studio parking lot of Dick Shock's show, Justine demanded that she get out of the car and give her some answers.

"Sherri, what is this all about? Why are we here?" Justine said.

"My brother said he told you the whole story last night, and, when I called and you were upset, I assumed it was because you knew the truth about Roc. When you decided to come along, I thought you were a part of the scheme my brother arranged to humiliate the superstar. "

"I wanted to come along because for some strange reason I thought you were going to have some kind of face-off with Roc or something, but I see that is not the case. So, again, I'm asking you, why are we here?"

"Well, you're almost right. I am going to have a face-off with Roc, but on national television. Finally I want the world to see him for the no good person that he is."

"On the Dick Shock Show? That sleaze-ball show...and what do you plan on doing with my kids?"

"Your kids"

"Yes, my kids"

When the two women got loud, Candice opened the car door and called Justine.

"Mama, why are we here? Is something wrong?"

"No, baby everything is all right. Get back in the car," Justine said reaching inside of her purse and getting out her phone. "If you want to expose Roc, then you do it on your own. You will not exploit my children in the process."

Justine walked away from Sherri to call her mother, and within minutes, she arrived. She didn't have the time to tell her what was going on, she just told her mother to take the children home.

Instantly, as she watched her mother's car disappear down the street Justine realized that she didn't want to be a part of Oakley and Sherri's plot to destroy Roc, especially to publicize his family's dark secret on television. Then, for the strangest reason, she felt obligated to warn him and she yelled for a cab.

Chapter Forty-Two

Deadbeat Dad

When Oakley arrived at the studio, he was angry when he found out Sherri did not have the kids.

"What do you mean Justine's mother came and got the kids?" he demanded.

"Like I said, Justine called her mother and the woman came and took the kids, but I was thinking maybe we can do this without the kids," Sherri replied.

Oakley looked at Sherri. Maybe her pitiful appearance would get the sympathy of a few women, but that was not enough. He wanted the world's compassion.

"Do you think her mother knows what's going on?"

"I'm not sure. They didn't have a conversation. The lady just got the kids and left. Justine didn't even get in the car with them."

Oakley took his cell phone from his pocket and dialed Justine's house number. When her mother answered the phone, he said, "Hello, it's Oakley. My mother would like to see the kids, and Justine said it'd be okay if I came over to get them. Will that be alright?" he asked.

Justine's mother did not think anything strange about it. Oakley had taken the kids many times to his parents' house for short visits. When she called to confirm the story with her daughter, Justine's phone went straight to her voicemail.

"I'll be there in ten minutes," Oakley said as he made a mad dash for the door.

"The show will start taping in thirty minutes," Sherri said before Oakley disappeared.

Meanwhile, when Sonya got up from bed, Roc rushed to her aid and put on her house shoes before her feet touched the floor. He'd waited on her hand and foot catering to her every need, hoping to alleviate any stress. More than anything, he wanted Sonya to have this baby and the doctor made it clear if Sonya was to carry the baby full term, she had to be as stress free as possible.

"Your mother looked good yesterday at the press conference," Sonya said, making her way to the kitchen for a glass of water.

"I thought you were going to stay in bed today. You know the doctor said you must try to get all the rest you can."

"Believe me—I'm going back to bed as soon as I take my vitamins. I don't want to do anything to jeopardize this pregnancy. But don't change the subject. I said your mother looked good yesterday. Do you think your parents are going to get back together?"

Roc avoided the question. He could not fathom the thought of his parents together again. He had no respect for Rockey and for all the pain he'd caused his mother to endure. To be truthful, Roc could not even believe how forgiving his mother was. Had she forgotten all the women, the verbal abuse, mental abuse and the pure misery associated with Rockey? In that moment, as much as Roc loved his mother, he had little respect for her, and even pitied her.

That was when Roc swore never to do anything else to jeopardize his family. He would be a better father and husband than his father ever was. He continued to watch Sonya as she slept. She looked so peaceful, and he could never again compromise her peace.

Justine had a general idea of where Roc stayed. He once told her he lived down the street from his mother. It was just Justine's luck when the cab driver got ready to pass Sadie Mae's house. He showed Justine where the famous Rocket lived. Justine paid the driver twenty extra dollars to take her to his house. When the cab driver dropped her off, Justine was amazed. She'd never seen a home so beautiful. Justine took in a deep breath to hold back the tears. She had to put aside her emotions. For the sake of her children, she had to tell Roc so he could stop Sherri and Oakley. When Justine knocked on the door, Roc answered. Justine started to run away until she heard his voice and knew there was no escape. The look in his eyes made her tremble in fear. She had never seen him look like that before, even when she kept showing up at his office insisting that he talk to her.

"Justine!" he said, alarmed and agitated. "What on earth are you doing here?"

Justine was frozen. The prepared speech she'd rehearsed in the cab ride was gone. When Roc repeated himself louder, Justine snapped out of her trance and responded nervously.

"I'm here, to warn you," she paused. "I know the whole story."

"What whole story?"

"The story about you, Sherri, and her babies!" Justine said with anger.

Suddenly, the same fire that shined from Roc's eyes blazed from hers. He'd lied to her about his marriage, forced her to fall in love with him, and now she found out that he was the father to her children—and a no good father at that!

"Don't you yell at me! You should be apologizing to me!"

Roc looked at Justine. It seemed as if she'd hired a private investigator to dig into his past and now she was trying to threaten him with what she'd found. Roc wasn't sure what Justine was up to, but one thing he did know was that he was not going to risk his wife waking up and seeing Justine on the doorstep. He grabbed her by the arm and practically dragged her to the side of his home—there he was safely out of Sonya's view.

"Look, it's over. As long as you live, don't you ever show up at my house again. I don't know what this is all about, but—"

"But it's not what you think. Just be quiet and listen. Oakley and your ex-girlfriend Sherri are brother and sister. Years ago when Oakley informed me that his sister was doing bad in California and was considering giving up her twins, I stepped in and adopted her two babies. Yes, Roc, the girl you thought just disappeared into thin air was in California and she didn't just have one child, she had two...Cordell and Candice. My children are your children!"

"Sherri had twins?" Roc said in amazement. His head started spinning as he thought about the picture Sherri had shown him in the hotel room. He wondered who that child was. At that crazy moment of confusion, Roc was feeling so many things he became numb and visibly confused. He then looked at Justine. She was the common factor in all of this. Was it true this crazy woman was actually raising his children?

"So you knew this all along, and you never told me that you were raising my children? Talk about living a low life. Were you trying to plot a scheme against me! Then, when you just about broke up my family, you tell me the big secret?!"

Justine could not believe her ears or her eyes. Suddenly standing before her, she saw the arrogant man Sherri and Oakley despised. At that moment, she understood why they felt the way that they did.

"How dare you accuse me of something like that. I just found out last night that you were the missing link in my children's life."

"This is some crazy stuff. Your children are actually my children," Roc said, nearly losing his balance before falling against the garage door. His head was pounding so hard he thought it would explode. How was he going to explain this to Sonya?

"To correct you Roc, the reason I'm here is to let you know that Oakley and Sherri are planning on exposing the whole story today on the Dick Shock show."

Oakley had achieved a lot of things in his life, but the thing he was most proud of today was his gift of charm.

On the way to the studio, he took the children to a neighborhood thrift store and purchased clothes two sizes too small for them to wear during taping. When the children became curious and questioned Oakley's peculiar behavior, he told them it was a game, and all they had to do was go along with their auntie Sherri. The practical joke was on her old friend Rocket, the basketball superstar. Still, Candice asked a slew of questions, but Cordell's curiosity was nipped once he found out who the joke was on—his idol—the one and only Rocket. Cordell was just thrilled to have anything to do with the whole thing and he even talked Candice out of calling their grandma and telling her about them going on television. He remembered Oakley saying it was their special secret, that everyone would find out sooner or later, and if they told anyone it would spoil the surprise. Oakley also told them that after the show he would give them their clothes back and some money. When he said money, Candice got on board.

When Sonya woke up from her catnap, she looked around the room and did not see Roc. Automatically she assumed he was downstairs eating or something. The poor man needed a break. He'd been so attentive to her needs, and hardly let her lift a finger. Sonya was not complaining; she'd never loved him as much as she did right now and she was basking in all the sudden interest. Whatever Roc was doing, Sonya did not want to disturb him. She knew how to entertain herself. From bed, she clicked on the TV with the remote, fluffed the pillows, adjusted her body in bed, and channel surfed until it stopped on the Dick Shock show. She always got a kick out of all the silly guests airing their dirty laundry in public. During the commercial, she wondered what kind of weirdos would be on the show today.

The recognizable theme song played as the audience stood up and clapped as Dick Shock strutted out on the stage, waving.

"Hello! As you know, my heart goes out to the less fortunate in our society and I feel it my assignment in life to call attention to those who most have forgotten. Today, I'm recognizing the unsung heroes on the battlefield of life facing each day as single mothers while deadbeat dads escape their responsibilities. On my panel today, I'm sitting with the mother of two. This woman has lived in the shadow of a famous man who refuses to acknowledge her and her children."

The cameras went in for a close-up on Sherri and the twins and the audience sighed at their pitiful appearance.

"Now who is this famous man, this scum of the earth that lurks about fleeing from his children? Well, hold on to your hats, ladies and gentlemen, this man we all love and call our hero is none other than Rockwell James, Jr., better known as the Rocket."

When Sherri opened up her mouth, the cameras went in for a close-up.

"I was only seventeen at the time when he violated me and promised to marry me. Then, when I became pregnant, he denied that the baby was his."

"Well, viewers, because of our connections, we were able to obtain Mr. James' DNA and we ran the necessary tests to prove if these are in fact his children," he paused, reaching for the test results. "And according to the test results, Mr. James, better known as the Rocket, and as of yesterday, the head coach of the Detroit Pistons, is the biological father to Cordell and Candice. Congratulations Rocket, you're a father sooner than you thought. However, we must put you into the hall of shame, for being the worst deadbeat dad yet," Dick Shock said before turning it over to the commercials.

"Roc! Roc!" Sonya yelled from her bedroom. She'd seen as much of the Dick Shock show as she could take, but her yelling was in vain because she never got an answer. She looked all throughout the house, checking everywhere, and when she opened the front door, she saw Roc and Justine talking. As far as she could tell, the two were trying to hide on the side of the house. "Roc!" she yelled again. Then, right there on the front porch, Sonya fainted.

When Roc saw Sonya on the concrete, his heart almost stopped. The day was like a nightmare, and it kept getting worse. He rushed to her side. Had God taken her and their baby away from him this time? Roc yelled for Justine to call an ambulance.

It took all Justine had not to have an emotional breakdown as she watched Roc cradling Sonya in his arms, praying that she would be all right. Quickly, Justine ran into the house and located the phone in the kitchen, made the 911 phone call. When she looked at her watch, she realized she was too late—the Dick Shock show was already in process. She turned on the television and flipped to the show. When she saw Sherri crying on the stage, Justine applauded at the sight.

"He abandoned us," Sherri said, wiping her eyes and then bowing her head in shame, looking as if someone had stripped her of her pride.

When the cameras did another close-up of her kids, Justine gasped in horror. Candice and Cordell looked like bums! As she ran out of the house, Roc raised his head, looked into the house at the television, and stared at the screen until hot tears began to roll uncontrollably down his face.

Chapter Forty-Three

Families that Pray Together…Stay Together!

After the doctor gave Sonya a complete examination, he was pleased to see everything was fine and he released her. He concluded that Sonya's collapsing was her body's own mechanism button, shutting her down to escape stress. In his practice, he'd learned the body was amazing and it had the ability to protect itself.

As Sonya was getting dressed and ready to leave, Roc walked into the waiting room. He was greeted by several people from Sonya's family and his family. Everyone was relieved when Roc gave them the good news; and after the crowd cleared away, with a sigh of relief, Roc fell into the arms of his mother.

"Mama, I almost lost my family. I can't believe that I thought the foolish things I did would not have any effect on my family, mostly Sonya. I love her so much and can't believe how close I've come to losing her, losing our child. And the saddest part of all, Mama, is I thought I was clever enough to get by with doing wrong, as if God and all of heaven were not watching my every move. If nothing else, I'm ashamed of all the dirt I exposed God to, thinking my power was above His authority. Mama," he paused, "Sonya says she forgives me.

Her mercy has me wondering who am I that she would love me so much to give me another chance. It scares me Mama, I'm so afraid I'm going to mess up again! I'm afraid," Roc said in his mother's arms.

"Of course you're going to mess up again, and again, and again if you try to be a good husband in your own strength. You're not strong enough to hold your family together, that's why marriage is a covenant with God. It is through Him that you will walk that straight and narrow path—through Him that your love will stay pure, youthful, and strong. Now I'm glad your family is on the road to recovery and I pray you will always treasure the good gift God has given you—your wife. I also pray that you will always respect her and honor her. If you do, God will bless you. Baby, do you understand?"

"Yes, Mama, finally, I understand."

When Roc and Sadie Mae embraced each other tighter, Roc looked up and saw his father. He did not want to hate his father anymore, but he wasn't sure of how to love him after all these years of feuding. At that moment, Roc prayed that God would take away the pain and the anger so that the hurt would go away.

"Roc, your father is here to pick me up. I'm glad that everything is all right with you and your wife, and now that you're addressing her needs, the next thing you need to address is your father. Pray that God will reconcile you and your father."

"To be truthful, Mama, I don't know if I can forgive him. I don't want to hate him anymore, but I don't want him to be a part of my life."

"Jesus Christ has forgiven him. Are you better than Him? And Christ has showed mercy to you. Are you less compassionate than Him? All I'm asking, Roc, is that you open up your heart to forgiveness so it will come," Sadie Mae said as she squeezed his hand, let go, and walked over to Rockey.

Roc watched his parents as they disappeared down the hall together. Still, his heart was hardened.

Three weeks later...

Justine sat across from Roc and Sonya in Roc's attorney's office. The stress of everything had caused Justine to gain almost twenty pounds. She'd spent all morning trying to find something to wear. Although her weight had gone up, she still wanted to look as good as possible.

Justine dreaded this meeting. She'd hoped that she did not have to face Roc and Sonya together, but there was no other way. She and Roc had agreed to joint custody of the twins. The meeting was just a formality to legalize the agreement.

Justine looked at Sonya. Her stomach was protruding

just a little from her clothes. She looked to be about four months along in her pregnancy. For the first time, Justine got a real good look at her, trying not to make eye contact. She was radiant and strikingly beautiful.

Justine could not believe how intense the pain still was in her heart. If it had not been for Pastor Mosley's constant prayers and counseling, she was not sure how she could've made it. He'd been a God-send in these last few weeks.

When the meeting was over, Sonya politely reached out to shake Justine's hand. "Hello, Justine, my name is Sonya. I understand that because of your past relationship with my husband, we are all put in an awkward position, but I have forgiven my husband, and in time, I pray that you can forgive him for the sake of the twins. I hope that we can get past our differences and concentrate on what is important—the children," Sonya said.

The knot in Justine's stomach tightened and she felt nauseated as she shook Sonya's hand.

"Well, I understand you completely and I have no plans of causing you and your husband any problems. So, from this moment on, we do not have to deal with each other unless it concerns the kids. Now, if you please excuse me," Justine said as she turned and left the office.

As Justine looked ahead, she remembered a saying she once heard: it is better to have loved and lost, than to never have loved at all. Well, she could not agree with that, because right now she felt like she was losing her life, and there was no good in that. Justine continued to look forward, as the tears fell down her face. As sad as it was, though, she realized she could never look back again.

Five months later....

When Rockey walked up the front walk to drop his wife off at Roc and Sonya's house for the baby shower, he heard the women laughing at the front door. Sonya saw who it was at the door and invited them both in. It was the first time Rockey had ever been invited in. He gladly accepted the invitation. Two months ago when he and Sadie Mae renewed their wedding vows, their son was on the road with the team and couldn't make it to the ceremony. Rockey had believed it was just a convenient excuse. When he saw his son coming down the stairs, Rockey kissed Sadie Mae goodbye and politely excused himself. As he neared the door, though, he heard Roc's voice welcoming his mother. Although the tension between them was diminishing, they had a long way to go. Because of their fragile relationship, Rockey did not expect his son to say anything to him other than hello. He would've been glad to hear that. Therefore, when Roc said, "So, you re going to leave me here alone with all these women?" Rockey was floored.

"Of course not," he replied.

"Well, there's a good game coming on. I wouldn't mind the company if you can stay." Sadie Mae rejoiced at the sight of her son and his father making peace and she silently thanked God.

Later on that night, when Sonya said goodbye to the last guest, the abdominal discomfort she was having was becoming unbearable. She just assumed it was something she ate, but as it worsened, she realized she was in labor.

One hour after they arrived at the hospital, Sonya gave birth to a beautiful baby boy. They named him Kaleb Daniel James. They carefully picked the name for their son from the Bible where Kaleb was a leader and Daniel was a praying young man. Roc and Sonya prayed that their son would be a leader who prayed for God's guidance.

As Sonya counted her baby's fingers and toes, she was pleased that God had finally allowed her to be a mother. And she felt double blessed. Her faithful God had not only given them one beautiful child, He blessed them with a set of twins as well. All she could say was, "What an awesome God we serve!"

The End

About the Author

Wanda J. Manning, a passionate Christian and native Detroiter, is the author of Inherited Sin and Harvesting the Fruit of the Spirit. The books emerged from her deep passion to spread God's Word and her strong desire to be a witness of His greatness. Her spiritual roots come from Second Chapel Hill Baptist Church, under the leadership of Pastor Robert J. Coverson. There she became a student of the Word as a faithful Bible class and Sunday school attendee. Then later, she became a Youth Christian Education instructor. She presently belongs to New St. Mark Baptist Church, where she continues to grow spiritually under the leadership of Pastor Larry Smith and Rev. Linda Smith.

Wanda is the mother of three sons, grandmother of two and has been married for twenty-one years. She hosts a radio broadcast, "A New Day is Dawning," on Rejoice 1440 WDRJ. When she's not busy with Zoe Life Publishing as a book outreach coordinator, Wanda enjoys writing, gardening, and cooking. She received an associate's degree in General Studies from Highland Park Community College and is currently pursuing a bachelor's degree in English through Baker College.

wmann30884@aol.com

www.wandajministries.com

Resource Page

To order additional copies of *Inherited Sin* or to find out about other books by Wanda Manning or Zoë Life Publishing, please visit our website at www.zoelifepub.com.

Quantity discounts are available directly from the publisher for bulk orders of *Inherited Sin.*

Zoë Life Publishing
P.O. Box 871066
Canton, MI 48187
(877) 841-3400
outreach@zoelifepub.com